LOST LIGHT

ALSO BY MICHAEL CONNELLY

The Black Echo

The Black Ice

The Concrete Blonde

The Last Coyote

The Poet

Trunk Music

Blood Work

Angels Flight

Void Moon

A Darkness More Than Night

City of Bones

Chasing the Dime

LOST LIGHT

MICHAEL CONNELLY

First published in Great Britain in 2003 by Orion,
an imprint of the Orion Publishing Group Ltd.

Published by arrangement with Little, Brown and Company (Inc.),
New York, NY, USA.

A CIP catalogue record for this book is available
from the British Library.

ISBNs: 0 75285 656 1 (hardback);
0 75285 657 X (trade paperback)

Printed in Great Britain by
Clays Ltd, St Ives plc

The Orion Publishing Group Ltd
Orion House
5 Upper Saint Martin's Lane
London, WC2H 9EA

This is for:

Noel
Megan
Sam
Devin
Maddie
Michael
Brendan
Connor
Callie
Rachel
Maggie
and
Katie

LOST LIGHT

There is no end of things in the heart.

Somebody once told me that. She said it came from a poem she believed in. She understood it to mean that if you took something to heart, really brought it inside those red velvet folds, then it would always be there for you. No matter what happened, it would be there waiting. She said this could mean a person, a place, a dream. A mission. Anything sacred. She told me that it is all connected in those secret folds. Always. It is all part of the same and will always be there, carrying the same beat as your heart.

I am fifty-two years old and I believe it. At night when I try to sleep but can't, that is when I know it. It is when all the pathways seem to connect and I see the people I have loved and hated and helped and hurt. I see the hands that reach for me. I hear the beat and see and understand what I must do. I know my mission and I know there is no turning away or turning back. And it is in those moments that I know there is no end of things in the heart.

1

The last thing I expected [illegible] his own door. [illegible] Hollowood. A man [illegible] guarded the door, for [illegible] uniformed man [illegible] would [illegible] my identity [illegible] hand [illegible] off to a [illegible] walls and the [illegible] were [illegible]

The [illegible] was [illegible] Road. The [illegible] in that [illegible] on the [illegible] it was [illegible] and [illegible] have been [illegible]

[illegible] was a large [illegible] around [illegible]

1

The last thing I expected was for Alexander Taylor to answer his own door. It belied everything I knew about Hollywood. A man with a billion-dollar box-office record answered the door for nobody. Instead, he would have a uniformed man posted full-time at his front door. And this doorman would only allow me entrance after carefully checking my identification and appointment. He would then hand me off to a butler or the first-floor maid, who would walk me the rest of the way in, footsteps falling as silent as snow as we went.

But there was none of that at the mansion on Bel-Air Crest Road. The driveway gate had been left open. And after I parked in the front turnaround circle and knocked on the door, it was the box-office champion himself who opened it and beckoned me into a home whose dimensions could have been copied directly from the international terminal at LAX.

Taylor was a large man. Over six feet and 250 pounds. He carried it well, though, with a full head of curly brown hair and contrasting blue eyes. The hair on his chin added the highbrow look of an artist to this image, though art had very little to do with the field in which he toiled.

He was wearing a soft blue running suit that probably cost more than everything I was wearing. A white towel was wrapped tightly around his neck and stuffed into the collar. His cheeks were pink, his breathing heavy and labored. I had caught him in the middle of something and he seemed a little put out by it.

I had come to the door in my best suit, the ash gray single-breasted I had paid twelve hundred dollars for three years before. I hadn't worn it in over nine months and that morning I had needed to dust off the shoulders after taking it out of the closet. I was clean-shaven and I had purpose, the first I had felt since I put the suit on that hanger so many months before.

"Come in," Taylor said. "Everybody's off today and I was just working out. Lucky the gym's just down the hall or I probably wouldn't have even heard you. It's a big place."

"Yes, that was lucky."

He moved back into the house. He didn't shake my hand and I remembered that from the time I first met him four years before. He led the way, leaving it to me to close the front door.

"Do you mind if I finish up on the bike while we talk?"

"No, that's fine."

We walked down a marble hallway, Taylor staying three steps ahead of me as if I were part of his entourage. He was probably most comfortable that way and that was all right with me. It gave me time to look around.

The bank of windows on the left gave a view of the opulent grounds — a soccer-field-sized rectangle of rolling green that led to what I assumed was a guest house or a pool house or both. There was a golf cart parked outside of the distant structure and I could see tracks back and forth across the manicured green leading to the main house. I had seen a lot in L.A., from the poorest ghettos to mountaintop mansions. But it was the first time I had seen a homestead inside the city limits so large that a golf cart was necessary to get from one side to the other.

Along the wall on the right were framed one sheets from the many films Alexander Taylor had produced. I had seen a few of them when they made it to television and seen commercials for the rest. For the most part they were the kind of action films that neatly fit into the confines of a thirty-second commercial, the kind that leave you no pressing need afterward to actually see the movie. None would ever be considered art by any meaning of the word. But in Hollywood they were far more important than art. They were profitable. And that was the bottom line of all bottom lines.

Taylor made a sweeping right and I followed him into the gym. The room brought new meaning to the idea of personal fitness. All manner of weight machines were lined against the mirrored walls. At center was what appeared to be a full-size boxing ring. Taylor smoothly mounted a stationary bike, pushed a few buttons on the digital display in front of him and started pedaling.

Mounted side by side and high on the opposite wall were three large flat-screen televisions tuned to competing twenty-four-hour news channels and the Bloomberg business report. The sound on the Bloomberg screen was up. Taylor lifted a remote control and muted it. Again, it was a courtesy I wasn't expecting. When I had spoken to his secretary to make the appointment, she had made it sound like I would be lucky to get a few questions in while the great man worked his cell phone.

"No partner?" Taylor asked. "I thought you guys worked in pairs."

"I like to work alone."

I left it at that for the moment. I stood silently as Taylor got up to a rhythm on the cycle. He was in his late forties but he looked much younger. Maybe surrounding himself with the equipment and machinery of health and youthfulness did the trick. Then again maybe it was face peels and Botox injections, too.

"I can give you three miles," he said, as he pulled the towel from around his neck and draped it over the handlebars. "About twenty minutes."

"That'll be fine."

I reached for the notebook in my inside coat pocket. It was a spiral notebook and the wire coil caught on the jacket's lining as I pulled. I felt like a jackass trying to get it loose and finally just jerked it free. I heard the lining tear but smiled away the embarrassment. Taylor cut me a break by looking away and up at one of the silent television screens.

I think it's the little things I miss most about my former life. For more than twenty years I carried a small bound notebook in my coat pocket. Spiral notebooks weren't allowed — a smart defense attorney could claim pages of exculpatory notes had been torn out. The bound notebooks took care of that problem and were easier on the jacket lining at the same time.

"I was glad to hear from you," Taylor said. "It has always bothered me about Angie. To this day. She was a good kid, you know? And all this time, I thought you guys had just given up on it, that she didn't matter."

I nodded. I had been careful with my words when I spoke to the secretary on the phone. While I had not lied to her I had been guilty of leading her and letting her assume things. It was a necessity. If I had told her I was an ex-cop working freelance on an old case, then I was pretty sure I wouldn't have gotten anywhere near the box-office champ for the interview.

"Uh, before we start, I think there might have been a misunderstanding. I don't know what your secretary told you, but I'm not a cop. Not anymore."

Taylor coasted for a moment on the pedals but then quickly worked back into his rhythm. His face was red and he was sweating freely. He reached to a cup holder on the side of the digital control board and took out a pair of half glasses and a slim card that had his production company's logo at the top — a square with a mazelike design of curls inside it — and several handwritten notations below it. He put on the glasses and squinted anyway as he read the card.

"That's not what I have here," he said. "I've got LAPD Detective Harry Bosch at ten. Audrey wrote this. She's been with me for eighteen years — since I was making straight-to-video dreck in the Valley. She is very good at what she does. And usually very accurate."

"Well, that *was* me for a long time. But not since last year. I retired. I might not have been very clear about that on the phone. I wouldn't blame Audrey if I were you."

"I won't."

He glanced down at me, tilting his head forward to see over the glasses.

"So then what can I do for you, Detective — or I guess I should say Mr. — Bosch? I've got two and a half miles and then we're finished here."

There was a bench-press machine to Taylor's right. I moved over and sat down. I took the pen out of my shirt pocket — no snags this time — and got ready to write.

"I don't know if you remember me but we have spoken, Mr. Taylor. Four years ago when the body of Angella Benton was found in the vestibule of her apartment building, the case was assigned to me. You and I spoke in your office over at Eidolon. On the Archway lot. One of my partners, Kiz Rider, was with me."

"I remember. The black woman — she had known Angie, she said. From the gym, I think it was. I remember that at the time you two instilled a lot of confidence in me. But then you disappeared. I never heard from —"

"We were taken off the case. We were from Hollywood Division. After the robbery and shooting a few days later, the case was taken away. Robbery-Homicide Division took it."

A low chime sounded from the stationary cycle and I thought maybe it meant Taylor had covered his first mile.

"I remember those guys," Taylor said in a derisive voice. "Tweedledumb and Tweedledumber. They inspired nothing in me. I remember one was more interested in securing a position as technical advisor to my films than he was in the real case, Angie. Whatever happened to them?"

"One's dead and one's retired."

Dorsey and Cross. I had known them both. Taylor's description aside, both had been capable investigators. You didn't get to RHD by coasting. What I didn't tell Taylor was that Jack Dorsey and Lawton Cross became known in Detective Services as the partners who had the ultimate bad luck. While working an investigation they drew several months after the Angella Benton case, they stopped into a bar in Hollywood to grab lunch and a booster shot. They were sitting in a booth with their ham sandwiches and Bushmills when the place was hit by an armed robber. It was believed that Dorsey, who was sitting facing the door, made a move from the booth but was too slow. The gunman cut him down before he got the safety off his gun and he was dead before he hit the floor. A round fired at Cross creased his skull and a second hit him in the neck and lodged in his spine. The bartender was executed last at point-blank range.

"And then what happened to the case?" Taylor asked rhetorically, not an ounce of sympathy in his voice for the fallen cops. "Not a damn thing happened. I guarantee it's been gathering dust like that cheap suit you pulled out of the closet before coming to see me."

I took the insult because I had to. I just nodded as if I agreed with him. I couldn't tell if his anger was for the never avenged murder of Angella Benton or for what happened after, the robbery and the next murder and the shutting down of his film.

"It was worked by those guys full-time for six months," I said. "After that there were other cases. The cases keep coming, Mr. Taylor. It's not like in your movies. I wish it was."

"Yes, there are always other cases," Taylor said. "That's always the easy out, isn't it? Blame it on the workload. Meantime, the kid is still dead, the money's still gone and that's too bad. Next case. Step right up."

I waited to make sure he was finished. He wasn't.

"But now it's four years later and you show up. What's your story, Bosch? You con her family into hiring you? Is that it?"

"No. All of her family was in Ohio. I haven't contacted them."

"Then what is it?"

"It's unsolved, Mr. Taylor. And I still care about it. I don't think it is being worked with any kind of . . . dedication."

"And that's it?"

I nodded. Then Taylor nodded to himself.

"Fifty grand," he said.

"Excuse me?"

"I'll pay you fifty grand — if you solve the thing. There's no movie if you don't solve it."

"Mr. Taylor, you somehow have the wrong impression. I don't want your money and this is no movie. All I want right now is your help."

"Listen to me. I know a good story when I hear it. Detective haunted by the one that got away. It's a universal theme, tried and true. Fifty up front, we can talk about the back end."

I gathered the notebook and pen from the bench and stood up. This wasn't going anywhere, or at least not in the direction I wanted.

"Thanks for your time, Mr. Taylor. If I can't find my way out I'll send up a flare."

As I took my first step toward the door a second chime came from the exercise bike. Taylor spoke to my back.

"Home stretch, Bosch. Come back and ask me your questions. And I'll keep my fifty grand if you don't want it."

I turned back to him but kept standing. I opened the notebook again.

"Let's start with the robbery," I said. "Who from your company knew about the two million dollars? I'm talking about who knew the specifics — when it was coming in for the shoot and how it was going to be delivered. Anything and anybody you can remember. I'm starting this from scratch."

2

Angella Benton died on her twenty-fourth birthday. Her body was found crumpled on the Spanish tile in the vestibule of the apartment building where she lived on Fountain near La Brea. Her key was in her mailbox. Inside the mailbox were two birthday cards mailed separately from Columbus by her mother and father. It turned out they were not divorced. They each just wanted to write their own birthday wishes to their only daughter.

Benton had been strangled. Before or after death, but most likely after, her blouse had been torn open and her bra jerked up to expose her breasts. Her killer then apparently masturbated over the corpse, producing a small amount of ejaculate that was later collected by forensic technicians for DNA typing. Her purse was taken and never recovered.

Time of death was established as between 11 P.M. and midnight. Her body was found by another resident in the apartment building when he left his home at 12:30 A.M. to take his dog for a walk.

That was where I came in. At the time I was a detective third grade assigned to the Hollywood Division of the

Los Angeles Police Department. I had two partners. We worked in threes instead of pairs back then as part of an experimental configuration designed to close cases quickly. Kizmin Rider and Jerry Edgar and I were alerted by pager and assigned the case at 1 A.M. We met at Hollywood Division, picked up two Crown Vics and then drove to the crime scene. We saw Angella Benton's body for the first time approximately two to three hours after she had been killed.

She lay on her side on brown tile that was the color of dried blood. Her eyes were open and bugged, distorting what I could tell had been a pretty face. The corneas were hemorrhaged. I noticed that her exposed chest was almost flat. It looked almost boyish and I thought maybe this had been a private embarrassment to her in a city where physical attributes seemed often to outweigh those on the inside. It made the tearing open of her blouse and lifting of her bra all the more of an attack, as if it were not enough to take her life, the killer also had to expose her most private vulnerability.

But it was her hands that I would remember the most. Somehow when her lifeless body was dropped to the tile, her hands fell together. Off to the left side of her body, they were directed upward from her head, as if she were reaching out to someone, almost beseechingly, begging for something. They looked like hands from a Renaissance painting, like the hands of the damned reaching heavenward for forgiveness. In my life I have worked almost a thousand homicides and no positioning of a fallen body ever gave me such pause.

Perhaps I saw too much in the vagaries of how she had fallen. But every case is a battle in a war that never ends. Believe me, you need something to carry with you every time you go into the fight. Something to hold on to, an edge that drives you or pulls you. And it was her hands that did it for me. I could not forget her hands. I believed they were reaching to me. I still do.

We got an immediate jump on the investigation because Kizmin Rider recognized the victim. They had been acquaintances. Rider knew her by first name from the gym on El Centro where they both worked out. Because of the irregular hours that came with her job on the homicide table Rider could not keep a regular workout schedule. She exercised at different times on different days, depending on her time and the case she was working. Often she had encountered Benton in the gym and they had struck up a conversational relationship while they worked side by side StairMasters.

Rider knew Benton was trying to establish a career in the film business on the production side. She worked as a production assistant for Eidolon Productions, the company headed by Alexander Taylor. Production schedules used all twenty-four hours on the clock, depending on the availability of locations and personnel. It meant that Benton had a gym schedule similar to Rider's. It also meant that Benton had little time for relationships. She told Rider that she'd had only two dates in the past year and that there was no man in her life.

It was only a surface friendship and Rider had never seen Benton outside of the gym. They were both young black women trying to keep their bodies from betraying them as they went about busy professional lives and attempted to scale steep ladders in different worlds.

Nevertheless, the fact Kiz knew her gave us a good jump. We knew right away who we were dealing with — a responsible and confident young woman who cared about both her health and her career. It eliminated a variety of lifestyle angles we might have mistakenly pursued. The negative from the break was that it was the first time Rider had ever come across someone she knew as the victim of a homicide she'd been assigned to investigate. I noticed right away at the scene that it put a pause in her step. She usually was quite vocal when breaking down a crime scene and developing an investigative theory. At this scene she was silent until spoken to.

There were no witnesses to the murder. The vestibule was hidden from street view and offered the killer a perfect blind. He would have been able to move into the small space and attack without fear of being seen from outside. Still, there had been a risk to the crime. At any moment another resident of the building could have come home or left and come upon Benton and her killer. If the dog walker had taken his pet out an hour earlier he possibly could have ventured into the crime in progress. He could have saved her, or possibly have become a victim himself.

Anomalies. So much of the work entailed study of the anomalies. The crime had the appearance of an attack of opportunity. The killer had followed Benton and waited for the moment she was in the blind. Yet there were aspects of the scene — its privacy, for example — that suggested that he already knew about the vestibule and may have been waiting there, like a hunter watching a bait trap.

Anomalies. Angella Benton was no more than five feet five but she was a strong young woman. Rider had witnessed her workout regimen and knew first-hand of her strength and stamina. Yet there was no sign of a struggle. Fingernail scrapings produced no skin or blood belonging to anyone else. Had she known her killer? Why hadn't she fought? The masturbation and the tearing open of the blouse suggested a crime of psychosexual motivation, a crime perpetrated alone. Yet the seeming lack of any fight for life suggested Benton had been completely and quickly overpowered. Had there been more than one killer?

In the first twenty-four hours our purpose had been to collect the evidence, make notifications and conduct first interviews of those immediately connected to the crime scene. It was in the second twenty-four that the sifting began and we began to work the anomalies, trying to crack them open like walnuts. And by the end of that second day we had concluded that it was a staged crime scene. That is, a scene designed by the perpetrator to convey false ideas about the crime. We concluded we had a killer who thought he was smarter than us, who was sending us down the psychosexual-predator road when the reality of the crime was something altogether different.

The thing that tilted us in this direction was the semen found on the body. In studying the crime scene photographs I noticed that drops of semen stretched across the victim's body in a line suggesting a trajectory. However, the individual drops were round. It was common investigative knowledge in regard to blood spatter evidence that round drops are formed when blood drops directly down to a surface. Elliptical-shaped drops occur when blood is spattered in a trajectory or at an angle to the surface. We consulted the department's blood spatter expert to see if the norms of blood evidence extended to other bodily fluids. We were told it did, and that for us cracked open an anomaly. We now theorized that the possibility was high that the killer or killers had planted the semen on the body. It had possibly been taken to the crime scene and then dripped onto the body as part of an intended misdirection.

We refocused the investigation. No longer did we view it as a case in which the victim wandered into the kill zone of a predator. Angella Benton *was* the kill zone. It had been something about her life and circumstances that had drawn the killer to her.

We attacked her life and work, looking for that hidden thing that had set the plan to kill her into motion. Someone had wanted her dead and thought they were clever enough to disguise it as the work of a hit-and-run psycho. While publicly we pumped the sex-slayer angle into the media machine, privately we began looking elsewhere.

On the third day of the investigation Edgar took the autopsy and the mounting paperwork duty while Rider and I took the field. We spent twelve hours in the offices of Eidolon Productions located at Archway Pictures on Melrose. Alexander Taylor had his moviemaking machine taking up nearly a third of the office space on the Archway lot. There were more than fifty employees. By virtue of her job as a production assistant, Angella Benton had interaction with them all. A PA stands at the bottom of the Hollywood totem pole. Benton had been a gofer, a runner. She had no office. She had a desk in the windowless mail room. But no matter, because she was always on the move, running between offices at Archway and back and forth from productions in the field. At that moment Eidolon had two movies and a television show shooting at separate locations in and around Los Angeles. Each one of those productions was a small city unto itself, a tent city that packed up and moved from location to location almost every night. A city with another hundred or more people who could have interacted with Angella Benton and needed to be interviewed.

The task we had was daunting. We asked for help — additional bodies to help with the interviews. The lieutenant could spare none. It took the whole day for Rider and me to cover the interviews at the company headquarters at Archway. And that was the one and only time I spoke to Alexander Taylor. Rider and I got a half hour with him and the conversation was perfunctory. He knew Benton, of course, but not well. While she was at the bottom of the totem pole, he was at the very top. Their interactions were infrequent and short. She had been with the company less than six months and he had not been the one who had hired her.

We got no hits during that first day of interviews. That is, no interview we conducted resulted in a new direction or focus for the investigation. We hit a wall. No one we talked to had an inkling of why someone would want to kill Angella Benton.

The following day we split up so each detective could visit a production location to conduct interviews. Edgar took the television production out in Valencia. It was a family-oriented comedy about a couple with an only child who connives to keep her parents from having more children. Rider took the movie production nearest her home in Santa Monica. It was a story about a man who takes credit for an anonymous valentine sent to a beautiful coworker and how their subsequent romance is built on a lie that grows inside him like a cancer. I had the second movie production, which was being shot in Hollywood. It was a high-action caper about a burglar who steals a suitcase with two million dollars in it, not knowing that the money belongs to the mob.

As a detective three I was the team leader. As such, I made the decision not to inform Taylor or any other administrators of his company that members of my team would be visiting the production locations. I didn't want advance notice to precede us. We simply split up the locations and the next morning we each arrived unannounced, using the power of the badge to force our way in.

What happened the next morning shortly after I arrived at the set is well documented. I sometimes review the moves of the investigation and wish I had gotten to the set one day sooner. I think that I would have heard somebody mention the money and that I would have been able to put it all together. But the truth is we handled the investigation appropriately. We made the right moves at the right time. I have no regrets about that.

But after that fourth morning the investigation was no longer mine. The Robbery-Homicide Division came in and bigfooted the case. Jack Dorsey and Lawton Cross ran with it. It had everything RHD likes in a case: movies, money and murder. But they got nowhere with it, moved on to other cases and then walked into Nat's for a ham sandwich and a jolt. The case more or less died with Dorsey. Cross lived but never recovered. He came out of a six-week coma with no memory of the shooting and no feeling below the neck. A machine did his breathing for him and a lot of people in the department figured his luck was worse than Dorsey's because he survived but was no longer really living.

Meantime, the Angella Benton case was gathering dust. Everything Dorsey and Cross touched was tainted by their luck. Haunted. Nobody worked the Benton case anymore. Every six months somebody in RHD would pull out the file and blow off the dust, write the date and "No New Developments" on the investigative log, then slide it back into its place until the next time. In the LAPD that is what is called due diligence.

Four years went by and I was now retired. I was supposedly comfortable. I had a house with no mortgage and a car that I'd paid cash for. I had a pension that covered more than I needed covered. It was like being on vacation. No work, no worries, no problems. But something was missing and deep down I knew it. I was living like a jazz musician waiting for a gig. I was staying up late, staring at the walls and drinking too much red wine. I needed to either pawn my instrument or find a place to play it.

And then I got the call. It was Lawton Cross on the line. Word had finally gotten to him that I had pulled the pin. He got his wife to call and then she held the phone up so he could speak to me.

"Harry, do you ever think about Angella Benton?"

"All the time," I told him.

"Me, too, Harry. My memory's come back, and I think about that one a lot."

And that's all it took. When I walked out of the Hollywood Division for the last time, I thought I'd had enough, that I'd walked around my last body, conducted my last interview with somebody I knew was a liar. But I'd hedged my bet just the same. I walked out carrying a box full of files — copies of my open cases from twelve years in Hollywood homicide.

Angella Benton's file had been in that box. I didn't have to open it to remember the details, to remember the way her body looked on the tile floor, so exposed and violated. It still drove the hook into me. It cut me that she had been lost in the fireworks that came after, that her life had not become important until after two million dollars was stolen.

I had never closed the case. It had been taken away from me by the big shots before I could. That was life in the LAPD. But that was then and this was now. The call from Lawton Cross changed all of that in me. It ended my extended vacation. It gave me a job.

3

I no longer carried a badge but I still carried a thousand different habits and instincts that came with the badge. Like a reformed smoker whose hand digs inside his shirt pocket for the fix that is no longer there, I constantly found myself reaching in some way for the comfort of my badge. For almost thirty years of my life I had been part of an organization that promoted isolation from the outside world, that cultivated the "us versus them" ethic. I had been part of the cult of the blue religion and now I was out, excommunicated, part of the outside world. I had no badge. I was no longer part of us. I was one of them.

As the months passed, there was not a day that I did not alternately regret and revel in my decision to leave the department behind. It was a period in which my main work was to separate the badge and what it stood for from my own personal mission. For the longest time I believed the two were inextricably entwined. I could not have one without the other. But over the weeks and months came the realization that one identity was greater, that it superseded the other. My mission remained intact. My job in this world, badge or no badge, was to stand for the dead.

When I hung up the phone after talking to Lawton Cross I knew I was ready and that it was time to stand again. I went to the closet in the hallway and pulled out the box that contained the dusty files and all the voices of the dead. They spoke to me in memories. In crime scene visions. Of all of them I remembered Angella Benton the most. I remembered her body crumpled on the Spanish tile, her hands held out in such a way, as if reaching to me.

And I had my mission.

4

The morning after I spoke to Alexander Taylor I sat at the dining room table in my house on Woodrow Wilson Drive. I had a pot of hot coffee in the kitchen. I had filled my five-disc changer with CDs chronicling some of Art Pepper's late work as a sideman. And I had the documents and photographs from the Angella Benton file spread in front of me.

The file was incomplete because the case was taken by RHD just as my investigation was beginning to come into focus and before many of the reports were written. It was merely a starting point. But after almost four years removed from a crime scene it was all I had. That and the list of names Alexander Taylor had given me the day before.

As I readied myself for a day of chasing down names and setting up interviews, my eyes were drawn to the small stack of newspaper clippings that had yellowed at the edges while closed in the file. I took these up and began looking through them.

Initially Angella Benton's murder rated only a short report in the *Los Angeles Times.* I remembered how this had frustrated me. We needed witnesses. Not only to the crime itself but possibly to the killer's car or getaway route. We needed to know the victim's movements before she was attacked. It had been her birthday. Where and with whom had she spent the evening before coming home? One of the best ways to stimulate citizen reports is through news stories. Because the *Times* decided to run only a short that was buried in the back of the B section, we got almost no help from the public. When I called the reporter to express my frustration, I was told that polling showed that customers were tired of stories about death and tragedy. The reporter said the news hole for crimes stories was shrinking and there was nothing she could do about it. As a consolation she wrote an update for the next day's edition which included a line about the police seeking the public's help in the case. But the story was even shorter than the first report and was buried deeper inside the paper. We got not one call from a citizen that day.

All of that changed three days later when the story hit the front page and was the lead story for every television station in the city. I picked up the first of the stories clipped from the front page and read it once again.

REAL-LIFE SHOOT-OUT ON FILM SET

1 DEAD, 1 HURT AS COPS AND ROBBERS INTERRUPT CELLULOID COUNTERPARTS

By Keisha Russell
Times Staff Writer

A deadly reality intruded on Hollywood fantasy Friday morning when Los Angeles police and security guards exchanged gunfire with armed robbers during a heist of $2 million in cash being used in the filming of a movie about a heist of $2 million in cash. Two bank employees were shot, one of them fatally.

The armed robbers escaped with the money after opening fire on security officers and a real-life police detective who happened to be on the set. Police said that blood found later in the abandoned getaway vehicle indicated that at least one of the robbers was also hit by gunfire.

The film's star, Brenda Barstow, was inside a nearby trailer at the time of the shooting. She was unhurt and did not witness the real-life shoot-out.

The incident occurred outside a bungalow on Selma Avenue shortly before 10 a.m., according to police spokesmen. An armored truck arrived at the filming location to deliver $2 million scheduled to be used as a prop in scenes to be shot inside the house. The film set was described as being under heavy security at the time, though the exact number of armed security guards and police on hand was not disclosed.

The victim who was fatally shot was identified as Raymond Vaughn, 43, director of security for BankLA, the bank that was delivering the money to the film set. Also shot was Linus Simonson, 27, another BankLA employee. He suffered a bullet wound to the lower torso and was listed late Friday in stable condition at Cedars-Sinai Medical Center.

LAPD Detective Jack Dorsey said that as two guards were moving the cash from the armored truck into the house, three heavily armed men jumped from a van parked nearby, while a fourth waited behind the wheel. The gunmen confronted the guards and took the money. As the suspects were retreating to the van with the four satchels containing the cash, one of them opened fire.

"That was when all hell broke loose," Dorsey said. "It turned into a firefight."

It was unclear Friday why the shooting started. Witnesses told police that the robbers encountered no resistance from the security people on the scene.

"As far as we can tell, they just opened up and started firing," said Detective Lawton Cross.

Police said several security guards returned fire, along with at least two off-duty patrol officers working as on-set security and a police detective, Harry Bosch, who had been inside a movie set trailer conducting a seemingly unrelated investigation.

Police yesterday estimated that more than a hundred gunshots were fired during the wild shoot-out.

Even so, the crossfire lasted no more than a minute, witnesses said. The robbers managed to get into the van and speed away. The van, riddled with bullet holes, was later found abandoned near the Sunset Boulevard entrance to the Hollywood Freeway. It was determined that it had been stolen from a movie studio equipment yard the night before.

"At this time we have no identities of the suspects," Dorsey said. "We are following a variety of leads that we think will prove useful to the investigation."

The shoot-out brought a sobering dose of reality to the encampment of moviemakers.

"At first I thought it was the prop guys just shooting blanks," said Sean O'Malley, a production assistant on the film project. "I thought it was like a joke. Then I heard people screaming to get down and real bullets started hitting the house. I knew it was real. I hit the deck, man, and just prayed. It was scary."

The untitled film is about a thief who steals a suitcase containing $2 million from the Las Vegas mob and runs to Los Angeles. According to experts, it is highly unusual for real money to be used in film productions, but the film's director, Wolfgang Haus, insisted on the use of real money because the scenes being shot in the Selma Avenue home entailed a variety of close-ups of the thief, played by Barstow, and the money.

Haus said the film's script called for the thief to dump the money on a bed and roll around in it, throwing it into the air and celebrating. Another scene involved the thief covering herself in a bathtub filled with the money. Haus said fake money would easily be noticeable in the finished film.

The German filmmaker also insisted that using real currency helped the actors perform better in scenes containing the money.

"If you are using play money, then you are playacting," Haus said. "We needed to get beyond that. I wanted this woman to feel she had stolen two million dollars. It would be impossible to do it any other way. My films rely on accuracy and truth. If we were to use Monopoly money, the film would be a lie and everybody who watched it would know it."

The film's producers, Eidolon Productions, arranged for a one-day loan of the cash and a phalanx of security guards to go with it, police detectives told reporters. The armored car was scheduled to remain on the scene during shooting, and the money was to be returned immediately after filming was completed. The largesse was entirely comprised of one-hundred-dollar bills wrapped in $25,000 packets.

Alexander Taylor, owner of the film's production company, declined comment on the robbery or the decision to use real money during the filming. It was unclear if the money was insured against robbery.

Police also declined to reveal why Detective Bosch was on the set when the shoot-out erupted. But sources told The Times that Bosch was investigating the death of Angella Benton, who was found strangled in her Hollywood apartment building four days earlier. Benton, 24, was an employee of Eidolon Productions, and police are now investigating the possibility of a connection between her murder and the armed robbery.

In a statement released by her publicist, Brenda Barstow said, "I am shocked by what has happened and my heart goes out to the family of the man who was killed."

A spokesman for BankLA said that Raymond Vaughn had been employed by the bank for seven years. Formerly he was a police officer who worked for departments in New York and Pennsylvania. Simonson, the injured employee, is an assistant to bank vice president Gordon Scaggs, who was in charge of the one-day cash loan to the movie set. Scaggs could not be reached for comment.

Production of the film was temporarily suspended. It was unclear Friday when the cameras would roll again, or if real currency would be used in the filming when it begins again.

I remembered the surreal scene of that day. The screaming, the cloud of smoke left after all of the shooting. People on the ground and me not knowing if they'd been hit or were just taking cover. No one got up for a long time, even after the getaway van was long gone.

I skimmed through a sidebar story that focused on how unusual it was to use real money — and so much of it — on a movie set, no matter what precautions had been taken. The story reported that the volume of the money took up four delivery satchels and correctly pointed out that it was unlikely that all $2 million would ever be contained in a single camera shot. Yet the producers of the film acceded to the director's demand that real money be used and that all $2 million be on hand for verisimilitude. But the unnamed insiders and Hollywood watchers quoted in the story seemed to suggest that it wasn't about the money or verisimilitude or even art. It was simply a power play. Wolfgang Haus did it because he could. The director was coming off of back-to-back films that had grossed more than $200 million each. In four short years he had risen from making small independent films to being a powerful Hollywood player. In demanding that $2 million in real cash be on hand for the filming of the rather routine scenes, he was exercising his newfound muscle. He had the power to ask for and get the $2 million on the set. Just another story about Hollywood ego. Only this time it involved murder.

I moved on to a follow-up story published two days after the robbery. It was a rehash of the first day's stories with little new information on the investigation. There were no arrests and no suspects. The most notable new information was that Warner Bros., the studio backing the film, had pulled the plug, canceling financing seven days into production after the film's star, Brenda Barstow, pulled out, citing safety concerns. The story cited unnamed sources within the production who suggested Barstow pulled out for other reasons but was using a personal safety clause in her contract to walk away. The other reasons suggested were her realization that a pall had been cast over the production that could shroud the film's box-office appeal as well, and her disappointment with the final script, which was finished after she signed on to the production.

The end of the follow-up story swung back to the investigation and reported that the investigation of the robbery and shooting had grown to encompass the murder of Angella Benton and that the Robbery-Homicide Division had taken over the case from Hollywood Division. I noticed that a paragraph had been circled near the bottom of the clip. Most likely by me four years before.

> Sources confirmed to The Times that the shipment of money stolen during the robbery was insured and contained marked bills. Investigators confided that tracing the cash may offer the best chance of identifying and capturing the suspects.

I didn't remember circling the paragraph four years before and wondered why I had — by the time the follow-up had been published I was off the case. I guessed that at the time I remained interested, whether on or off it, and was curious as to whether the reporter's source had given her accurate information or was simply hoping the robbers would read the story and panic over the possibility of the cash being traceable. Maybe it would make them hold on to it longer and increase the chance of a full recovery.

Wishful thinking. It didn't matter now. I folded the clips and put them aside. I thought about the trailer I was in that day when it began. The newspaper stories were just a blueprint, as distant as an aerial view. Like trying to figure out Vietnam in 1967 by watching Walter Cronkite at night. The stories carried none of the confusion, the smell of blood and fear, the searing charge of adrenaline dumping into the pipes like paratroopers going down the ramp of a C-130 over hostile territory, *"Go! Go! Go!"*

The trailer was parked on Selma. I was talking to Haus, the director, about Angella Benton. I was searching for anything to grab on to. I was obsessed with her hands, and suddenly in that trailer I thought maybe the hands had been part of the staging of the crime scene. Staged by a director. I was pressing Haus, pushing him, wanting to know his whereabouts on the night in question. And then there was a knock and the door opened and everything changed.

"Wolfgang," a man in a baseball cap said. "The armored truck's here with the money."

I looked at Haus.

"What money?"

And then I knew, instinctively, what was about to happen.

I look back at the memory now and see everything in slow motion. I see all the moves, all the details. I came out of the director's trailer to see the red armored truck in the middle of the street two houses down. The back door was open and a man in uniform inside was handing money satchels to two men on the ground. Two men in suits, one much older than the other, stood nearby watching.

As the money carriers turned toward the house, the side door of a van parked across the street slid open and three armed men in ski masks emerged. Through the open door of the van I saw a fourth behind the wheel. My hand went inside my coat to the gun on my hip but I held it there. The situation was too volatile. Too many people around and in the possible crossfire. I let things go.

The robbers came up behind the money carriers, surprised them and took the satchels without a shot. Then, as they backed into the street toward the van, the inexplicable happened. The cover man not carrying a satchel stopped, spread his stance and leveled his weapon in a two-handed grip. I didn't get it. What had he seen? Where was the threat? Who had made a move? The gunman opened fire and the older man in the suit, his hands raised and no threat, went down backwards on the street.

In less than a second the full firefight erupted. The guard in the truck, the security men and the off-duty cops on the front lawn all opened up. I pulled my gun and moved down the lawn toward the van.

"Down! Everybody down!"

As crew members and technicians dove for ground cover I moved in closer. I heard someone start screaming and the van's engine begin revving. The smell of spent gunpowder invaded and burned my nostrils. By the time I had a clear, safe shot the robbers were to the van. One threw his satchels through the open door and then turned back, drawing two pistols from his belt.

He never got a shot off. I opened up and watched him fly backwards into the van. The others then dove in after him and the van took off, its tires screaming and the side door still open, the wounded man's feet protruding. I watched the van round the corner and head toward Sunset and the freeway. I had no chance of pursuit. My Crown Vic was parked more than a block away.

Instead, I opened up my cell phone and called it in. I told them to send ambulances and lots of people. I gave them the direction of the van and told them to get to the freeway.

The whole while the background screaming never stopped. I closed the phone and walked over to the screaming man. It was the younger man in the suit. He was on his side, his hand clamped over his left hip. Blood was leaking between his fingers. His day and his suit were ruined but I knew he was going to make it.

"I'm hit!" he yelled as he squirmed. "I'm fucking hit!"

I came out of the memory and back to my dining room table as Art Pepper started playing "You'd Be So Nice to Come Home To," with Jack Sheldon on trumpet. I had at least two or three versions of Pepper performing the Cole Porter standard on disc. On each one he always attacked it, tore its guts out. It was the only way he knew how to play and that relentlessness was what I liked best about him. It was the thing that I hoped I shared with him.

I opened my notebook to a fresh page and was about to write a note about something I had seen in my memory of the shoot-out, when someone knocked on the door.

5

I got up and went down the hall and looked through the peephole. I then quickly came back to the dining room and got a tablecloth from the cabinet against the wall. The tablecloth had never been used. It had been bought by my ex-wife and put in the cabinet for when we entertained. But we never entertained. I no longer had the wife but now the tablecloth would come in handy. There was another knock on the door. Louder this time. I quickly finished covering the photos and documents and went back to the door.

Kiz Rider had her back to me and was looking out at the street when I opened the door.

"Kiz, sorry. I was on the back deck and didn't hear the first knock. Come on in."

She walked past me and down the short hallway toward the living and dining room areas. She probably saw that the sliding door to the deck was closed.

"Then how did you know there was a first knock?" she asked as she went by.

"I, uh, just thought that the knock I heard was so loud it must've meant that whoever was out there had —"

"Okay, okay, Harry, I got it."

I hadn't seen her in almost eight months. Since my retirement party, which she had organized and held at Musso's, renting out the whole bar and inviting everybody from Hollywood Division.

She moved into the dining room and I saw her eyes run over the rumpled tablecloth. It was clear that I was covering something and I immediately regretted doing it.

She was wearing a charcoal gray business suit with the skirt below the knee. The outfit took me by surprise. Ninety percent of the time we worked together as partners she wore black jeans and a blazer over a white blouse. It allowed her freedom to move, to run if necessary. In the suit she looked more like a bank vice president than a homicide detective.

Her eyes still on the table, she said, "Oh, Harry, you always set such a nice table. What's for lunch?"

"Sorry. I didn't know who was at the door and I just sort of threw that over some stuff I have out."

She turned to face me.

"What stuff, Harry?"

"Just stuff. Old case stuff. So tell me, how are things down at RHD? Better than last time we talked?"

She had been promoted downtown about a year before I split the department. She'd had trouble with her new partner and others in RHD and had confided in me about it. I'd had a mentoring relationship with her that continued after she transferred to RHD. But it ended when I chose retirement over a reassignment that would have put us back together as partners in RHD. I knew it hurt her. Her organizing of the retirement party had been a nice gesture but it was also the big good-bye from her.

"RHD? RHD didn't work out."

"What? What are you talking about?"

I was genuinely surprised. Rider had been the most skilled and intuitive partner I had ever worked with. She was made for the mission. The department needed more like her. I had thought for sure that she would be able to adjust to life in the department's highest-profile squad and do good work.

"I transferred out at the beginning of the summer. I'm in the chief's office now."

"You're kidding. Oh, man . . ."

I was stunned. She had obviously chosen a career path through the department. If she was working for the chief as an adjutant or on special projects, then she was being groomed for command staff administration. There was nothing wrong with that. I knew Rider was as ambitious as the next cop. But homicide was a calling, not a career. I had always thought she understood and accepted that. She had heard the call.

"Kiz, I don't know what to say. I wish . . ."

"What, that I had talked to you about it? You split the gig, Harry. Remember? What were you going to tell me, to tough it out in RHD when you bailed out yourself?"

"It was different for me, Kiz. I had built up too much resistance. I was pulling too much baggage. You were different. You were the star, Kiz."

"Well, stars burn out. It was too petty and political on the third floor. I changed directions. I just took the lieutenant's exam. And the chief is a good man. He wants to do good things and I want to be right there with him. It's funny, things are less political on the sixth floor. You'd think it would be the other way around."

It sounded as though she was trying to convince herself more than me. All I could do was nod as a sense of guilt and loss flooded me. If I had stayed and taken the RHD job, she would have stayed also. I went into the living room and dropped onto the couch. She followed me but remained standing.

I reached over to turn down the music but not too much. I liked the song. I stared out through the sliding doors and across the deck to the vista of mountains across the Valley. It was no smoggier out there than most days. But the overcast somehow seemed to fit as Pepper took up the clarinet to accompany Lee Konitz on "The Shadow of Your Smile." There was a sad wistfulness to it that I think even gave Rider pause. She stood silently listening.

I had been given the discs by a friend named Quentin McKinzie, who was an old jazzman who knew Pepper and had played with him decades earlier at Shelly Manne's and Donte's and some of the other long-gone Hollywood jazz clubs spawned by the West Coast sound. McKinzie had told me to listen and study the discs. They were some of Pepper's last recordings. After years spent in jails and prisons because of his addictions, the artist was making up for lost time. Even in his work as a sideman. That relentlessness. He never stopped it until his heart stopped. There was a kind of integrity in that and the music that my friend admired. He gave me the discs and told me never to stop making up for lost time.

Soon the song ended and Kiz turned to me.

"Who was that?"

"Art Pepper, Lee Konitz."

"White guys?"

I nodded.

"Damn. That was good."

I nodded again.

"So what's under the tablecloth, Harry?"

I shrugged.

"First time you've come around in eight months, I suppose you know."

She nodded.

"Yeah."

"Let me guess. Alexander Taylor's tight with the chief or the mayor or both and he called to check me out."

She nodded. I had gotten it right.

"And the chief knew you and I were close at one time, so . . ."

At one time. She seemed to stumble while saying that part.

"Anyhow, he sent me out to tell you that you're barking up the wrong tree."

She sat down on the chair opposite the couch and looked out across the deck. I could tell she wasn't interested in what was out there. She just didn't want to look at me.

"So this is what you gave up homicide for, to run errands for the chief."

She looked sharply at me and I saw the injury in her eyes. But I didn't regret what I said. I was just as angry with her as she was with me.

"It's easy for you to say that, Harry. You've already been through the war."

"The war never ends, Kiz."

I almost smiled at the coincidence of the song that was now playing while Rider was delivering her message. The piece was "High Jingo," with Pepper still accompanying Konitz. Pepper would be dead six months after laying down the track. The coincidence was that when I was young in the department, "high jingo" was a way old-guard detectives would describe a case that had taken on unusual interest from the sixth floor or carried other unseen political or bureaucratic dangers. When a case had high jingo on it, you had to be careful. You were in murky water. You had to watch your back because nobody else was watching it for you.

I got up and went to the window. The sun was reflecting off a billion particles that hung in the air. It was orange and pink and looked beautiful. It didn't seem like it could be poison.

"So what's the word from the chief — lay off it, Bosch? You're a citizen now. Leave it to the professionals?"

"More or less."

"The case is gathering dust, Kiz. Why does he care that I'm poking around when nobody in his own department does? Is he afraid I'll embarrass him or something by closing it?"

"Who says it's gathering dust?"

I turned around and looked at her.

"Come on, don't give me the due diligence dance. I know how that goes. A signature every six months on the log, 'Uh yup, nothing new here.' I mean, don't you care about this, Kiz? You knew Angella Benton. Don't you want to see this thing cleared?"

"Of course I do. Don't think for one moment that I want anything less. But things are happening, Harry. I was sent out here as a courtesy to you. Don't get involved. You might wander into something you shouldn't. You might hurt rather than help."

I sat back down and looked at her for a long moment as I tried to read between the lines. I wasn't convinced.

"If it is actively being worked, who is working it?"

She shook her head.

"I can't tell you that. I can only tell you to leave it alone."

"Look, Kiz, this is me. Whatever anger you have because I pulled the pin shouldn't stop you —"

"From what? Doing what I am supposed to do? Following orders? Harry, you no longer have a badge. People with badges are actively working on this. *Actively.* You understand? Leave it at that."

Before I could speak she fired another round at me.

"And don't trouble yourself about me, okay? I have no anger toward you anymore, Harry. You left me high and dry but that was a long time ago. Yeah, I had anger but it's a long time gone. I didn't even want to be the one who came here today but he made me come. He thought I could convince you."

He being the chief, I assumed. I sat silently for a moment, waiting to see if there was more. But that was all she had. I spoke quietly then, almost as if I was putting a confession through the screen to a priest.

"And what if I can't leave it alone? What if for reasons that have nothing to do with this case I need to work this? Reasons for myself. What happens then?"

She shook her head in annoyance.

"Then you are going to get hurt. These people, they don't fuck around. Find some other case or some other way to work out your demons."

"What people?"

Rider stood up.

"Kiz, what people?"

"I've told you enough, Harry. Message delivered. Good luck."

She headed toward the hallway and the door. I got up and followed, my mind churning through what I knew.

"Who is working the case?" I asked. "Tell me."

She glanced back at me but kept moving toward the door.

"Tell me, Kiz. Who?"

She stopped suddenly and turned to me. I saw anger and challenge in her eyes.

"For old time's sake, Harry? Is that what you want to say?"

I stepped back. Her anger was a force field around her body that was pushing me back. I held my hands out wide in surrender and didn't say anything. She waited a moment and then turned back to the door.

"Good-bye, Harry."

She opened the door and stepped out, then pulled it closed behind her.

"Good-bye, Kiz."

But she was already gone. For a long time I stood there thinking about what she had said and not said. There had been a message within a message but I couldn't yet read it. The water was too murky.

"High jingo, baby," I said to myself as I locked the door.

6

The drive out to Woodland Hills took almost an hour. It used to be in this place that if you waited, picked your spots and went against the grain of traffic, you could get somewhere in a decent amount of time. Not anymore. It seemed to me that the freeways, no matter what time and what location, were always a nightmare. There was never any respite. And having done little long-distance driving in the past months, being re-immersed in the routine was an annoying and frustrating exercise. When I'd finally hit my limit, I got off the 101 at the Topanga Canyon exit and worked my way on surface streets the rest of the way. I was careful not to try to make up for lost time by speeding through the mostly residential districts. In my inside coat pocket was a flask. If I got pulled over, it could be a problem.

In fifteen minutes I got to the house on Melba Avenue. I pulled my car in behind the van and got out. I walked up the wooden ramp that started next to the van's side door and had been built over the front steps of the house.

At the door I was met by Danielle Cross, who beckoned me in silently.

"How's he doing today, Danny?"

"Same as always."

"Yeah."

I didn't know what else to say. I couldn't imagine what her view of the world was, how it had changed from one set of hopes and anticipations to something completely different overnight. I knew she couldn't be much older than her husband. Early forties. But it was impossible to tell. She had old eyes and a mouth that seemed permanently tight and turned down at the corners.

I knew my way and she let me go. Through the living room and down the hallway to the last room on the left. I walked in and saw Lawton Cross in his chair — the one bought along with the van after the fund-raiser run by the police union. He was watching CNN on a television mounted on a bracket hanging from the ceiling in the corner. Another report on the Mideast situation.

His eyes moved toward me but his face didn't. A strap crossed above his eyebrows and held his head to the cushion behind it. A network of tubes connected his right arm to a bag of clear fluid that hung from a utility tree attached to the back of his chair. His skin was sallow, he weighed no more than 125 pounds, his collarbones jutted out like shards of broken pottery. His lips were dry and cracked, his hair was an uncombed nest. I had been shocked by his appearance when I'd come by after his call to me. I tried not to show it again.

"Hey, Law, how are you doing?"

It was a question I hated to ask but felt I owed it to him to ask.

"About what you'd expect, Harry."

"Yeah."

His voice was a harsh whisper, like a college football coach's who has spent forty years screaming from the sidelines.

"Listen," I said. "I'm sorry to come back so soon but there were a few other things."

"Did you go see the producer?"

"Yeah, I started with him yesterday. He gave me twenty minutes."

There was a low hissing sound in the room that I had noticed when I came by earlier in the week. I think it was the ventilator, pumping air through the network of clear tubes that ran under Cross's shirt and out of his collar and up either side of his face before plugging into his nose.

"Anything?"

"He gave me some names. Everybody from Eidolon Productions who supposedly knew about the money. I haven't had a chance to run them down yet."

"Did you ever ask him what Eidolon means?"

"No, I never thought to ask. What is it, like a family name or something?"

"No, it means phantom. That's one of the things that's come back to me. Just sort of popped into my head while I've been thinking about the case. I asked him once. He said it came from a poem. Something about a phantom sitting on a throne in the dark. I guess he figures that's him."

"Strange."

"Yeah. Hey, Harry, you can turn off the monitor. So we don't have to bother Danny."

He had asked me to do the same thing on the first visit. I moved around his chair to a nearby bureau. On the top of it was a small plastic device with a small green light glowing on its face. It was an audio monitor manufactured for parents to listen in on their sleeping babies. It helped Cross call to his wife when he needed to change the channel or wanted anything else. I switched it off so we could speak privately and came back around to the front of the chair.

"Good," Cross said. "Why don't you close the door now."

I did as instructed. I knew what this was leading to.

"Did you bring me something this time?" Cross said. "Like I asked?"

"Uh, yeah, I did."

"Good. Let's start with that. Go into the bathroom behind you and see if she left my bottle in there."

In the bathroom the counter surrounding the sink was crowded with all manner of medicines and small medical equipment. Sitting on a soap dish was a plastic bottle with an open top. It looked like something normally found on a touring bike but a little different. The neck was wider and it was slightly curved. Probably to make the drinking angle a little more comfortable, I thought. I quickly took the flask out of my jacket and then poured a couple ounces of Bushmills into the bottle. When I took it out to the bedroom Cross's eyes widened in horror.

"No, not that! That's a piss bottle! It goes under the chair."

"Ah, shit! Sorry."

I turned around and went back to the bathroom, pouring the booze out into the sink just as Cross yelled, "No, don't!"

I looked back out at him.

"I would've taken it."

"Don't worry. I've got more."

After the piss bottle was rinsed and returned to the soap dish I went back out to the bedroom.

"Law, there's no drinking bottle in there. What do you want me to do?"

"Goddamn, she probably took it. She knows what I'm up to. You have the flask?"

"Yeah, right here."

I tapped it from the outside of my sport coat.

"Bring it out. Let me have a taste."

I pulled the flask out and opened it. I brought the mouth to his and let him take a swallow. He coughed loudly and some of it spilled down his cheek and neck.

"Ah, Jesus!" he gasped.

"What?"

"Jesus . . ."

"What? Law, you all right? I'll get Danny."

I made a move toward the door but he stopped me.

"No, no. I'm fine. I'm fine. I just . . . it's been a long time, is all. Give me another."

"Law, we've got to talk."

"I know that. Just give me another taste."

I held the flask to his mouth again and poured in a good jolt. He took it down well this time and closed his eyes.

"Black Bush . . . Jesus, is that good."

I smiled and nodded.

"Fuck the meds," he said. "Give me Bushmills anytime, Harry. Any fucking time."

He was a man who couldn't move but I could still see the whiskey work into his eyes and soften them.

"She won't give me anything," he said. "Doctor's orders. Only time I get a nip is when one of you guys comes by and visits. And that ain't often. Who wants to come and see this sorry sight . . .

"You gotta keep coming, Harry. I don't care about the case, clear it, don't clear it, but keep comin' to see me."

His eyes moved to the flask.

"And bring your friend there. Always bring a friend."

It was beginning to dawn on me. Cross had held back on me. I had come to him the day before I went to Taylor. Cross had been the place to start. But he had held back in order to bring me back — with a flask. Maybe the whole thing, his call to reawaken the case in me had all been about one thing. The flask.

I held the wallet-size container up.

"You held back on me, Law, so I'd bring you this."

"No. I was going to have Danny call you. There was something I forgot."

"Yeah, well, I already know it. I go talk to Taylor and the next thing I know I get a visit from the sixth floor telling me to lay off, it's being worked. By people who don't fuck around."

Cross's eyes were darting back and forth in his frozen face.

"No," he said.

"Who came to see you before me, Law?"

"No one. Nobody's come about the case."

"Who did you call before you called me?"

"Nobody, Harry, I promise."

I must have raised my voice because the door to the bedroom suddenly opened and Cross's wife stood there.

"Is everything okay?"

"Everything is fine, Danny," her husband said. "Leave us alone."

She stood in the doorway for a moment and I saw her eyes go to the flask in my hand. For a moment, I thought about taking a drink from it myself, so she might think it was there for me. But in her eyes I could see she knew exactly what was going on. She didn't move for a long moment and then her eyes came up to mine and held for a moment. She then took a step back and closed the door. I looked back at Cross.

"If she didn't know she knows now."

"I don't care. What time is it, Harry? I can't see the screen too good."

I looked up at the corner of the television screen where CNN always carried the time.

"It's eleven-eighteen. Who came out to see you, Law? I want to know who is working the case."

"I'm telling you, Harry, nobody came. As far as I knew, the case was deader than these goddamn legs of mine."

"Then what was it you didn't tell me when I was here before?"

His eyes went to the flask and he didn't have to ask. I held it to his chapped and peeling lips and he drank deeply from it. He closed his eyes.

"Ah, God . . . ," he said. "I've got . . ."

His eyes opened and they jumped on me like wolves taking down a deer.

"She's keeping me alive," he whispered desperately. "You think this is what I want? Sitting in my own shit half the time? She's getting a full ride while I'm alive — full pay and medical. If I'm gone she gets the widow's pension. And I wasn't in that long, Harry. Fourteen years. It's about half of what she gets with me alive."

I looked at him for a long moment, the whole time wondering if she was outside the door listening.

"So what do you want from me, Law? To pull the plug? I can't do that. I can get you a lawyer if you want, but I'm not —"

"And she doesn't treat me right, either."

I paused again. I felt a tugging sensation in the pit of my guts. If what he was saying was true, then his life was more of a hell than I could imagine. I lowered my voice when I spoke.

"What does she do to you, Law?"

"She gets mad. She does things. I don't want to talk about it. It's not her fault."

"Listen, you want me to get a lawyer in here? I could also get a social services investigator."

"No, no lawyers. That'll take forever. No investigators. I don't want that. And I don't want you to get in any trouble, Harry, but what am I going to do? If I could pull the plug myself I would . . ."

He blew out a burst of air. The only gesture his body would allow him to make. I could only imagine his horrible frustration.

"This is no way to live, Harry. It isn't living."

I nodded. None of this had come up on the first visit. We had talked about the case, what he could remember about it. His case memory was coming back in chunks. It had been a difficult interview but there was no sense of self-loathing or desperation. No more depression than would be expected. I wondered if it had been the alcohol that had suddenly brought it out.

"I'm sorry, Law."

It was all I could say. His eyes looked away, up to the television screen which was over my left shoulder.

"What time is it now, Harry?"

This time I checked my watch.

"Twenty after. What's your hurry, Law? You expecting somebody else?"

"No, no, nothing like that. There's just a show I like to watch on Court TV. Comes on at twelve. Rikki Klieman. I like her."

"Then you've still got time to talk to me. Why don't you get a bigger clock in here?"

"She won't give me one. She says the doctor says it's bad for me to be watching a clock."

"She's probably right."

It was the wrong thing to say. I saw anger flood his eyes and I immediately regretted the words.

"I'm sorry. I shouldn't —"

"You know what it's like not to be able to raise your own goddamn wrist to look at your fucking watch?"

"No, Law, I don't have any idea."

"You know what it's like to shit in a bag and have your wife take it to the toilet? To have to ask her for every goddamn thing, including a taste of whiskey?"

"I'm sorry, Law."

"Yeah, you're sorry. Everybody's fucking sorry but nobody's —"

He didn't finish. He seemed to bite off the end of the sentence like a dog getting a hold of raw meat. He looked away and was silent and I was silent for a long moment, until I thought the anger had drained back down his throat into the seemingly bottomless well of frustration and self-pity that was down there.

"Hey, Law?"

His eyes came back to me.

"What, Harry?"

He was calm. The moment had passed.

"Let's go back. You said you were going to call me because there was something you forgot. You know, when we went over the case before. What was it you forgot to tell me?"

"Nobody's come here and talked to me about the case, Harry. You're the only one. I mean that."

"I believe you. I was wrong about that. But what was it that you forgot before? Why were you going to call me?"

He closed his eyes for a moment but then opened them. They were clear and focused.

"I told you that Taylor insured the money, right?"

"Right, you told me that."

"What I forgot was that the insurance company — offhand I can't remember the name of —"

"Global Underwriters. You remembered the other day."

"Right. Global Underwriters. As a condition of contract Global required that the lender — that was BankLA — scan all the bills."

"Scan the bills? What do you mean?"

"Record the serial numbers."

I remembered the paragraph I had circled on the newspaper clip. It had apparently been true. I started doing the math in my head. Two million divided by a hundred. I almost had it and then lost the number.

"That would be a lot of numbers."

"I know. The bank balked — said it would take four people a week, something like that. So they negotiated and compromised. They sampled. They took ten numbers from every one of the stacks."

I remembered from the *Times* story that the money was delivered in $25,000 bundles. That math I could do. Eighty bundles made $2 million.

"So they took eight hundred numbers. Still a lot."

"Yeah, I remember the printout was like six pages long."

"And what did you do with it?"

"Let me have another taste of that Black Bush, would you?"

I gave it to him. I could tell the flask was just about empty. I needed to get what he had and get out of there. I was getting sucked into his miserable world and I didn't like it.

"Did you put out the numbers?"

"Yeah, we put out the list. Gave it to the feds. And used the robbery guys to get the list out to all the banks in the county. I also sent it to Vegas Metro so they could get it into the casinos."

I nodded, waiting for more.

"But you know how that goes, Harry. A list like that is only good if the people are checking it. Believe it or not, there are a hell of a lot of hundred-dollar bills out there, and if you use them in the right places people don't raise an eyebrow. They aren't going to take the time to run the number down a six-page list. They don't have the time or the inclination."

It was true. Recorded money was most often used as evidence when it was found in the possession of a suspect in a financial crime such as a bank robbery. I could not remember working on or even hearing about a case where marked or recorded money was actually traced by transaction to a suspect.

"You were going to call me back because you forgot to tell me that?"

"No, not just that. There's more. Anything left in that little flask of yours?"

I shook the flask so he could hear that it was almost empty. I gave him what was left and then capped it and put it back in my pocket.

"That's it, Law. Until next time. Finish what you were going to tell me."

His tongue poked out of his horrible hole of a mouth and licked a drop of whiskey from the corner. It was pathetic and I turned away as if to check the time on the television so he didn't have to know I saw it. On the tube was a financial news report. A graph with a red line trending down was on the screen to the side of the anchorman's concerned and puffy face.

I looked back at Cross and waited.

"Well," he said, "about, I don't know, ten months or so into the case, close to a year — this is after me and Jack had moved on and were working other things — Jack got a call from Westwood about the serial numbers. It all came back to me the other day after you left."

I assumed Cross was talking about an FBI agent calling his partner. It was not an uncommon practice within the LAPD for investigators to never refer to FBI agents as FBI agents, as if denying them their title somehow knocked them down a notch or two. There had never been any love lost between the two competing organizations. But the main federal building in Los Angeles was on Wilshire Boulevard in Westwood and it housed the whole sandbox of federal law enforcement. All jurisdictional biases aside, I needed to be sure.

"An FBI agent?" I asked.

"Yeah, an agent. A woman, in fact."

"Okay. What did she tell you guys?"

"She only spoke to Jack, and then Jack told me. The agent said that one of the serial numbers was wrong and Jack said, 'Is that right? How so?' And the agent told him that the list had wound through the building and eventually across her desk and she'd taken the time to scan the numbers into her computer and there was a problem with one of them."

He stopped as if to catch his breath. He licked his lips again and it reminded me of some sort of underwater creature poking out of a crevice.

"I sure wish you had more in that flask, Harry."

"Sorry, I don't. Next time. What was the problem with the number?"

"Well, as far as I remember, this gal, she told Jack that she collects numbers. Know what I mean? Whenever a flier comes across the desk with currency numbers on it, she puts them into her computer, adds them to the data bank. She can run cross-matches, things like that. It was a new program she was working on. She'd been doing it for a few years and had a lot of numbers in the box. Tell you what, I need some water. My throat — too much talking."

"I'll go get Danny."

"No, no, that's not — tell you what, just go to the sink and put some water in that thing you got and I can drink from that. That'll be fine. Don't bother Danny. She's been bothered enough."

In the bathroom I filled the flask halfway with water from the faucet. I shook it and brought it out to him. He took it all. After a few moments he finally continued the story.

"She said one of the numbers on our list was on somebody else's list and that was impossible."

"What do you mean? I'm not tracking this."

"Let me see if I remember this right. She said that one of the hundreds that was on our list had a serial number that belonged to a hundred that was part of a bait packet taken in a bank robbery about six months before our movie set robbery went down."

"Where was the bank robbery?"

"Marina del Rey, I think. I'm not sure about that, though."

"Okay, so what was the problem? Why couldn't the hundred from the earlier bank robbery get recirculated, land back in a bank and then become part of the two million sent to the movie set?"

"That's what I said and Jack told me that it was impossible. He said the agent said the guy who took that bill in Marina del Rey in the first place got caught. He had the bait pack on him and he went to the federal clink and the bill was held as evidence."

I nodded and thought about this, trying to get it right.

"You're saying that she was telling you that it would have been impossible for the hundred on your list to have been part of the movie delivery because at that time that hundred-dollar bill was in evidence lockup in regard to the Marina del Rey bank robbery."

"Exactly. She even went in and checked the evidence to make sure the hundred was still there. It was."

I tried to think about what this could mean, if it meant anything at all.

"What did you and Jack do?"

"Well, not much. There were a lot of numbers — six pages' worth. We figured maybe we just got a bad one. You know, maybe the guy who recorded it all had messed up, transposed a number or whatever. We were running on a new case by then. Jack said he'd make some calls to the bank and Global Underwriters. But I don't know if he did. Then, soon after that, we walked into the shit in that bar and everything else sort of drifted away . . . until I thought about Angella Benton and called you. Things are starting to come back to me now, you know?"

"I understand. Do you remember the agent's name?"

"Sorry, Harry, I don't remember the name. I might've never had it. I didn't talk to her and I don't think Jack even told me."

I was silent while I considered whether this was a lead worth pursuing. I thought about what Kiz Rider had said about the case being worked. Maybe this was the angle. Maybe the people she told me about were FBI agents. While I was working it over, Cross started talking again.

"For what it's worth, I got the idea from Jack that this agent, whoever she was, sort of came up with this thing on her own. It was her own little program she was running. Almost like a hobby. Not on the official computer."

"Okay. Do you remember if you ever got any other hits on the numbers? Before this one?"

"There was one but it didn't go anywhere. It came up pretty soon, in fact."

"What was that?"

"It came up in a bank deposit. I think it was Phoenix. My memory's like Swiss cheese. A lot of holes."

"You remember anything about that one at all?"

"Just that it was a deposit from a cash business. Like a restaurant. Something we weren't going to be able to trace any further back."

"But it was pretty soon after the heist?"

"Yeah, I remember we jumped on it. Jack went out there. But it was a dead end."

"How soon after the heist, can you remember?"

"Maybe a few weeks. I don't know for sure."

I nodded. His memory was coming back but it still wasn't reliable. It served to remind me that without the murder book — the case documentation — I was severely handicapped.

"Okay, Law, thanks. If you remember or think of anything else, have Danny call me. And whether that happens or not I'll be back to see you."

"And you'll bring the . . ."

He didn't finish and didn't need to.

"Yeah, I'll bring it. You sure you don't want me to bring somebody else? Maybe a lawyer that could talk to you about —"

"No, Harry, no lawyers, not yet."

"You want me to talk to Danny?"

"No, Harry, don't talk to her."

"You sure?"

"I'm sure."

I nodded my good-bye and left the room. I wanted to get to my car so I could quickly write some notes about the call Jack Dorsey had gotten from the bureau agent. But when I came from the hallway into the living room Danielle Cross was sitting there waiting for me. She was on the couch and looked at me with accusing eyes. I threw the look right back at her.

"I think it's almost time for a show he wants to watch on Court TV."

"I'll take care of it."

"Okay. I'm leaving now."

"I wish you would not come back."

"Well, I may have to."

"The man is on a delicate balance — mentally and physically. The alcohol upsets it. It takes days for him to recover."

"Looked to me like it improved things for him."

"Then come back tomorrow and have another look."

I nodded. She was right. I spent a half hour with the man, not my life. I waited. I could tell she was working up toward something.

"I assume he told you that he wants to die and that I'm the one keeping him alive. For the money."

I hesitated but then nodded.

"He said I mistreat him."

I nodded again.

"He tells that to everybody that comes visit. All the cops."

"Is it true?"

"The part about wanting to die? Some days. Some days it's not."

"What about the part about being mistreated."

She looked away from me.

"It's frustrating, dealing with him. He's not happy. He takes it out on me. One time I took it out on him. I turned off the television. He started crying like a baby."

She looked up at me.

"That's all I've ever done but it was enough. I hate what I did, what I became in the moment. Everything got the better of me."

I tried to read her eyes, the set of her jaw and mouth. She had her hands together in front of her, the fingers of one hand working the rings on the other set. A nervous gesture. I watched her chin start to quiver and then the tears started to come.

"What am I supposed to do?"

I shook my head. I didn't know. The only thing I knew was that I had to get out of there.

"I don't know, Danny. I don't know what any of us are supposed to do."

It was all I could think of to say. I walked quickly to the front door and left. I felt like a coward walking away and leaving them alone together in that house.

7

Loose lips sink ships. The theory of the case pursued by Cross and Dorsey four years earlier was simple. They believed that Angella Benton had intimate knowledge through her job about the $2 million that was to be delivered to the film location and had set the robbery and her own death in motion by either intentionally or mistakenly talking about the money. Her loose lips planted the seed of the robbery and, consequently, her own demise. Being the inside link to the robbers, she had to be eliminated to cover their tracks. Because she was murdered four days before the robbery, it was believed by the two investigators that her involvement was unintentional. She had somehow furnished the information that led to the robbery and needed to be eliminated before she realized what she had done. She also needed to be eliminated in a way that would not draw suspicion to the impending cash delivery. Thus the psychosexual aspects of the crime scene — the tearing of the clothes and the evidence of masturbation — were in a way simply window dressing on the misdirection.

Conversely, if she had been a willing participant in the robbery scheme, it seemed likely to the investigators that her death would have come after the robbery had been successfully accomplished.

It seemed like a solid theory to me as Lawton Cross had recounted it during my first visit to his home. It was probably the way I would have gone if I had been allowed to stay on the case. But ultimately the theory didn't pay off. Cross told me that he and his partner had worked a full field investigation on Benton but never came across the one clue that opened up the case. They spent five solid months on her. They traced her movements, personal habits and daily-life routines. They studied her credit-card, banking and telephone data. They interviewed and re-interviewed all family members and known friends and associates. They spent eight days in Columbus alone. Dorsey went to Phoenix to chase down a single hundred-dollar bill. They spent so much time at Eidolon Productions that for one month they were given their own office at Archway Pictures in which to conduct interviews.

And they got nothing.

As is often the case with a homicide, they amassed a wealth of knowledge about the victim but not the key piece of information that led to the identity of her killer. They ended up knowing who she had slept with in college but not where she had spent the last evening of her life. They knew her last meal had been Mexican — the corn tortillas and beans were still in her digestive tract — but not which one of the city's thousands of such establishments had served her.

And after six months on the case they found absolutely no link between Angella Benton and the robbery, aside from the surface connection of her job as a production assistant for the company that was making the film in which the cash was to play a starring role.

Six months in and they were at a dead end. What they did have in the way of evidence were the forty-six slugs and shell casings collected after the shoot-out, the blood collected from the getaway van and the semen collected from the murder scene. It was all good evidence to have; ballistics and DNA could tie a suspect to a crime with zero doubt — unless your lawyer was Johnnie Cochran. But it was the kind of evidence that was icing on a cake; the kind that links a suspect and weapon already identified and usually in custody. It didn't do much as far as getting you that suspect. After half a year on it they had the icing but no cake to put it on.

When they reached this dead end it was time to evaluate the case at the six-month mark. This is the point where hard choices are made. The probability of clearing the case is weighed against the need for the pair of investigators to work other cases and help shoulder the caseload of the division. Their supervisor took the case off full-time status and Dorsey and Cross went back into rotation at RHD. They were free to work the Benton case as often and as much as possible, but they also drew new investigations. As could be expected, the Benton case suffered for it. Cross had readily admitted this to me. He said it became a part-time investigation, with Dorsey doing most of the follow-up while Cross concentrated on the new cases they were assigned.

Then it all became academic when the pair got shot up in Nat's bar in Hollywood. The Benton case went into the OU files. Open-Unsolved. And it was orphaned. No detective likes a hand-me-down file, which the Benton case was. No one likes the idea of going into a file and proving his colleagues were wrong or misguided or possibly even incompetent or lazy. Added to this deterrent was the fact that the Benton case was now haunted. Cops are a superstitious species. The fate of the two original investigators — one dead, the other in a chair for life — was somehow inextricably bound to the cases they had worked, whether directly related or not. Nobody, and I mean nobody, was going to take on the Benton case now.

Except me. Now that I was out of the official game.

And four years later, I had to trust that Cross and Dorsey had done their job well in the investigation of Angella Benton's death and its connection to the robbery. I had no choice really. Covering the ground they had already trod to a dead end didn't seem to be the way to go. That was why I went to see Taylor. My plan was to accept their investigation as thorough if not flawless and approach it from a different direction. I was operating on the belief that Cross and Dorsey found nothing linking Benton to the robbery because there was nothing to find. Her death had been part of a plan, a carefully planned misdirection within a misdirection. I now had a list with nine names on it that had come out of my three-mile ride with Taylor. All the people involved in the planning of the money shoot. Everyone — as far as he knew — with knowledge that the cash was coming, when it was coming and who would bring it. I would go from there.

But now I had been thrown a curveball of sorts; what Cross had told me about the serial numbers and how at least one of them had been wrong. He said he had left it to Dorsey to pursue and didn't know what had happened.

Shortly thereafter Dorsey was dead and the case died with him. But now I was interested. It was an anomaly and it had to be dealt with. Coupled with Kiz Rider's warning and oblique reference to "these people," I felt something stirring inside that had been absent for a long time. A small tug toward the darkness I one time knew so well.

8

I drove back into Hollywood and ate a late lunch at Musso's. A Ketel One martini for openers, followed by chicken pot pie, creamed spinach on the side. A good combination, but not good enough to make me forget about Lawton Cross and his situation. I asked for a second martini to help with that and tried to concentrate on other things.

I hadn't been back to Musso's since my retirement party and I missed the place. I had my head down and was reading and writing some notes when I heard a voice in the restaurant that I recognized. I looked up and saw Captain LeValley being led to a table with a man I didn't recognize. She was commander of the Hollywood Division, which was only a few blocks away. Three days after I'd left my badge in a desk drawer and walked out she called to ask me to reconsider. She almost convinced me but I said no. I told her to send in my papers and she did. She didn't come to my retirement party and we hadn't spoken since.

She didn't see me and sat with her back to me in a booth far enough away that I could not hear her conversation. I left by the back way without finishing the second martini. In the lot I paid the attendant and got in my car, a Mercedes Benz ML55 that I'd bought used from a guy moving to Florida. It had been the one big extravagance I allowed myself after retiring. In my mind the ML55 stood for Money Lost: $55,000, because that was what I paid for it. It was one of the fastest sport utility vehicles on the road. But that wasn't really why I bought it. The low mileage on it wasn't the reason either. I bought it because it was black and it blended in. Every fifth car in L.A. was a Mercedes, or so it seemed. And every fifth one of them was a black M-class SUV. I think maybe I knew where I was going long before I started the journey. Eight months before I would need it I'd bought an automobile that would serve me well as a private investigator. It had speed and comfort, it had dark smoked windows, and if you looked in your mirror and saw one of these behind you in L.A. it wouldn't cause a second thought.

The Mercedes took some getting used to. In terms of comfort as well as routine operation and maintenance. In fact, I had already run out of gas on the road twice. It was one of those little things that came with giving up the badge. For several years before my retirement I had been a detective third grade, a supervisory-level position that came with a take-home car. That car was a Ford Crown Victoria, the Police Interceptor model that rode like a tank, had vinyl wash-off seats, heavy-duty suspension and the expanded gas tank. I never needed gas when on the job. And the car was routinely refueled at the station by the guys from the motor pool. As a citizen I had to re-learn to watch the needle. Or else I found myself sitting on the side of the road.

From the center console I retrieved my cell phone and turned it on. I'd had little need for a cell phone but had kept the one I carried on the job. I don't know, maybe I thought somebody from the division would call and ask my advice on a case or something. For four months I kept it charged and turned it on every day. Nobody ever called. After the second time I ran out of gas I plugged it into the charger in the center console and left it there for the next time I would need roadside assistance.

Now I needed assistance but not of the roadside variety. I called information and got the number for the Federal Bureau of Investigation in Los Angeles. I called the number and asked for the supervisory agent in the bank squad. I figured the agent that had contacted Dorsey might have worked in the unit that handled bank robberies. It was the unit that most often dealt with currency numbers.

My call was transferred and picked up by someone who simply said, "Nunez."

"Agent Nunez?"

"Yes, what can I help you with?"

I knew that handling a supervising FBI agent would not be the same as handling the secretary of a movie mogul. I had to be as up-front as I could with Nunez.

"Yes, my name is Harry Bosch. I just retired from the LAPD after about thirty years and I —"

"Good for you," he said curtly. "What can I do for you?"

"Well, that's what I'm trying to tell you. About four years ago I was working a homicide case that was connected to a large cash robbery involving currency that had been recorded."

"What case?"

"Well, you probably won't recognize it by case name but it was the murder of Angella Benton. The murder preceded the robbery, which took place on a movie set in Hollywood. It made a big splash. The bad guys got away with two million dollars. Eight hundred of the hundred-dollar bills had been recorded."

"I remember it. But we did not work it. We had noth—"

"I know that. Like I told you, I worked the case."

"Then go on, what can I do for you?"

"Several months into the case an agent from your office contacted the LAPD to report an anomaly in the recorded numbers. She had received the list of serials because we had sent it all over."

"An anomaly, what is that?"

"An anomaly is a deviation, something that doesn't —"

"I know what the word means. What anomaly are you talking about?"

"Oh, sorry. This agent called and said one of the numbers was a misprint or a couple of the numbers got inverted, something like that. But that's not what I'm calling about. She said she had a computer program that cross-referenced and cross-matched numbers from these sorts of cases. I think it was her own program, something that she worked up on her own. Does any of this ring a bell? Not the case but the agent. An agent who had this program. A female agent."

"Why?"

"Well, because I have misplaced her name. Actually, I never got it because she spoke to one of the other investigators on the case. But I would like to speak to her, if I could."

"Speak to her about what? You said you are retired."

I knew it would come to this, and this is where I was weak. I had no station, no validity. You either had a badge that opened all doors or you didn't. I didn't.

"Some cases die hard, Agent Nunez. I'm still working it. Nobody else is, so I figured I'd take the shot. You know how it is."

"No, actually, I don't. I'm not retired."

A real hard-ass. He was silent after that and I found myself getting angry with this faceless man who was probably trying to balance a burdensome caseload with a lack of manpower and funding. L.A. was the bank robbery capital of the world. Three a day was the norm and the FBI had to respond to every one of them.

"Look, man," I said. "I don't want to waste your time. You can either help me or not. You either know who I am talking about or you don't."

"Yeah, I know who you're talking about."

But then he was silent. I tried one last angle. I had held it back because I wasn't sure I wanted it known in some circles what I was doing. But the visit from Kiz Rider sort of shot that down anyway.

"Look, you want a name, somebody you can check me out with? Call over to Hollywood detectives and ask for the lieutenant. Her name is Billets and she can vouch for me. She won't know anything about this though. As far as she knows, I'm swinging in a hammock."

"All right, I'll do that. Why don't you call me back? Give me ten minutes."

"Right. I will."

I closed the phone and checked my watch. It was almost three. I started the Mercedes and drove down to Sunset and headed east. I turned on the radio but didn't like the fusion that was playing. I turned it back off. At the ten-minute mark I pulled to the curb in front of the Splendid Age Retirement Home. I picked up the phone to call Nunez back and it rang in my hand. I thought maybe Nunez had caller ID on his line and had gotten the number. But then I remembered I had been transferred to his line. I didn't think an ID record could jump with a transfer.

"Harry Bosch."

"Harry, it's Jerry."

Jerry Edgar. It was turning into old home week. First Kiz Rider and now Jerry Edgar.

"Jed, how you doing?"

"I'm fine, man. How's the retiring life?"

"It's very restful."

"You don't sound like you're on the beach, Harry."

He was right. The Splendid Age was just yards from the Hollywood Freeway and the din of gas-combustion machinery was ever present. Quentin McKinzie told me that they house the Splendid Age residents with hearing loss in the rooms on the west side because they are closer to the noise.

"I'm not a beach guy. What's up? Don't tell me that eight months after I'm gone you actually want to ask my advice on something?"

"Nah, it's not that. I just got a call from somebody who was checking you out."

I was immediately embarrassed. My pride had led me to conclude that Edgar needed me on a case.

"Oh. Was it a bureau agent named Nunez?"

"Yeah, he didn't say what it was about, though. You starting a new career or something, Harry?"

"Thinking about it."

"You ever get your private ticket?"

"Yeah, about six months ago, just in case. I stuck it in a drawer somewhere. What did you tell Nunez? I hope you said I was a man of high moral standing and courage."

"Absolutely not. I gave him the straight dope. I said you could trust Harry Bosch about as far as you could throw him."

I could hear the smile in his voice.

"Thanks, man. You're a pal."

"I just thought you should know. You want to tell me what's going on?"

I was silent for a moment as I thought about this. I didn't want to tell Edgar what I was doing. Not that I didn't trust him. I did. But as a rule I operated under the belief that the fewer people who know your business the better.

"Not right now, Jed. I'm late for an appointment and have to get going. But I'll tell you what — you want to catch lunch one of these days? I'll tell you all about my exciting life as a pensioner."

I sort of laughed as I said the last line and I think it worked. He agreed to lunch but said he'd have to call me back about it. I knew from experience it was difficult to schedule a lunch ahead of time when you were working homicide. What would happen was that he would call on the morning he had a lunch free. That was the way it worked. We said we'd stay in touch and ended the call. It was nice to know that he apparently wasn't carrying the same anger as Kiz Rider over my abrupt departure from our partnership and the department.

I called the bureau back and was put through to Nunez.

"You get a chance to make that call?"

"Yeah, but she wasn't there. I talked to your old partner."

"Rider?"

"No, his name was Edgar."

"Oh, yeah. Jerry. How is he doing?"

"I don't know. I didn't ask. I'm sure you did when he just called you."

"Excuse me?"

He had nailed me.

"You can skip the bullshit, Bosch. Edgar told me he felt obligated to call you and let you know someone was checking you out. I said that was fine with me. I asked him for your number so that way I would know I was dealing with the real Harry Bosch. He gave it to me and when I tried to call a couple minutes ago it was busy. I figure you were talking to Edgar, so I don't appreciate your little dumb-guy dance."

My embarrassment over being cornered turned to anger. Maybe it was the vodka in my stomach or the hammering reminder that I was an outsider now, but I was tired of dealing with this guy.

"Man, you are a great investigator," I said into the phone. "A brilliant deductive mind. Tell me, do you ever use it on cases or do you reserve it only for busting the chops of people who are just trying to get something done in the world?"

"I have to be careful about who I give information to. You understand that."

"Yeah, I understand that. I also understand why law enforcement works about as well as the freeways in this town."

"Hey, Bosch, don't go away mad. Just go away."

I shook my head in frustration. I didn't know if I had blown it or if I was never going to get anything from him in the first place.

"So that's your little dance, huh? You call me on my act but you were acting the whole time, too. You never were going to give me the name, were you?"

He didn't answer.

"It's just a name, Nunez. No harm no foul."

Still nothing from the agent.

"Well, I'll tell you what. You've got *my* name and number. And I think you know what agent I am talking about. So go to her and let her decide. Give her my name and number. I don't care what you think about me, Nunez.

You owe it to your fellow agent to give it to her. Just like Edgar. He was obligated. So are you."

That was it. That was my pitch. I waited in the silence, this time deciding not to speak again until Nunez did.

"Look, Bosch, I would tell her you were calling for her. I would have told her before I even talked to Edgar. But obligations only go so far. The agent you were asking about? She's not around anymore."

"What do you mean not around? Where is she?"

Nunez said nothing. I sat up straight, my elbow hitting the wheel, drawing a blast from the horn. Something was in my memory, something about a female agent in the news. I couldn't quite get to it.

"Nunez, is she dead?"

"Bosch, I don't like this. This talking on the phone with somebody I've never met. Why don't you come in and maybe we can talk about this."

"Maybe?"

"Don't worry, we'll talk. When can you come in?"

The dashboard clock said it was five after three. I looked at the front door of the retirement home.

"Four o'clock."

"We'll be here."

I closed the phone and sat there unmoving for a long moment, working at the memory. It was there, just out of reach.

I reopened the phone. I didn't have my phone book with me, and numbers I once knew by heart had washed away in the past eight months like they had been written in sand on the beach. I called information and got the number for the *Times* newsroom. I then was connected to Keisha Russell. She remembered me like I had never left the department. We'd had a good relationship. I fed a number of exclusives to her over the years and she returned the favor by helping me with clip searches and keeping stories in the paper when she could. The Angella Benton case had been one of the times she couldn't.

"Harry Bosch," she said. "How are you?"

I noticed that her Jamaican accent was now almost completely gone. I missed it. I wondered if that was intentional or just the product of living ten years in the so-called melting pot.

"I'm fine. You still on the beat?"

"Of course. Some things never change."

She had once told me that the cop beat was an entry-level position in journalism but that she never wanted to leave it. She thought moving up to cover city hall or elections or almost anything else would be terminally boring compared with writing stories about life and death and crime and consequences. She was good and thorough and accurate. So much so she had been invited to my retirement party. It was a rarity for an outsider of any ilk, especially a journalist, to earn such an invitation.

"Unlike *you,* Harry Bosch. You, I thought, would always be there in Hollywood Division. Almost a year later now and I still can't believe it. You know, I called your number out of habit on a story a few months ago and a strange voice answered and I just had to hang up."

"Who was it?"

"Perkins. They moved him over from autos."

I hadn't kept up. I didn't know who had taken my slot. Perkins was good but not good enough. But I didn't tell Russell that.

"So what's up with you, mon?"

Every now and then she would turn on the accent and

the patter. It was her way of making a transition, getting to the point.

"Sounds like you're busy."

"A bit."

"Then I won't bother you."

"No, no, no. No bother. What can I do for you, Harry? You're not working a case are you? Have you gone private?"

"Nothing like that. I was just curious about something that's all. It can wait. I'll check you later, Keisha."

"Harry, wait!"

"You sure?"

"I am not too busy for an old friend, you know? What are you curious about?"

"I was just wondering, remember a while back there was an FBI agent, a woman, who disappeared? I think it was in the Valley. She was last seen driving home from —"

"Martha Gessler."

The name brought it all back. Now I remembered.

"Yeah, that's it. Whatever happened with her, do you know?"

"As far as I know she's still missing in action, presumed dead probably."

"There hasn't been anything about her lately? I mean, any stories?"

"Nope, because I would've written them and I haven't written about her in, oh, two years at least."

"Two years. Is that when it happened?"

"No, more like three. I think I did a one-year-later story. An update. That was the last time I wrote about her. But thanks for the reminder. It may be time for another look."

"Hey, if you do that, hold off a few days, would you?"

"So you are working on something, Harry."

"Sort of. I don't know if it's related to Martha Gessler or not. But give me till next week, okay?"

"No problem if you come clean and talk to me then."

"Okay, give me a call. Meantime, could you pull the clips on her? I'd like to read what you wrote back then."

I knew they still called it pulling clips even though it was all on computer now and actual newspaper clippings were a thing of the past.

"Sure, I can do that. You have a fax or an e-mail?"

I had neither.

"Maybe you can just mail them to me. Regular mail, I mean."

I heard her laugh.

"Harry, you won't make it as a modern private detective like that. I bet all you have is a trench coat."

"I've got a cell phone."

"Well, that's a start then."

I smiled and gave her my address. She said the clips would go out in the afternoon mail. She asked for my cell number so she could call me the following week and I gave her that, too.

Then I thanked her and closed the phone. I sat there for a moment considering things. I had taken an interest in the Martha Gessler case at the time. I didn't know her but my former wife had. They had worked together in the bureau's bank robbery unit many years before. Her disappearance had held in the news for several days, then the reports were more sporadic and then they just dropped off completely. I had forgotten about her until now.

I felt a burning in my chest and I knew it wasn't the midday martini backing up. I felt like I was closing in on something. Like when a child can't see something in the dark but is sure it is there just the same.

9

I got the instrument case out of the back of the Benz and carried it up the sidewalk to the double doors of the retirement home. I nodded to the woman behind the counter and walked by. She didn't stop me. She knew me by now. I went down the hallway to the right and opened the door to the music room. There was a piano and an organ at the front of the room and a small grouping of chairs lined up for watching performances, but I knew that those were few. Quentin McKinzie was sitting on a seat in the front row. He was slouched and his chin was down, his eyes closed. I gently nudged his shoulder and immediately his face and eyes came up.

"Sorry, I'm late, Sugar Ray."

I think he liked that I called him by his stage name. He had been known professionally as Sugar Ray McK because when he played he would dodge and weave on the stage like Sugar Ray Robinson in the ring.

I pulled a chair out of the front row and brought it around so it faced him. I sat down and put the case on the ground. I flipped up the snaps and opened it, revealing the shining instrument held snug in its maroon velvet lining.

"This has got to be short today," I said. "I've got an appointment at four in Westwood."

"Retired guys don't have appointments," Sugar Ray said, his voice sounding like he grew up just down the street from Louis Armstrong. "Retired guys have all the time in the world."

"Well, I've got something working and I might . . . well, I'm going to try to keep our schedule but the next couple weeks might be tough. I'll call the desk and get a message to you if I can't make the next lesson."

We had been meeting two afternoons a week for six months. I had first seen Sugar Ray play on a hospital ship in the South China Sea. He had been part of the Bob Hope entourage that came to entertain the wounded during Christmastime 1969. Many years later, in fact one of my last cases as a cop, I was working a homicide and came across a stolen saxophone with his name engraved inside the mouth. I tracked him to Splendid Age and returned it. But he was too old to play it anymore. His lungs no longer had the push.

Still, I had done the right thing. It was like returning a lost child to a parent. He invited me to Christmas dinner. We stayed in touch and after I pulled the pin I came back to him with a plan that would save his instrument from gathering dust.

Sugar Ray was a good teacher because he didn't know how to teach. He told me stories and told me how to love the instrument, how to draw from it the sounds of life. Any note I could sound could bring out a memory and a story. I knew I was never going to be any good at playing the sax but I came twice a week to spend an hour with him and hear his stories about jazz and feel the passion he still carried for his deathless art. Somehow it got inside me and came out in my own breath when I held the instrument to my mouth.

I lifted the saxophone out of the case and held it in position, ready to play. We always began each lesson with me trying to play "Lullaby," a song by George Cables that I had first heard on a Frank Morgan disc. It was a slow ballad and easier for me to play. But it was also a beautiful composition. It was sad and steadfast and uplifting all at the same time. The song wasn't even a minute and a half long but to me it said all that ever needed to be said about being alone in the world. Sometimes I believed that if I could learn to play this one song well, then that would be enough for me. I would not be wanting.

Today it felt like a funeral dirge. I thought about Martha Gessler the whole time I played. I remembered her picture in the paper and on the TV at eleven. I remembered my ex-wife talking about how they had been the only two females on the bank robbery squad at one time. They took a constant ration of abuse from the men until they proved themselves by working together and taking down a robber known as the Two Step Bandit because he always did a little dance as he left a bank with the loot.

As I played, Sugar Ray watched my finger work and nodded approvingly. Halfway through the ballad he closed his eyes and just listened, nodding his head with the beats. It was a high compliment. When I finished the piece he opened his eyes and smiled.

"Gettin' there," he said.

I nodded.

"You still got to get the smoke out of your lungs. Get your capacity up."

I nodded again. I hadn't had a cigarette in more than a year, but I had spent most of my life as a two-pack-a-day man and the damage was done. Sometimes putting air into the instrument was like pushing a boulder up a hill.

We talked and I played for another fifteen minutes, taking a hopeless shot at "Soul Eyes," the Coltrane standard, and then working the bridge of Sugar Ray's own signature song, "The Sweet Spot." It was a complicated riff but I had been working on it at home because I wanted to please the old man.

At the end of the abbreviated lesson I thanked Sugar Ray and asked if he needed anything.

"Just music," he said.

He answered that way every time I asked. I put the instrument back into the case — he always insisted I keep it with me for practicing — and left him there in the music room.

As I was heading back down the hallway to the main entrance a woman named Melissa Royal was approaching from the other way. I smiled.

"Melissa."

"Hi, Harry, how was the lesson?"

She was there to see her mother, an Alzheimer's victim who never knew who she was. We had met at the Christmas dinner and then had run into each other during our separate visits. She started timing her visits to her mother with my three o'clock lessons. She didn't tell me this but I knew. We had coffee a few times and then I asked her out to hear some jazz at the Catalina. She said she had fun but I knew she didn't know or care much about the music. She was just lonely and looking for someone. That was okay with me. We're all that way.

That was how it stood. Each of us waiting for the other to make the next move, though her showing up when she knew I was scheduled to be there was a move in some way. But seeing her now was a problem. I had to get rolling if I was going to make it to Westwood on time.

"Gettin' there," I said. "At least that's what my teacher tells me."

She smiled.

"Great. Someday you're going to have to perform for us here."

"Believe me, that day is a long way off."

She nodded good-naturedly and waited. My turn now. She was in her early forties, divorced like me. She had light brown hair with lighter streaks in it that she told me she had added in the beauty shop. Her smile was the thing, though. It took over her whole face and was infectious. I could tell that being with her would mean working night and day to keep that smile going. And I didn't know if I could do it.

"How's your mother doing?"

"I'm about to go find out. Are you leaving? I thought maybe I could check in with her and we could get some coffee in the cafeteria."

I put a pained look on my face and checked my watch.

"I can't. I have to be in Westwood at four."

She nodded like she understood. But I could see in her eyes that she was taking it as a rejection.

"Well, don't let me hold you up. You'll probably be late as it is."

"Yeah, I should go."

But I didn't. I stood looking at her.

"What?" she finally asked.

"I don't know. I'm kind of involved in this case at the moment but I was trying to think of when we could get together."

Suspicion entered her eyes and she gestured toward the saxophone case in my hand.

"You told me you were retired."

"I am. I'm kind of working this on the side. Freelance, you could say. That's where I have to go now, to go talk to an investigator at the FBI."

"Oh. Well, go. Be careful."

"I will. So can we get together maybe one night next week or something?"

"Sure, Harry. I'd like that."

"Okay, good. I want to, Melissa."

I nodded and she nodded and then she made a move toward me and came up on her toes. She put one hand on my shoulder and kissed me on the cheek. Then she continued down the hallway. I turned and watched her go.

I walked out of that place wondering what I was doing. I was holding out hope of something to that woman that I knew deep down I could not deliver. It was a mistake that was born of good intentions but that would ultimately hurt her. As I got into the Mercedes I told myself I had to end it before it started. Next time I saw her I would have to tell her I was not the man she was looking for. I couldn't keep that smile on her face.

10

It was 4:15 by the time I got to the federal building in Westwood. As I was heading through the parking lot toward the security entrance my cell phone rang. It was Keisha Russell.

"Hey, Harry Bosch," she said. "Wanted to let you know, I printed out everything and put it in the mail. But I was wrong about something."

"What was that?"

"There was an update on the case. It ran a couple months ago. I was on vacation. You stick around here long enough and they give you four weeks paid vacation. I took it all at once and went to London. While I was gone it was the third anniversary of Martha Gessler's disappearance. People were poaching on my beat right and left, I tell you. David Ferrell did an update. Nothing new, though. She's still in the wind."

"In the wind? That suggests you — or the bureau — think she's still alive. Before, you said she was presumed dead."

"Just an expression, mon. I don't think anybody's holding their breath for her, if you know what I mean."

"Yeah. Did you put that update in the clips you're sending me?"

"It's all there. And you remember who sent it. Ferrell's a nice guy but I don't want you calling him if something you're doing breaks big."

"Never happen, Keisha."

"I know you are up to something. I did my homework on you."

That made me pause as I was halfway across the building's front plaza. If she had called the bureau and spoken to Nunez, the agent wasn't going to be happy about me involving a nosy reporter.

"What do you mean?" I asked calmly. "What did you do?"

"I did more than just check the clips. I called Sacramento. The state licensing board. I found out that you applied for and received a private investigator's license."

"Yeah, so? Every cop who retires does that. It's part of the process of letting go of the badge. You think, *Oh, well, I'll just get a PI ticket and keep on catching the bad guys.* My ticket is in a drawer in my house, Keisha. I'm not in business and I'm not working for anybody."

"Okay, Harry, okay."

"Thanks for the clips. I've gotta go."

"Bye, Harry."

I closed the phone and smiled. I liked sparring with her. Ten years covering cops and she seemed no more cynical than the first day I talked to her. That was amazing for a journalist, even more so for a black journalist.

I looked up at the building. It was a concrete monolith that eclipsed the sun from the angle I had. I was thirty feet from the entrance. But I walked over to a row of benches to the right of the entranceway and sat down. I checked my watch and saw that I was very late for my appointment with Nunez. The trouble was I didn't know what I was walking into up there and that made me reluctant to go through the doors. The federals always had a way of putting you off balance, of making it clear that it was their world and you were only an invited visitor. I assumed that now without a badge I would be treated more like an uninvited visitor.

I opened the phone back up and called the general number for Parker Center, one of the few numbers I still remembered. I asked for Kiz Rider in the chief's office and was transferred. She picked up immediately.

"Kiz, it's me, Harry."

"Hello, Harry."

I tried to read something in her tone but she had flatlined her response. I couldn't tell how much of the morning's anger and animosity remained.

"How are you doing? You feeling any . . . uh, better?"

"Did you get my message, Harry?"

"Message? No, what did it say?"

"I called your house a little while ago. I apologized. I shouldn't have let personal feelings get mixed in with the reason I had come out there. I'm sorry."

"Hey, it's okay, Kiz. I apologize, too."

"Really? For what?"

"I don't know. For the way I left, I guess. You and Edgar didn't deserve that. Especially you. I should have talked about it with you guys. That's what partners do. I guess I wasn't a very good partner at that moment."

"Don't worry about it. That's what I said on the message. Water under the bridge. Let's just be friends now."

"I'd like to. But . . ."

I waited for her to pick up the invitation.

"But what, Harry?"

"Well, I don't know how friendly you'll want to be after this because I've got to ask you a question and you're probably not going to like it."

She groaned into the phone so loud that I had to hold it away from my ear.

"Harry, you're killing me. What is it?"

"I'm sitting outside the federal building in Westwood. I'm supposed to go in and see some guy named Nunez. A bureau man. And something's not feeling right about this. So I was wondering, are these the people you warned me were working the Angella Benton case? A guy named Nunez? Is it connected to Martha Gessler, the agent who disappeared a few years ago?"

There was a long silence on the phone. Too long.

"Kiz?"

"I'm here. Look, Harry, it's just like I told you at your house. I can't talk to you about the case. All I can tell you is what I *did* tell you. It is open and active and you should stay away from it."

Now it was my turn not to respond. She was like a complete stranger. Less than a year earlier I would have gone into combat with her and trusted her to take my back while I took hers. Now I wasn't sure I could trust her to tell me if the sun was out, unless she cleared it first with the sixth floor.

"Harry, you there?"

"Yeah, I'm here. I'm just kind of speechless, Kiz. I thought if there was somebody in the department who would always level with me, it was going to be you. That's all."

"Look, Harry, have you done anything illegal while running this little freelance operation of yours?"

"No, but thanks for asking."

"Then you have nothing to worry about with Nunez. Go in and see what they want. I don't know anything about Martha Gessler. And that's all I can tell you."

"Okay, Kiz, thanks," I said, putting my voice on a flat line now. "You take care of yourself up there on the sixth floor. And I'll talk to you later."

Before she could throw in the last word I closed the phone. I got up from the bench and headed to the building's entrance. Inside, I had to go through a metal detector, take off my shoes and spread my arms wide for a search with the magic wand. I could barely understand the man with the wand when he told me to raise my arms. He looked more like a terrorist than I did, but I didn't protest. You have to pick your battles. Finally, I got to the elevator and took it to the twelfth floor, which was really the thirteenth since the elevator didn't count the lobby. I stepped into a waiting area where there was a large glass and presumably bullet-proof window separating the public area from the bureau's inner sanctum. I said my name and who I wanted to see into a microphone and the woman on the other side of the glass told me to have a seat.

Instead I walked over to the window and looked down at the veterans cemetery across Wilshire Boulevard. I recalled that I was in the exact same position more than twelve years earlier when I first met the woman who would later become my wife, ex-wife and lasting infatuation.

I turned away from the window and sat down on the plastic couch. There was a magazine with Brenda Barstow's photo on its cover on a beat-up coffee table. Under the picture the caption read "Brenda, America's Sweetheart."

I was reaching for the magazine when the door to the interior offices opened and a man with a white shirt and tie stepped out.

"Mr. Bosch?"

I stood up and nodded. He reached his right hand forward while he used the left to keep the security door from closing and locking.

"Ken Nunez, thanks for coming in."

The handshake was quick and then Nunez turned and led the way inside. He said nothing as he walked. He wasn't what I had expected. On the phone he had sounded like a tired veteran who had seen it all twice. But he was young, just a year or two past thirty. And he didn't really walk down the hallway. He strode. He was a young go-getter, still out to prove something to himself and others. I wasn't sure which — old or new agent — I would have preferred.

He opened a door on the left and stepped back to allow me in. When I saw that the door opened outward and that there was a peephole I knew I was going into an interrogation room. And I knew then that this was not going to be a polite little meet-and-greet. More likely, I was about to get my ass kicked — federal style.

11

As I made the turn into the doorway I saw a square table positioned in the middle of the interrogation room. Sitting at the table, his back to me, was a man wearing a black shirt and jeans. He had close-cropped blond hair. As I entered I looked over his heavily muscled shoulder and saw he was reading an open investigative file. He closed it and looked up as I moved around the table to the other chair, opposite him.

It was Roy Lindell. He smiled at my reaction.

"Harry Bosch," he said. "Long time no see there, *podjo*."

I paused for a moment but then pulled the chair out and sat down. Meantime, Nunez closed the door, leaving me alone with Lindell.

Roy Lindell was about forty now. The heavy muscles I remembered were still in place, pressing his shirt to its boundaries. He still had the Las Vegas tan and the bleached teeth to go with it. I had first met him on a case that took me to Vegas and right into the middle of an undercover FBI operation. Forced to work together, we had managed to put aside jurisdictional and agency animosities to a certain extent and we closed the case, the bureau taking all the credit of course. That had been six or seven years earlier. I ran into him on a case in L.A. once after that, but we never stayed in touch. Not because the bureau had thieved the credit on that first case. Because cops and feds just don't mix.

"Almost didn't recognize you without the ponytail, Roy."

He stuck his big hand across the table and I slowly reached out and shook it. He had the confident demeanor that big men often have. And he had the rascal's smile that often comes with it. The ponytail line had been a crack. When I first met him — and before I knew his status as an undercover agent — I took the liberty of cutting the tail off the back of his head with a penknife.

"How you been? You told Nunez you're retired, huh? I hadn't heard about that."

I nodded but otherwise didn't respond. This was his play. I wanted to let him make all the first moves.

"So what's it like being retired from the force?"

"I'm not complaining."

"We ran a check. You're a licensed private eye now, huh?"

Big day in Sacramento.

"Yeah, I got a license. For the hell of it."

I almost gave him the same story I gave Keisha Russell about it being part of the letting-go process but decided not to bother.

"Must be nice to have a little business, make your own hours, work for whoever you want to work for."

That was enough for me as far as preliminaries went.

"Tell you what, let's not talk about me, Roy. Let's get to the point. What am I doing here?"

Lindell nodded as if to say fair enough.

"Well, what happened is that you called up and asked

about an agent who used to work here, and doing that sort of raised a bunch of flags for us."

"Martha Gessler."

"That's right. Marty Gessler. So you knew who you were calling about when you told Nunez you didn't know who you were calling about?"

I shook my head.

"No. I put it together off his reaction. I remembered a female agent who went missing without a trace. Took me a while, then I remembered her name. What's the latest with her? Gone but not forgotten, I suppose."

Lindell leaned forward and brought his massive arms together over the closed file. His wrists were as thick as the legs of the table. I remembered the struggle I had putting cuffs on them. Back in Vegas when he was under and I still didn't know it.

"Harry, I consider us to be like old friends. We haven't talked in a while but we've sort of been through a battle or two together so I don't want to jerk you around too bad here. But the way this is going to work is that I'm going to ask you the questions. That okay?"

"To a point."

"We're talking about a missing agent here. A female."

"And you're not fucking around."

Paraphrasing the warning from Kiz Rider. Lindell didn't seem to appreciate it.

"Let's start with the reason you called," he said. "What are you up to?"

I waited for a long moment, trying to work out how I should handle this. I wasn't working for anybody other than myself. There was no confidentiality agreement. But I had always been resistant to bending over for the imperialist forces of the FBI. It had been part of the inbred

LAPD culture. It wasn't going to change now. I respected Lindell — like he said, we had been in the trenches together and I knew he ultimately would deal fairly with me. But the agency he worked for liked to play with a marked deck. I had to be careful. I had to remember that.

"I told Nunez what I was doing when I called. I'm just checking out a case that I worked a few years back and that has always sort of stuck with me. There a problem with that?"

"Who's your client?"

"I don't have one. I got the private license right after I pulled the pin to keep my options open. But I started looking into this thing for myself."

He didn't believe me. I could read it in his eyes.

"But this movie caper thing wasn't even your case."

"It was. For about four days. Then I got pulled. But I still remember the girl. The victim. I didn't think anybody cared anymore so I started poking around."

"So who told you to call the bureau?"

"Nobody."

"You just thought it up on your own."

"Not exactly. But you asked me who told me to call. Nobody told me to call. I did it all on my own, Roy. I learned about the call Gessler made to one of the detectives on the case. This was information that was new to me and I'm not sure it was ever followed up. It may have sort of fallen through the cracks. So I made a call to check it out. I didn't have a name at the time. I talked to Nunez and here I am."

"How do you know that Gessler called one of the detectives on the case?"

It seemed to me that the answer would be obvious. It also would mean nothing to Lawton Cross if I told Lindell about something that he freely had told me and that was probably part of the official investigative file.

"I was told about your agent's call by Lawton Cross. He was one of the Robbery-Homicide guys who took the case from me once it blew up big. He told me his partner, Jack Dorsey, was the one who got the call from your agent."

Lindell was writing the names down on a piece of paper he had pulled out of the file. I continued.

"This was well into the case when Gessler called him up. Months. Cross and Dorsey weren't even working it full-time at that point. And it didn't sound like they were too impressed with whatever it was Gessler had to say."

"You talk to Dorsey about this?"

"No, Roy. Dorsey's dead. Killed in a robbery in a bar in Hollywood. Cross was hit, too. He's in a wheelchair with tubes in his arms and up his nose."

"When was this?"

"About three years ago. It was big news."

Lindell's eyes showed his mind working. He was doing the math, checking dates. It reminded me that I had to put together a timeline for the case. It was getting too unwieldy.

"What's the prevailing theory on Gessler? Dead or alive?"

Lindell looked down at the file on the table and shook his head.

"I can't answer that, Harry. You are not a cop, you have no standing. You're just some guy who can't let go of his badge and gun, out there running around like a loose cannon. I can't bring you into this."

"Fine. Answer me one question then. And don't worry. It won't be giving anything away."

He shrugged his shoulders. His answer would depend on the question.

"Was my call today the first connection you've come across between the movie money thing and Gessler?"

Lindell shrugged again and it seemed he was surprised by the question. It was as if he had been expecting something a little tougher.

"I'm not even saying there is a connection, you understand?" he said. "But yes, this is the first time this came up. And that's exactly why I want you to back off and let us check it out. Just leave it to us, Harry."

"Yeah, I've heard that before. I think it was the FBI who said it to me, too."

Lindell nodded.

"Don't put us on a collision course. You'll regret it."

Before I could come up with an answer he stood up. He reached into one of his pockets and pulled out a package of cigarettes and a yellow plastic lighter.

"I'm going to go down and have a smoke," he said. "That will give you a few minutes to think about things and remember anything else you forgot to tell me."

I was about to take another verbal shot at him when I noticed that he was turning around and leaving without the file. It was left there on the table and I instinctively knew he was doing this on purpose. He wanted me to see the file.

I realized then that we were being taped. What he had been saying to me was for a record of some sort or perhaps a supervisor listening in. What he was allowing me to do was something different.

"Take your time," I said. "It's a lot to think about."

"Fuckin' federal building. I have to go all the way downstairs."

As he opened the door he looked back at me and gave me the wink. The moment the door was closed I slid the file across the table and opened it.

12

The file was marked with Martha Gessler's name on the tab. I took out my notebook and wrote that down at the top of a fresh page before opening the inch-thick file folder and seeing what Lindell had left me. I figured I had maybe fifteen minutes tops to look through the file.

On top of the documents stacked in the file was a single page with nothing on it but a phone number. I figured this was left specifically for me so I folded it and put it in my pocket. The rest of the file was a collection of investigative reports, most of which had Lindell's name and signature on them. It listed him as working for the OPR. I knew that was the Office of Professional Responsibility, the bureau's version of Internal Affairs.

The file contained the reports detailing the investigation into Special Agent Martha Gessler's disappearance without a trace on March 19, 2000. This date was immediately significant to me because I knew Angella Benton was murdered the night of May 16, 1999. This put Gessler's disappearance roughly ten months later, about the same time that Cross said the agent had called Dorsey about the currency number.

According to the investigative file, Gessler was working as a crime analyst, not a field agent, at the time of her disappearance. She had long since transferred from the bank robbery unit where she had known my wife and into a cyber unit. She worked Internet investigations and was developing computer programs for tracking criminal patterns. I assumed the program Cross told me about was something that came out of this assignment.

On the evening of March 19, 2000, Gessler left work in Westwood after a long day. Fellow agents remembered her being in the office until at least 8:30 P.M. But she apparently never made it to her home in Sherman Oaks. She was unmarried. Her disappearance was not discovered until the next day, when she did not show up for work and did not answer phone calls or pages. A fellow agent went to her home to check on her and discovered her missing. He found her home partially ransacked but later determined her two dogs, crazed with hunger and inattention, had spent the night tearing the place apart. I noticed in the incident report that the fellow agent who made this discovery happened to be Roy Lindell. I wasn't sure if this meant anything. Possibly as an agent assigned to the OPR he would be sent to check on a fellow agent's well-being. Nevertheless, I wrote his name under hers in my notebook.

Gessler's personal car, a 1998 Ford Taurus, was not found at the house. Eight days later it was located in a long-term parking lot at LAX. The key was left on top of one of the rear tires. The rear bumper showed an eighteen-inch surface scratch and a broken taillight, damages acquaintances of the agent said were new. Again, Lindell was listed in the reports as one of these acquaintances.

The trunk of the car was empty and the interior offered no immediate clues as to where Gessler was or what had happened. The briefcase containing her laptop computer that she was known to have left the office with was gone as well.

Forensic analysis of the entire car found no evidence of foul play. No record of Gessler taking any flight from LAX was ever found. Agents checked flights at Burbank, Long Beach, Ontario and Orange County airports and also found no flight with her name on the passenger list.

Gessler was known to carry an ATM card, two gas credit cards as well as American Express and Visa cards. On the night of her disappearance she used the Chevron card to buy gas and a Diet Coke at a station on Sepulveda Boulevard near the Getty Museum. The receipt indicated she purchased 12.4 gallons of midgrade unleaded gasoline at 8:53 P.M. Her car's tank held a maximum of 16 gallons.

The purchase was significant because it placed Gessler in the Sepulveda Pass — her normal route home from Westwood to Sherman Oaks — at a time that coordinated with her leaving the bureau offices in Westwood. The night-shift cashier at the Chevron also identified Gessler from a photo lineup as a regular customer who had bought gas on the night of March 19. Gessler was an attractive woman. He knew and remembered her. He had told her she didn't need to drink Diet Coke and she seemed pleased by the compliment.

This confirmed sighting was important for several reasons. First, if Gessler was going from Westwood to LAX, where her car was later found, it was unlikely that she would have traveled north into the Sepulveda Pass to buy gas. The airport was southwest of the bureau office. The service station was directly to the north.

The next significance was that Gessler's Chevron card was used a second time the same night at a Chevron service station off Highway 114 in the north county. The card was used at point of purchase to buy 29.1 gallons of gasoline, more than Gessler's and most other cars could hold. Highway 114 was the main route to the desert areas of the northeast county. It was also a major trucking route.

Last but not least in terms of significance was the fact that none of Gessler's credit cards were ever found or used again.

There was no summary or conclusion in the reports I scanned. This would be something the investigator — Lindell — would draw for himself and keep to himself. You don't write a report concluding that your fellow agent is dead. You don't say the obvious and you always speak about the missing agent in the present tense.

But it was clear to me from what I had read what the conclusion had to be. Sometime after Gessler pumped gas into her car in the Sepulveda Pass she was stopped and abducted and it didn't look like she was coming back. She had probably been rear-ended. She then pulled to the side of the road to check damage and possibly to exchange insurance information with the other driver.

What happened next was unknown. But she was likely abducted by force and her car was dumped at the LAX lot — a move that probably guaranteed it would not be located for several days, thereby allowing the trail to go cold and the memories of potential witnesses to fade.

The second gas purchase was the curiosity. Was it a mistake, a clue pointing to the direction of the agent's abductors? Or was it misdirection, an intentional move by the abductors to point the investigation the wrong way? And the amount of gasoline purchased raised a whole other question. What kind of vehicle were they looking for? A tow truck? A pickup? A moving van?

Bureau agents descended on the station but there were no exterior video cameras and no credible witnesses to the use of the credit card because it had been a pay-at-the-pump purchase. It was the last blip on the radar screen, but nothing more than that.

Nevertheless, an agent was still missing. There was no choice. The file contained the short summaries of three days of aerial searches over the desert of the northeast county. It was a needle-in-the-haystack operation but it had to be done. It proved fruitless.

Agents also spent several days on the likely routes that Gessler would have taken through the Sepulveda Pass on her way home. The Pass cut through the Santa Monica Mountains. While the south slope offered few choices besides the 405 Freeway and Sepulveda Boulevard, the northern slope offered a network of shortcuts pioneered over fifty years of rush hours. Agents traveled all of these roads looking for witnesses to an accident involving a blue Ford Taurus, an accident scene that might have seemed routine but was actually the abduction of a federal agent.

They got nothing.

The Sepulveda Pass had been the location of similar crimes in the past. The son of popular entertainer Bill Cosby had been robbed and murdered on the dark side of the road one night just a few years before. And over the last decade a handful of women had been abducted and raped, one of them stabbed to death, after pulling off the road when their vehicles were rear-ended or became disabled. These incidents were not thought to be the work of one person. But rather that the Pass, with its hillsides, dark, winding roads and anonymity, was a place that drew predators. Like lions keeping watch on a water hole, the human predators would not need to wait long in the Sepulveda Pass. The cut through the mountains was one of the busiest traffic corridors in the world.

It was possible Gessler was the victim of a random crime, the very thing she sought to categorize and make sense of in her job. She could have drawn a predator at the service station, maybe opening her purse too wide when she pulled out her credit card. Maybe drawing a tail for some other unknown reason. She was an attractive woman. If a service station attendant had noticed it and acted on it in a subtle way, a predator could have just as likely seen what he needed in her as well.

Still, the team of agents initially assigned to the case had doubts about Gessler falling into the profile of prior victims in the Pass. Gessler's car advertised no personal riches. And she would have been a formidable opponent. She was a highly trained federal agent after all. She was also tall, standing almost six feet tall and weighing a hundred and forty pounds. She worked out regularly at the L.A. Fitness Club on Sepulveda and had been taking Tai-Bo training for several years. Her charts at the club showed she had four percent body fat. She was mostly muscle and she knew how to use it.

Gessler was also known to wear her service weapon while off duty. On the night she disappeared she had been wearing black slacks and blazer with a white blouse. Her pistol, a Smith & Wesson 9mm, was holstered on her right hip. The service station attendant recalled seeing the weapon because Gessler was not wearing her blazer when she put gas in her car at the self-pump station. The blazer was later found on a hanger hooked above the rear driver's side window in the Taurus.

All of this meant that when Gessler's car was rear-ended somewhere in the Pass that night, she got out of the car with a weapon clearly showing on her hip. She got out of that car a woman who was competent and confident in her physical skills. It was a combination that would have likely been a high deterrent to attack, that would seemingly convince any predator to find another victim.

So while the bureau never gave an inch on the possibility that Gessler was the randomly chosen victim of a crime, Lindell headed a parallel investigation into the possibility that Gessler had been specifically targeted because of her job as an FBI agent.

The reports on this branch of the investigation accounted for more than half of the documents in the file in front of me. Though I could tell that I did not have the complete investigative file, it was clear that agents on the case left no stone uncovered in seeking a possible link to Gessler's disappearance. Cases ranging back to Gessler's first years in the Los Angeles field office were examined for potential links to the investigation. Partners and colleagues from all her years in the bureau were questioned about potential enemies and threats she might have received. Among these reports was a summary of an interview with former agent Eleanor Wish, my former wife, conducted in Las Vegas. She had not spoken with Gessler in nearly ten years before the disappearance. She had no recollection of any threats or anything else that might help in the investigation.

Every criminal Gessler ever put in jail or testified against was run down and checked. Most were cleared through alibis. None surfaced as a prime suspect.

According to the reports, Gessler had become the go-to agent in the L.A. field office for any and all requests for computer-related searches and investigations. It was to be expected in a giant bureaucracy like the FBI. Most requests by L.A. agents for computer-based expertise would be shipped to bureau offices in Washington and Quantico, sometimes taking days before being approved and then weeks before any results were shipped back. But Gessler was part of a growing breed of agents with high computer skills who liked to do things for herself. The special agent in charge of the L.A. office became aware of this and, consequently, Gessler was taken off the street, where she had worked for several years in the bank robbery unit. She was placed in a newly formed computer unit, where she handled requests from street agents while developing her own computer programs.

This meant Gessler had her finger in a lot of investigative pies at the time she disappeared. I checked my watch and quickly skimmed through dozens of reports detailing work she had done on different cases in just the month before her disappearance. Lindell and other agents working for him backtracked on these jobs, looking for anything that was a clue to why Gessler had disappeared. The closest it appeared they came to finding something was when they reviewed Gessler's work on an investigation of an escort service that advertised women for hire on a website. Gessler's work was part of the organized crime unit's investigation into the eastern mob's ties to prostitution in Los Angeles.

According to what I read, Gessler was able to find Internet connections between websites advertising women in more than a dozen cities. Women were being moved from city to city and client to client. Money generated by the escort services flowed to Florida and then to New York. Seven weeks before Gessler disappeared a grand jury indicted nine men under the federal Racketeering Influenced and Corrupt Organization Act. Exactly one week before her disappearance, Gessler testified about her part in the investigation during a pretrial hearing in the case. Her testimony was described as effective and it was assumed she would testify when the case went to trial. She was not, however, a key witness. Her testimony was seemingly part of the linkage between the websites and the defendants. The key witness was one of the members of the ring who had cut a deal with prosecutors to escape a stiff sentence.

The possibility that Gessler was targeted because she was a witness was a long shot but it seemed to be the best thing going. Lindell worked it hard, judging by the number of reports and the details they contained. But apparently nothing came of it. The last report in the file pertaining to the RICO case described this branch of the investigation as "open and active but without substantive leads at this time." I recognized it as bureauspeak meaning this path of investigation had hit a dead end.

I closed the file and checked my watch again. Lindell had been gone seventeen minutes. There was nothing in the file about Gessler filing a report or notifying a supervisor or colleague that she had run a computer cross-reference check on the currency numbers contained on the flier put out by Cross and Dorsey. Nothing that said she had gotten a hit and had called the LAPD to report that one of the numbers on the currency report was bad.

After putting away my notebook I stood up and stretched my back and paced a little bit in the small room. I checked the door and found it unlocked. That was good. They weren't holding me like a suspect. At least, not yet.

After a few more minutes I got tired of waiting and stepped out into the hallway. I looked both ways and saw no one, not even Nunez. I went back into the room and picked up the file and then started walking out the way I had come in. I got all the way to the front waiting room without anyone stopping me or asking where I was going. I nodded to the receptionist through the glass and took the elevator down.

13

Roy Lindell was sitting on the same bench I had used before entering the building. There were three cigarettes crushed on the pavement between his feet. A fourth was between his fingers.

"You took your sweet-ass time," he said.

I sat down next to him and put the file between us.

"Putting you in the OPR — isn't that like putting the fox in charge of the henhouse?"

I was thinking about the case I had met him on six years before. I'd had no clue he was law enforcement. This was mostly because he was running a strip club in Vegas and bedding the strippers two and three at a time. His front was so convincing that even after I learned he was an undercover I entertained the idea that he had crossed over. Eventually and completely, I was convinced otherwise.

"Once a smart-ass always a smart-ass, eh, Bosch?"

"Something like that, I guess. So who was listening to our little conversation up there?"

"I was told to tape it. That the tape would be forwarded."

"To who?"

He didn't say anything. It was like he was still deciding something.

"Come on, Roy, you want to give me a clue about what's going on? I looked through your file. It's pretty thin, not much that helps me."

"That's just the highlights — stuff I kept in a backup file. The real file used to fill a whole drawer."

"Used to?"

Lindell looked around as if realizing for the first time he was sitting outside a building that housed more agents and spooks than anywhere west of Chicago. He looked down at the file lying there between us for the world to see.

"I don't like sitting out here. Where's your car? Let's take a ride."

We walked out into the parking lot without talking. But seeing Lindell acting the way he was unnerved me and made me think again about Kiz Rider's warning about some sort of higher authority being involved in the case. Once we got inside the Benz, I put the file on the backseat and keyed the engine. I asked him where he wanted to go.

"I don't care, just drive."

I went west on Wilshire, thinking I'd cut over to San Vicente and cruise through Brentwood. It would be a nice drive on a street lined with trees and joggers, even if the conversation wasn't nice.

"Were you being square on the tape?" Lindell asked. "That's your real story about not working on this for anybody?"

"Yeah, that's the square story."

"Well, you better watch your ass, *podjo*. There are larger forces at work here. People that don't —"

"Fuck around. Yeah, I know. I've been told that but

nobody wants to tell me who this higher authority is and why this connects to Gessler or means anything to the movie money heist four years after it went down."

"Well, I can't tell you because I don't know. All I know is that after you called today I made a few calls myself and the next thing I know the walls came down on me. Hard, man, they came down hard."

"This came out of Washington?"

"No, right here."

"Who, Roy? There's no use in us driving around and talking if you're not talking. What do we have here? Organized Crime? I read the report on Gessler's RICO case. It looked like the only thing you had going on it."

Lindell laughed as though I had suggested something absurd.

"Organized crime. Shit, I wish this was just an OC deal."

I pulled to the side of San Vicente. We were a couple blocks from where Marilyn Monroe had OD'd, one of the city's lasting scandals and mysteries.

"Then what, Roy? I'm tired of talking to myself."

Lindell nodded and then looked over at me.

"Homeland security, baby."

"What do you mean? Somebody thinks there's a terrorist connection to this?"

"I don't know what they think. I wasn't made privy. All I know is that I was told to shut you down, tape it and send it down to the ninth floor."

"The ninth floor . . ."

I said it just to be saying something. I was trying to think. My mind scanned quickly through the images of the case, Angella Benton on the tile, the gunman waving weapons and firing, the impact of one of my shots catching one of them in the body and knocking him — at least I think it was a him — backward into the van. Nothing seemed to fit with what Lindell was telling me.

"The ninth is where they put the REACT squad," Lindell said, pulling me out of the reverie. "They're heavy hitters, Bosch. You walk out in front of them in the street and they won't stop. They won't even tap the brakes."

"What's REACT?"

I knew it had to be another federal acronym. All law enforcement agencies are good for putting together acronyms. But the feds are the best at it.

"Regional Response . . . no, it's Rapid Enforcement Against something Terrorism. I forget the whole thing — oh, I got it, Rapid Response Enforcement And Counterterrorism. That's it."

"That one must've come straight out of the director's office in D.C. That took some thought."

"Funny. Basically, it's a multi-agency gang bang. You've got us, Secret Service, DEA, everybody."

I figured that last "everybody" was a catchall for the agencies that didn't like their initials bandied about. NSA, CIA, DIA and so on through the federal alphabet.

A man on a bike rode by the Benz and slapped the side view mirror hard, making Lindell jump. The biker kept going, keeping his gloved hand up and giving me the finger. I realized I had pulled over in the bike lane and pulled the Benz back out onto the street.

"These fucking bikers think they own the road," Lindell said. "Pull up next to him and I'll give *him* a whack."

Ignoring the request, I sped past the biker, giving him a wide berth.

"I don't get it, Roy. What does the ninth floor have to do with my case?"

"First of all, it's not your case anymore. Secondly, I don't know. They ask me the questions. I don't get to ask them."

"When did they start asking?"

"Today. You call up and ask about Marty Gessler and tell Nunez it has something to do with the movie money case. He comes to me and I tell him to have you come in. Meantime, I start doing some checking. Turns out, we've got the movie money caper listed on our computer. With a REACT flag on it. So I call down to the ninth and say, 'What's up, fellas?' and two seconds later I get crapped on pretty good."

"You were told to find out what I know, then shut me down and send me on my way. Oh, and to tape it so they could listen and make sure you were a good little agent and did what you were told to do."

"Yeah, something like that."

"So why'd you let me read the file? And take it? Why are we driving around talking?"

Lindell took his time before responding. We had made the curve onto Ocean Boulevard in Santa Monica. I pulled off the road again next to the cliffs that look down to the beach and the Pacific. The horizon was blurred white by the marine layer. The Ferris wheel on the Pacific Park pier stood still, and without its neon blazing.

"I did it because Marty Gessler was a friend of mine."

"Yeah, I could sort of tell from the file. Close friends?"

My meaning was obvious.

"Close," he said.

"Wasn't that sort of a conflict, you leading the case?"

"Let's just say my relationship with her was not known until we were down the road a ways on the investigation. I then cashed in every chip I had to stay on it. Not that it did a hell of a lot of good. Here we are three-plus years later and I still have no idea what happened to her. Then you call up and tell me something that was brand-fucking-new to me."

"So you were being square. There was no record of her talking to Dorsey about the currency number?"

"Nothing we found. But she kept a lot of stuff on her computer and that's gone, man. There had to be stuff she hadn't backed up on the office box. You know, the rule is back everything up every night before going home, but nobody does that. Nobody has the time."

I nodded and thought about things. I was gathering a lot of information but had little time to process it. I tried to think about what else I needed to ask Lindell while I was with him.

"I'm still not tracking something," I finally said. "Why was it one way up in the interrogation room and another way out here? Why are you talking to me, Roy? Why let me see the file?"

"REACT is a BAM squad, Bosch. By Any Means. There are no rules with these guys. The rules went out the window September eleventh, two thousand one. The world changed, so did the bureau. The country sat back and let it happen. They were watching the war over there in Afghanistan when they were changing all the rules here. Homeland security is what it's all about now and everything else can take a back-fucking-seat. Including Marty Gessler. You think the ninth floor took over this case because an agent is missing? They couldn't care less. There is something else and whether or not they find out what happened to her doesn't matter. To them, that is. It's not the same for me."

Lindell stared straight ahead as he spoke. I understood a little better what was happening now. The bureau told him to cease and desist. It could keep him in check but I was a free agent. Lindell would help me when and if he could.

"So you've got no idea what their interest is in this case."

"Not a clue."

"But you want me to keep going."

"If you ever repeat it I'll deny it. But the answer is yes. I want to be your client, *podjo.*"

I put the Benz in drive and pulled back onto the roadway. I headed back toward Westwood.

"I can't pay you, of course," Lindell said. "And I probably can't contact you after today, either."

"Tell you what. Stop calling me *podjo* and we'll call it even."

Lindell nodded as though I had been serious and to say that he had agreed to the deal. We drove in silence while I dropped down the California Incline to the coast highway and took it up to Santa Monica Canyon and then back up to San Vicente.

"So what did you think about what you read up there?" Lindell finally asked.

"Looked like you made all the right moves to me. What about the gas station guy who saw her that night? He checked out?"

"Yeah, we came down on him six ways till Sunday. He was clean. The place was busy and he was there till midnight. We have him on the security video. And he never left the booth after she came and went. His alibi for after midnight checked out, too."

"Anything else from the video? I didn't see anything in the file."

"Nah, the video was worthless. Other than the fact it shows her and it was the last time she was ever seen."

He looked out the window. Three years later and Lindell

was still hooked in deeply on this one. I had to remember that. I had to filter everything he said and did through that prism.

"What are the chances of me getting a look at the whole investigative file?"

"I'd say somewhere between zero and none."

"The ninth floor?"

He nodded.

"They came up and popped the drawer out and took it. I won't see that stuff again. I probably won't even get the goddamn drawer back."

"Why didn't they put the freeze on me? Why you?"

"Because I knew you. But mostly because you're not supposed to even know about them."

I nodded as I turned onto Wilshire, the federal building in sight up ahead.

"Look, Roy, I don't know if the two things are connected, know what I mean? I'm talking about Martha Gessler and the thing in Hollywood. Angella Benton. Martha made a call on it but it doesn't mean that they are connected. I've got other things I'll be chasing down. This is just one of them. Okay?"

He looked out the window again and mumbled something I couldn't hear.

"What?"

"I said nobody ever called her Martha until she disappeared. Then it was in the papers and on TV that way. She hated that name, Martha."

I just nodded because there was nothing else to do. I turned into the federal parking lot and drove up to the plaza to drop him off.

"That phone number in the file, it's okay to call you on that?"

"Yeah, anytime. Make sure your own phones are safe before you do."

I thought about that until I brought the Benz to a stop at the curb in front of the plaza. Lindell looked out the window and surveyed the plaza as if he was judging whether it was safe to get out.

"You get back to Vegas much?" I asked him.

He answered without looking back at me. He kept his eyes on the plaza and the windows of the building looming above.

"Whenever I get the chance. Have to go in disguise. A lot of people over there don't like me."

"I can imagine."

His undercover work coupled with my team's homicide investigation had toppled a major underworld figure and most of his minions.

"I saw your wife over there about a month ago," he said. "Playing cards. I think it was at the Bellagio. She had a nice stack of chips in front of her."

He knew Eleanor Wish from that first casc in Vcgas. That was when and where I had married her.

"Ex-wife," I said. "But that wasn't why I was asking."

"Sure, I know."

Seemingly satisfied with the view he opened the door and got out. He looked back in at me and waited for me to say something. I nodded.

"I'll take your case, Roy."

He nodded back.

"Then call me anytime. And watch yourself out there, *podjo.*"

He gave me the rogue's got-you-last smile and closed the door before I could say anything.

14

Around the detective squad rooms of the LAPD's numerous stations the state of Idaho is called Blue Heaven. It's the goal line, the final destination for a good number of the detectives who go the distance, put in their twenty-five years and then cash out. I hear there are whole neighborhoods up there full of ex-cops from L.A. living side by side by side. Realtors from Coeur d'Alene and Sandpoint run business-card-size ads in the police union newsletter. In every issue.

Of course some cops turn in the badge and set out for Nevada to bake in the desert and pick up part-time work in the casinos. Some disappear into northern California — there are more retired cops in the backwoods of Humboldt County than there are marijuana growers, only the growers don't know it. And some head south to Mexico, where there are still spots where an air-conditioned ranch house with an ocean view is affordable on an LAPD pension.

The point is, few stick around. They spend their adult lives trying to make sense of this place, trying to bring a small measure of order to it, and then can't stand to stay here once their job is done. The work does that to you. It robs you of the ability to enjoy your accomplishment. There is no reward for making it through.

One of the few men I knew who turned in the badge but not the city was named Burnett Biggar. He gave the city its twenty-five years — the last half of it in South Bureau homicide — and then retired to open up a small business with his son near the airport. Biggar & Biggar Professional Security was on Sepulveda near La Tijera. The building was nondescript, the offices unpretentious. Biggar's business was primarily geared toward providing security systems and patrols to the warehouse industries around the airport. The last time I had spoken to him — which was probably two years earlier — he had told me he had more than fifty employees and business was going good.

But out of the other side of his mouth he confided that he missed what he called the real work. The vital work, the work that made a difference. Protecting a warehouse full of blue jeans made in Taiwan could be profitable. But it didn't even begin to touch what you got out of putting a stone killer on the floor and the cuffs on his wrists. It wasn't even close, and that was what Biggar missed. It was because of that I thought I could approach him for help with what I wanted to do for Lawton Cross.

There was a small waiting room with a coffee machine but I wasn't there that long. Burnett Biggar came down a hallway and invited me back to his office. As befitting his name, he was a large man. I had to follow him down the hallway rather than walk next to him. His head was shaved, which was a new look for him as far as I knew.

"So Big, I see you traded the Julius for the Jordan, huh?"

He rubbed a hand over his polished scalp.

"Had to do it, Harry. It's the style. And I'm getting gray."

"Aren't we all."

He led me into his office. It wasn't small and it wasn't big. It was basic, with wood paneling and framed commendations, news clips and photos from his days with the department. It was probably all very impressive to the clients.

Biggar swung around behind a cluttered desk and pointed me to a chair in front of it. As I sat down I noticed a framed slogan on the wall behind him. It said "Biggar & Biggar is getting Better & Better."

Biggar leaned forward and folded his arms on his desk.

"So, Harry Bosch, I don't think I was expecting to see you maybe ever again. It's funny seeing you in that chair."

"Funny seeing you, too. I don't think I was expecting it either."

"You come here for a job? I heard you quit last year. You were the last guy I ever thought about quitting."

"Nobody goes the distance, Big. And I appreciate the offer but I already have a job. I'm just looking for a little help."

Biggar smiled, the skin pulling tight around his eyes. He was intrigued. He knew I wasn't ever going to be the corporate or industrial security type.

"I never heard you ask for help on a goddamn thing. What do you need?"

"I need a setup. Electronic surveillance. One room, nobody can know the camera is there."

"How big's the room?"

"Like a bedroom. Maybe fifteen by fifteen."

"Ah, man, Harry, don't go down that road. You start that sort of snooping and you'll lose sight of yourself. Come work for me. I can find some —"

"No, it's nothing like that. It's actually an offshoot of a homicide I'm working. The guy's in a wheelchair. He sits and watches TV all day. I just want to be able to make sure he's okay, you know? There's something going on with the wife. At least I think so."

"You mean like abuse?"

"Maybe. I don't know. Something."

"Does the guy know you're going to do this?"

"No."

"But you've got access to the room?"

"Pretty much. Think you can help me out?"

"Well, we got cameras. But you have to understand most of our work is industrial application. Heavy-duty stuff. Sounds to me like all you need is a nanny cam, something that you can just pick up at Radio Shack."

I shook my head.

"I don't want to be too obvious about it. The guy was a cop."

Biggar nodded, digested it quickly and stood up.

"Well, come on back to the tech room and take a look at what we've got. Andre's back there and he can fix you up."

He led me back into the hallway and toward the back of the building. We entered the tech room, which was about the size of a double garage and was crowded with workbenches and shelves of all manner of electronics equipment. There were three men gathered around one of the workbenches. They were looking at the screen of a small television. A grainy black-and-white surveillance tape was playing. I recognized one of the men, the largest, as Andre Biggar, Burnett's son. I had never met him but I knew it was him by his size and resemblance to Burnett. Right down to the shaved scalp.

Introductions were made and Andre explained that he was reviewing a tape showing a burglary of a client's warehouse. His father explained what I was looking for and the son led me to another workbench, where he could display and review equipment. He showed me cameras housed in a vase, a lamp, a picture frame and finally a clock. Thinking about how Lawton Cross had complained about not being able to see the time on his television, I stopped Andre right there.

"This will do. How does it work?"

It was a round clock about ten inches across.

"This is a classroom clock. You want to put this on the wall of a bedroom? It will stick out like tits on a —"

"Andre," his father said.

"It's not being used as a bedroom," I said. "It's like a TV room. And the subject told me he can't see the time on the corner of the screen on CNN. So this will make sense when I bring it in."

Andre nodded.

"Okay. You want sound? Color?"

"Sound, yes. Color would be good but not necessary."

"All right. Are you going to transmit, or you want to go self-contained?"

I looked at him blankly and he knew I didn't understand.

"I build these two ways. One is you have a camera in the clock and you transmit picture and sound to a receiver that records it on video. You would have to find a secure place for the recorder within about a hundred feet to be sure. Are you going to be outside the house in a van or something?"

"I wasn't planning on it."

"Okay, the second option is to go digital and put everything in the camera and record internally to a digital tape or memory card. The drawback is capacity. With a digital tape you get about two hours real time, then you have to change it out. With a card you get even less."

"That won't work. I was only planning to check on it every few days."

I started thinking of how I would be able to hide the receiver inside the house. Maybe the garage. I could pretend I was going to the garage to throw something away and I could hide the receiver somewhere Danny Cross wouldn't see it.

"Well, we can slow the recording down if we need to."

"How?"

"A number of different ways. First off we put the camera on a clock. Turn it off, say, midnight to eight. We can also stagger the FPS and lengthen —"

"FPS?"

"The recorded frames per second. It makes the image jump, though."

"What about sound? Does that jump, too?"

"No, sound is separate. You'd get full sound."

I nodded but wasn't sure I wanted to lose any of the visual recording.

"We can also put it on a motion sensor. This guy you say is in a wheelchair, does he move around a lot?"

"No, he can't. He's paralyzed. Most of the time I think he just sits there staring at the TV."

"Any pets?"

"I don't think so."

"So the only time there is real movement in the room is when the caregiver comes in, and that's who you want to watch. Am I right?"

"Right."

"No problem then. This will work. We put a motion sensor on it and a two-gig memory card and you'll probably stretch it out a couple days."

"That'll work."

I nodded and looked at Burnett. I was impressed with his son. Andre looked like he should be out breaking quarterbacks in half. But he had found a specialty in life dealing with circuits and microprocessors. I could see the pride in Burnett's eyes.

"Give me fifteen minutes to put it together and then I'll come show you how to install it and how to switch out the memory card."

"Sounds good."

I sat with Burnett in his office and we talked about the department and a couple of the cases that we had worked together. One case had involved a hired killer who had murdered both the intended target in South L.A. and then his employer in Hollywood when the employer failed to pay the second half of the agreed-upon fee. We had worked it together for a month, my team and Biggar and his partner, who was named Miles Manley. We broke it when Big and Manley, as the pair were called, came up with a witness in the target victim's neighborhood who remembered seeing a white man on the day of the shooting and could describe his car, a black Corvette with red leather interior. The car matched the vehicle used by the second victim's next-door neighbor. He confessed after a lengthy interrogation conducted alternately by Biggar and me.

"It's always something small like that," Biggar said while leaning back behind his desk. "That's what I loved best about it. Not knowing where that little break was going to come from."

"I know what you mean."

"So you miss it?"

"Yeah. But I'll get it back. I'm starting to now."

"You mean the feeling, not the job."

"Right. How about you, you still missing it?"

"I'm making more money than I need here but, yeah, I miss the juice. The job gave me the juice and I don't get it shuffling rent-a-cops around and setting up cameras. Be careful what you do, Harry. You might end up successful like me and then you sit around remembering the old days, thinking they were a lot better than they were."

"I'll be careful, Big."

Biggar nodded, pleased that he had dispensed his dose of advice for the day.

"You don't have to tell me if you don't want to, Harry, but I'm guessing this guy in the chair is Lawton Cross, huh?"

I hesitated but decided it didn't matter.

"Yeah, it's him. I'm working something else and it crossed his path. I went to see him and he said some stuff. I just want to make sure. You know."

"Good luck with it. I remember his wife, saw her a couple times at things. She was a nice lady."

I nodded. I knew what he was saying, that he hoped Cross wasn't being victimized by his wife.

"People can change," I said. "I'm going to find out."

Andre Biggar came in a few minutes later carrying a toolbox, a laptop computer and the camera clock in a box. He took me to school on electronic surveillance. The clock was rigged and ready. All I needed to do was mount it on a wall and plug it in. When I adjusted the time, I would activate the surveillance by pushing the dial all the way in. To switch out the memory card I just had to remove the backing of the clock and pop the card out of the camera. Easy.

"Okay, so once I take the card out, how do I look at what I've got?"

Andre nodded and showed me how to plug the memory card into the side of the laptop computer. He then went through the keyboard commands that would bring up the surveillance recording on the computer's screen.

"It's simple. Just take care of the equipment and bring it all back. We've got a lot of bread invested in it."

I didn't want to tell him that it wasn't simple enough for me. I seized on the financial side of the equation as a way of avoiding revealing my technical shortcomings.

"Tell you what," I said. "I think I'll leave your laptop here and just come back with the memory card when I want to look at it. I don't want to risk all your equipment. I like to travel light, anyway."

"Whatever suits you. But the beauty of this setup is the immediacy. You can pull the card and watch it in your car right outside the guy's house if you want. Why come all the way back here?"

"I don't think there's that kind of urgency. I'll leave the laptop and bring you back the card, okay?"

"Whatever."

Andre put the clock back in its cushioned box, then shook my hand and left the office, taking the laptop with him but leaving me the toolbox along with the clock. I looked at Burnett. It was time to go.

"He looks like he's more than helping you."

"Andre's the heart of this place."

He gestured toward the wall of framed memorabilia.

"I bring the clients in, impress them, sign them up. Andre's the one who gets it done. He figures out the needs and gets it done."

I nodded and stood up.

"You want to charge me something for this?" I said, holding up the box with the clock in it.

Biggar smiled.

"Not if you bring it back."

Then his face turned serious.

"It's the least I can do for Lawton Cross."

"Yeah," I said, knowing the feeling.

We shook hands and I went out, carrying the clock and the toolbox, hoping the hidden camera would be the piece of equipment that would show me the world wasn't as bad as I thought it could be.

15

From Biggar & Biggar I drove back to the Valley, taking the Sepulveda Pass and catching the first brutal wave of rush hour. It took me almost an hour just to get to Mulholland Drive. At that point I jumped off the freeway and drove west along the crest of the mountains. I watched the sun drop behind Malibu and leave a burning sky in its trail. At the low angles the sun often reflected off the smog caught in the bowl of the Valley and turned it brilliant shades of orange and pink and purple. It was like some sort of reward for putting up with having to breathe the poisoned air every day. This evening it was mostly a smooth orange color with wisps of white mixed in. It was what my ex-wife used to call a Creamsicle sky when she watched sunsets off the back deck of the house. She had a descriptive label for each one and that always made me smile.

The memory of her on the deck seemed like such a long time ago and such a different part of my life. I thought about what Roy Lindell had said about seeing her in Las Vegas. He knew I had been asking about her even though I told him I hadn't. If not a day then at least not a week went by that I didn't think about going out there, finding her and asking for another chance. A chance of making a go of it on her terms. I had no job holding me to L.A. anymore. I could go where I wanted. This time I could go to her and we could live there together in the city of sin. She could still be free to find what she needed on the blue felt poker tables of the city's casinos. And at the end of each day she could come home to me. I could do whatever came up. There would always be something in Vegas for a person with my skills.

One time I had packed a box, put it in the back of the Benz and had gotten as far as Riverside before the familiar fears started rising in my chest and I pulled off the freeway. I ate a hamburger at an In-N-Out and then headed back home. I didn't bother unpacking the box when I got there. I put it on the floor in the bedroom and took out the clothes I had packed as I needed them over the next two weeks. The empty box was still there on the floor, ready for the next time I wanted to pack it and make that drive.

The fear. It was always there. Fear of rejection, fear of unrequited hope and love, fear of feelings still below the surface in me. It was all mixed in the blender and poured smooth as a milkshake into my cup until it was filled to the very edge. So full that if I were to move even a step it would spill over the sides. Therefore I couldn't move. I stood paralyzed. I stayed home and lived out of a box.

I'm a believer in the single-bullet theory. You can fall in love and make love many times but there is only one bullet with your name etched on the side. And if you are lucky enough to be shot with that bullet then the wound never heals.

Roy Lindell might have had Martha Gessler's name on a bullet. I don't know. What I do know is that Eleanor Wish had been my bullet. She had pierced me through and through. There were other women before and other women since but the wound she left was always there. It would not heal right. I was still bleeding and I knew I would always bleed for her. That was just the way it had to be. There is no end of things in the heart.

16

On the way into Woodland Hills I made a quick stop at a Vendome Liquors and then headed to the house on Melba Avenue. I didn't call ahead. With Lawton Cross I knew the chances were always good he'd be at home.

Danielle Cross answered the door after three knocks, and her already strained face took on a deeper scowl when she saw it was me.

"He's sleeping," she said, holding her body tightly in the door's opening. "He's still recovering from yesterday."

"Then wake him up, Danny, because I need to talk to him."

"Look, you can't just barge in here. You're not a cop anymore. You have no right."

"Do you have the right to decide who he does and doesn't see?"

That seemed to stall her anger a little bit. She looked down at the toolbox in one hand and the box I had under my arm.

"What is all of that?"

"I got him a gift. Look, Danny, I need to talk to him. People are going to be coming to see him. I have to talk to him about it so he'll be ready."

She relented. Without further word she stepped back and opened the door wide. She signaled me in with an outstretched arm and I stepped over the threshold. I found my way to the bedroom.

Lawton Cross was asleep in his chair, his mouth open and a spill of medicinal-looking drool curved down his cheek. I didn't want to look at him. He was too much of a reminder of what could happen. I put the toolbox and the clock box down on the bed. I went back to the door and closed it, making sure it banged in the jamb loud enough to hopefully startle Cross awake. I didn't want to have to touch him to wake him up.

When I turned back to the chair I noticed his eyes flutter and then go still at half mast.

"Hey, Law? It's me, Harry Bosch."

I noticed the green light on the monitor on the bureau and moved behind the chair to turn it off.

"Harry?" he said. "Where?"

I came back around the chair and looked down on him with a frozen smile on my face.

"Right here, man. You awake now?"

"Yeah . . . mmm 'wake."

"Good. There's some stuff I need to tell you. And I got you something."

I went to the bed and started pulling the clock out of the box Andre Biggar had packed for me.

"Black Bush?"

His voice was alert now. Once again I regretted my choice of words to him. I came back into his field of vision holding the clock up.

"I got you this clock for the wall. Now you'll be able to tell the time when you need it."

He blew a burst of air out through his lips.

"She'll just take it down."

"I'll tell her not to. Don't worry."

I opened the toolbox and pulled out the hammer and a drywall nail from a plastic package that contained a variety of nails for different purposes. I surveyed the wall to the left of the television and picked a spot at center. There was an electrical outlet directly below. I held the nail up high on the wall and drove it halfway in with the hammer. I was hanging the clock when the door opened and Danny looked in.

"What are you doing? He doesn't want a clock in here."

I finished hanging the clock, lowered my hands and looked at her.

"He told me he did want a clock."

We both looked at Law to settle it. His eyes flitted from his wife to me and then back again.

"Let's try having a clock for a while," he said. "I'd like to know the time of day so I know when my shows are coming on."

"Fine," she said in a clipped tone. "Whatever you want."

She left the room, closing the door behind her. I leaned over and plugged the clock's line into the outlet. Then I checked my watch and reached up to set the time and turn on the camera. When I was finished I put the hammer back into the toolbox and snapped the latch.

"Harry?"

"What?" I asked, though I knew what the question would be.

"Did you bring me some?"

"A little."

I reopened the toolbox and took out the flask I had filled in the parking lot at the Vendome.

"Danny said you're hung over. You sure?"

"'Course I'm sure. Give me a taste, Harry. I need it."

I went through the same routine as the day before and then waited to see if he could tell I had watered down the whiskey.

"Ah, that's the good stuff, Harry. Give me another, would you?"

I did and then I closed the flask, feeling somehow guilty about giving this broken man the one joy he seemed to have left in life.

"Listen, Law, I'm here to give you a heads-up. I think I sort of kicked over a can of worms with this thing."

"What happened?"

"I tried to run down that agent you said had called Jack Dorsey about the currency numbers. You know, about the problem?"

"Yeah, I know. Did you find her?"

"No, Law, I didn't. The agent was Martha Gessler. That ring a bell with you?"

His eyes moved across the ceiling as if that was where he kept his memory banks.

"No, should it?"

"I don't know. She's missing. She's been missing for three years, since right about the time she called Jack."

"Holy shit, Harry."

"Yeah. So I kind of walked into that when I called up to try to track that call."

"They're going to come talk to me?"

"I don't know. But that's the heads-up. I think they might. Somehow, they've got this whole thing tied into a terrorism angle. It's one of these post–September eleven crews running with it now. And I hear they like to kick ass and read the rule book later."

"I don't want them coming here, Harry. What did you start?"

"I'm sorry about that, Law. If they come, just let them ask their questions and you answer them the best you can. Get their names and tell Danny to call me after they leave."

"I'll try. I just want to be left alone."

"I know, Law."

I moved closer to his chair and held the flask up into his field of vision.

"You want more?"

"Does the pope shit in the woods?"

I poured a good slug into his mouth, then a chaser. I waited for it to go down and then work its way back up into his eyes. They seemed to glaze over.

"You okay?"

"Fine."

"There are a few more questions I have for you. They sort of came to me after I talked to the bureau."

"Like what?"

"Like about the phone call Jack got. The FBI says there was no record of Gessler calling about the currency list."

"That's simple. Maybe it wasn't her. Like I said, I didn't get a name from Jack. Or if I did it's gone. I don't remember it."

"I'm pretty sure it was her. Everything else you described about it fits. She had a program like you described on her laptop. It went missing with her."

"There you go. There probably was a record of her calling. It just disappeared with her."

"I guess so. What about the time of the call? Can you remember anything more about that, about when it came in?"

"Ah, jeez, I don't know, Harry. It was just one of those things. It was just a call. I'm sure Jack put it on the log."

He was talking about the chronological log. Everything was always entered on the log. Or was supposed to be.

"Yeah, I know," I said. "But I don't have access to that. I'm on the outside, remember?"

"Yeah."

"You told me you thought it was ten or so months into the case, remember? You said you were working other cases by then and Jack took over lead on Angella Benton. Her murder was May sixteenth of 'ninety-nine. Martha Gessler disappeared the following March nineteenth. That's almost exactly ten months later."

"So I remembered it right. What else you want from me?"

"It's just that . . ."

I didn't finish. I was trying to figure out what to ask and how to say it. Something wasn't right about the chronology.

"It's just what?"

"I don't know. It seems to me if Jack had recently talked to this agent he would have said something about it when she went missing. It was a big story, you know? In the papers and on the TV every night. Is there any way the call could have come earlier? Closer to the beginning of the case? That way Jack might have forgotten about it and her by the time she hit the news."

Cross didn't say anything for a while as he considered this. I considered other possibilities, too, but kept hitting logic walls.

"Give me another shot of that stuff, would you, Harry?"

He tried to suck too much of it down and it backed up

and burned his throat. When he spoke again his voice was hoarser than usual.

"I don't think so. I think it was ten months."

"Close your eyes for a second, Law."

"What are you talking about?"

"Just close your eyes and concentrate on that memory. Whatever it is that you have, that you're keying on, concentrate on that."

"You trying to hypnotize me, Harry?"

"I'm just trying to focus your thoughts, help you remember what Jack said."

"It won't work."

"Not if you don't let it. Relax, Law. Relax and try to forget everything. Like your mind's a blackboard and you're erasing it. Think about what Jack said about the call."

His eyes moved under the thin, pale eyelids but after a few moments they slowed and stopped. I watched his face and waited. It was years since I had tried any hypnotic techniques, and that had been to draw out visual descriptions of events and suspects. What I wanted from Cross now was a memory of a time and place and the dialogue that went with it.

"You see the blackboard, Law?"

"Yeah, I see it."

"Okay, go to the board and write Jack's name on it. Write it at the top so you have room underneath it."

"Harry, this is stupid. I —"

"Just humor me, Law. Write Jack's name at the top of the board."

"Okay."

"Okay, Law, that's good. Now look at the board and underneath Jack's name write the words 'phone call.' Okay?"

"Okay, did it."

"Good. Now look at those three words and concentrate on them. Jack. Phone call. Jack. Phone call."

The silence that followed my words was punctuated by the barely discernible ticking of the new clock.

"Now, Law, I want you to concentrate on the black around those words. Around those letters. Go through the letters, Law, into the black. Go through the letters."

I waited and watched his eyelids. I saw the retinal movement begin again.

"Jack is talking to you, Law. He's telling you about the agent. He says she has new information on the movie set heist."

I waited for a long moment, wondering if I should have mentioned Gessler by name, then deciding it was better that I hadn't.

"What is he saying to you, Law?"

"There's something wrong with the numbers. They don't match."

"Did she call him?"

"She called him."

"Where are you when he is telling you this, Law?"

"We're in the car. We've got court."

"Is it a trial?"

"Yes."

"Whose trial is it?"

"It's that little Mexican kid. The little gangbanger who killed the Korean jeweler on Western. Alejandro Penjeda. It's the verdict."

"Penjeda is the defendant?"

"That's right."

"And Jack got the call from the agent before you went to court to hear the verdict?"

"That's right."

"Okay, Law."

I had gotten what I wanted. I tried to think what else I could ask him.

"Law? Did Jack say what the agent's name was?"

"No, he didn't say."

"Did he say he would check out the information she gave him?"

"He said he'd do some checking but that he thought it was a bullshit call. He said he didn't think it meant anything."

"Did you believe him?"

"Yes."

"Okay, Law, I'm going to tell you to open your eyes in a moment. And when you open them, I want you to feel like you just woke up but I want you to remember what we just talked about. Okay?"

"Okay, yes."

"And the other thing is I want you to feel better. I want you to be . . . okay about things in your life. I want you to be as happy as you can be, Law. Okay?"

"Yes."

"Okay, Law, open your eyes now."

The eyelids fluttered once and then they were open. They strafed the ceiling and then came to me. They seemed brighter than before.

"Harry . . ."

"How do you feel, Law?"

"Okay."

"You remember what we were talking about?"

"Yeah, that little Mex. Penjeda. We called him Pin-Heada. He didn't take the deal the DA floated. Life with. He took his chances with the jury and got snake eyes. Life without."

"Live and learn."

What sounded like what might have been a laugh gurgled from deep in his throat.

"Yeah, that was a good one," he said. "I remember when we were going over to court that day was when Jack told me about the call from Westwood."

"Right. You remember when that verdict came in on Penjeda?"

"End of February, beginning of March. My last trial, Harry. A month later I took the bullet in that shithole bar and I was history. I remember watching PinHeada's face when he heard that verdict and knew he was facing life *without* parole. Fucker got what he deserved."

The laugh came up again and then I saw the light go out of his eyes.

"What is it, Law?"

"He's up there at Corcoran playing handball in the yard or getting his ass rented out by the Mexican Mafia on an hourly basis. And I'm here. I got life without, too, I guess."

His eyes looked into mine. I nodded because it was the only thing I could think of to do.

"It's not fair, Harry. Life isn't fair."

17

The downtown library was on Flower and Figueroa. It was one of the oldest buildings in the whole city. Therefore it was dwarfed by the modern glass-and-steel structures that surrounded it. Inside it was a beauty, centered around a domed rotunda with 360-degree mosaics depicting the founding of the city by the *padres*. The place had been twice burned by arsonists and closed for years, then restored to its original beauty. I had come after the restoration was completed, the first time back since I was a child. And I continued to come. It brought me close to the Los Angeles I remembered. Where I felt comfortable. I would take my lunch in the book rooms or the upper-level patios while reading case files and writing notes. I got to know the security guards and a few of the librarians. I had a library card, though I rarely checked out a book.

I went to the library after leaving Lawton Cross because I no longer could call on Keisha Russell to help me with clip searches. Her call to Sacramento to run a check on me when I had asked her to simply run a clip search on Martha Gessler was the warning. Her journalistic curiosity would lead her further than my requests, to places I didn't want her to go.

The main reference desk was on the second floor. I recognized the woman behind the counter, though I had never spoken to her before. I could tell she recognized me as I approached. I used a library card where a police shield used to do. She read it and recognized the name.

"Do you know that you have the same name as a famous painter?" she asked.

"Yes, I know."

Her face flushed. She was midthirties with an unattractive hairstyle. She wore a name tag that said Mrs. Molloy.

"Of course you do," she said. "You must know that. How can I help you?"

"I need to look for stories that were in the *Times* from about three years ago."

"You want to do a key word search?"

"I guess so. What is that?"

She smiled.

"We have the *Los Angeles Times* on computer going back to nineteen eighty-seven. If what you are looking for was published after that, all you have to do is go online on one of our computers, type in a key word or phrase, like a name, for example, that you think is in the story and it will search for it. There is a five-dollar-per-hour fee for accessing the newspaper archives."

"Fine, that's what I want to do."

She smiled and reached beneath the counter. She handed me a white plastic device that was about a foot long. It looked like no computer I had ever seen.

"How do I use this?"

She almost laughed.

"It's a pager. All our computers are being used at the moment. I will page you as soon as one becomes available."

"Oh."

"The pager doesn't work outside of the building. It also does not emit an audible page. It vibrates. So keep it on your person."

"I will. Any idea how long it will be?"

"We set one-hour use limits, which right now would mean one won't be available for another thirty minutes. However, people often don't require the full hour."

"Okay, thank you. I'll be nearby."

I found an empty table in one of the reading rooms and decided to work on the case chronology. I got out my notebook and on a fresh page wrote down the three key dates and events I knew.

Angella Benton — murdered — May 16, 1999
Movie set heist — May 19, 1999
Martha Gessler — missing — March 19, 2000

I then began adding the things I was missing.

Gessler/Dorsey — phone call — ?????

And after a few moments I thought of something else that might help explain something that bothered me.

Dorsey/Cross — murder/shooting — ?????

I looked around to see if anyone was using a cell phone. I wanted to make a call but wasn't sure it would be allowed in a library. When I turned and looked behind me I saw a man standing by a magazine rack quickly turn away and take a magazine off the display without seeming to look at what it was first. He was dressed in blue jeans and a flannel shirt. Nothing about him said FBI but it still seemed to me that he had been looking directly at me until I had looked at him. His reaction had been too quick, almost furtive. There had been no eye contact, nothing that suggested any sort of overture. The man clearly didn't want me to know he was watching me.

Putting my notebook away, I got up from the table and headed toward the magazine racks. I passed the man and noticed that the magazine he had grabbed was called *Parenting Today.* It was another strike against him. He didn't look like the parenting type to me. I was pretty sure I was being watched.

Back at the reference desk I put my hands on the counter and leaned over to whisper to Mrs. Molloy.

"Can I ask you a question? Is it okay to use a cell phone in the library?"

"No, it's not. Is somebody bothering you by using a phone?"

"No, I was just wondering what the rule was. Thank you."

Before I could turn away she said she was just about to page me because a computer was now available. I gave her back the pager and she led me to a cubicle where the glowing screen of a computer was waiting.

"Good luck," she said as she headed back to the desk.

"Excuse me," I said, beckoning her back. "Um, I don't know how to get to the *Times* stuff on this."

"There's an icon on the desktop."

I turned back around and scanned the desk. There was nothing on it but the computer and the keyboard and the mouse. The librarian started to laugh behind me but then covered her mouth with her hand.

"I'm sorry," she said. "It's just . . . you don't know the first thing about how to do this, do you?"

"Or the second or the third. Can you just help get me started?"

"Hold on. Let me just go check the front desk and make sure there is no one waiting for me."

"Fine. Thank you."

She was gone thirty seconds and then came back and leaned over me to work the mouse and click through screens until she was inside the *Times* archives and at what she called the key word search template.

"So now you type in the key word for the story you are looking for."

I nodded that I understood that much and typed in the name "Alejandro Penjeda." Mrs. Molloy reached across and hit the ENTER key and the search began. In about five seconds I had the results on the screen. There were five hits. The first two were from 1991 and 1994 and the final three were all from 2000. I dismissed the first two as being unrelated to the Penjeda I was interested in. The next three were all from March 2000. I moved the mouse to the first one — March 1, 2000 — and clicked on the READ button. The story filled the top half of the screen. It was a short report on the opening of the trial of Alejandro Penjeda, who was charged with the murder of a Korean jeweler named Kyungwon Park.

The second story was also short and it was the one I wanted. It was the verdict story in the Penjeda case. It was dated March 14 and reported events from the day before. I took the notebook out of my pocket and completed that part of the chronology, putting the new information in the right time slot.

Angella Benton — murdered — May 16, 1999
Movie set heist — May 19, 1999
Gessler/Dorsey — phone call — March 13, 2000
Martha Gessler — missing — March 19, 2000

I looked at what I had. Martha Gessler disappeared and presumably was murdered six days after talking to Jack Dorsey about the currency list anomaly.

"If there isn't anything else, I'm going to go back up front."

I had forgotten that Mrs. Molloy was still standing behind me. I stood up and signaled her to the seat.

"Actually, this might be faster if you could do it," I said. "I need to do a couple more searches."

"We are not supposed to do the searches. You are supposed to be proficient with the computer if you are going to use it."

"I understand. I am going to learn but at the moment I'm not that proficient and these searches are very important."

She seemed to be wavering on whether to continue to help me. I wished I'd had the small wallet-size copy of the private investigator's license I had gotten from the state. Maybe that would have impressed her. She leaned backwards to look down the row of cubicles to the front desk to see if anyone was waiting for help. The *Parenting Today* guy was milling about, trying to act as though he was either waiting for someone or waiting for help.

"I'll come back after I ask this gentleman if he needs help," Mrs. Molloy said.

She walked off without waiting for a response from me. I watched as she asked Parenting Today if he needed something and he shook his head and then glanced back at me before walking off. Mrs. Molloy then came back down the aisle to me. She took the seat in front of the computer.

"What is the next search?"

She moved the mouse smoothly and quickly and got back to the key word template.

"Try 'John Dorsey,'" I said. "And to narrow it down, can you also add 'Nat's bar'?"

She typed in the information and started the search. It came back with thirteen hits and I asked her to bring up the first one. It was dated April 7, 2000, and reported events from the day before.

One Cop Dead, One Hurt in Hollywood Bar Shooting

By Keisha Russell
Times Staff Writer

Two Los Angeles police detectives on a lunch break and a bartender were gunned down in a Hollywood bar yesterday when a man entered the establishment and attempted to rob it at gunpoint.

The 1 p.m. shooting at Nat's on Cherokee Avenue left Detective John H. Dorsey, 49, dead of multiple gunshot wounds and his partner, Lawton Cross Jr., 38, in critical condition with head and neck wounds. Donald Rice, 29, a bartender working in the lounge, was shot multiple times and also died at the scene.

The suspect, who wore a black ski mask, escaped with an undisclosed amount of cash from the cash register, said Lt. James Macy, of the Officer Involved Shooting unit.

"It appears this was about a few hundred dollars at most," Macy said at a press conference staged outside of the bar where the shooting took place. "We can find no reason for this guy to have started shooting."

Macy went on to say that it was unclear whether Dorsey and Cross had attempted to stop the robbery, thereby causing the shooting to start. He said both detectives were shot while sitting in a booth in the dimly lit bar area. Neither had drawn his weapon.

The detectives had been conducting an interview in a business near Nat's bar when they decided to take a lunch break in the bar, according to Macy. There was no indication that either man had been consuming alcohol in the bar.

"They went there as a matter of convenience," Macy said. "It was the unluckiest decision they could have made."

No other patrons or employees were in the bar at the time of the incident. A person who was not in the bar saw the gunman fleeing after the shooting and was able to provide police with a limited description of the suspect. As a safety precaution the witness was not identified by police.

I stopped reading to ask the librarian if I could simply print the story out.

"It's fifty cents a page," she said. "Cash only."

"Okay, do it."

She hit the PRINT command and then leaned backwards in her seat to see if she could see down the aisle to the reference desk. Standing, I could see it better.

"You're still clear. Can you do one more for me?"

"If we hurry. What is it?"

I raced through my memory banks trying to come up with a name that would work for what I wanted to do next.

"How about the word 'terrorism'?"

"Are you kidding me? Do you know how many stories that word's been used in during the last two years?"

"Right, right, what am I thinking? Let's cut it down. The search words don't have to be connected, like in a sentence, right?"

"No. Listen, I need to get back to my —"

"Okay, okay, how about the words 'FBI' and 'suspected terrorist' plus 'Al Qaeda' and 'cell' spelled with a 'c.' Could you try that?"

"That will probably break the bank, too."

She typed in the information and we waited, and then the computer reported that there were 467 hits, all but six of them since September 11, 2001. Beneath this number the computer printed out the headline of each story. The screen displayed the first of forty-two pages of headline listings.

"You're going to have to look through this yourself," Mrs. Molloy said. "I need to go back to my post now."

I had started the last search almost as a joke. My assumption was that Parenting Today would either interview Mrs. Molloy after I left or send another agent while he continued the tail. I wanted to add a terrorism angle to my search just so they would have something to puzzle over. Now I realized I might be able to find out about what the bureau was doing.

"Okay," I said. "That's fine. Thanks for all of your help."

"Remember, we close the library at nine this evening. That gives you about twenty-five more minutes."

"Okay, thanks. Where did that printout go, by the way?"

"The printer is at the front desk. Anything you print will come out there. You come to me and pay for it and I give it to you."

"A well-oiled machine."

She didn't answer. She walked off and left me alone with the computer. I took a look around and didn't see Parenting Today anywhere. I then dropped back down into the cubicle and began scrolling through the story list. I clicked on a few and started to read them but stopped each time I discerned that the story had not even a remote connection to Los Angeles. I realized I should have included Los Angeles in the key word search. I stood up to see if Mrs. Molloy was at the front desk but she was not there. The front desk was abandoned.

I went back to the computer and on the third page of the story list a headline caught my eye.

TERRORISM MONEY MAN CAPTURED
AT BORDER CROSSING

I clicked the READ button and pulled up the entire story. The box above the body of the story said it had been published a month earlier on page A13 of the newspaper. It was accompanied by a mugshot of a man with deeply tanned skin and wavy blond hair.

By Josh Meyer
Times Staff Writer

A suspected money courier for supporters of global terrorism was arrested yesterday as he attempted to cross the Mexican border at Calexico with a satchel of cash, the Justice Department reported.

Mousouwa Aziz, 39, who has been on the FBI's terrorist watch list for four years, was apprehended by Border Patrol agents as he attempted to cross from the United States into Mexico.

Aziz, who the FBI claims has ties to a Philippine cell of Al Qaeda terrorists, was carrying a large quantity of U.S. currency in a satchel found hidden under the seat of the car he was attempting to drive across the border. Aziz, who was alone in the car, was arrested without a struggle. He was being held in an unknown location under federal guidelines as an enemy combatant.

Agents said Aziz had attempted to disguise himself by dyeing his hair blond and shaving the beard he had been known to wear.

"This is a significant arrest," said Abraham Klein, an assistant U.S. attorney in the Los Angeles anti-terrorism unit. "Our efforts around the world have been geared toward cutting off funding for terrorists. This suspected terrorist is believed to be a person intimately involved in financing terrorist activities here and abroad."

Klein and other sources said Aziz could be a key figure in efforts to stop the movement of money — the lifeblood of long-term terrorism activity — to those targeting American interests.

"Not only did we take away a good chunk of cash with this arrest but, perhaps more importantly, we took a person who was in the business of delivering money to terrorists out of circulation," said a Justice source who spoke on the condition he would not be identified.

Aziz is a Jordanian national who attended high school in Cleveland, Ohio, and speaks fluent English, the Justice source said. He had a passport and an Alabama driver's license in his possession that both identified him as Frank Aiello.

Aziz's name was placed on an FBI watch list four years ago after information was developed that connected him to money deliveries made to terrorists involved in the bombings of U.S. embassies in Africa. Aziz was nicknamed "Mouse" by federal agents because of his small stature, ability to stay hidden from authorities in recent months and the difficulty agents had in pronouncing his first name.

After the terrorist attacks of September 11, 2001, a higher alert status was issued in regard to Aziz, though sources said there was no evidence directly linking Aziz to the 19 terrorists who carried out those suicide attacks.

"This guy is a money man," the Justice source said. "His job is to move money from point A to point B. The money is then used to buy materials to make bombs and weapons, to support the lifestyles of terrorists while they plan and carry out their operations."

It was unclear why Aziz was apparently attempting to take U.S. currency out of the country.

"The U.S. dollar is good anywhere," Klein said. "In fact, it is stronger than the currency in most of the countries where these terrorist cells exist. The U.S. dollar goes a lot further. It could be that this suspect was taking the money to the Philippines to simply help pay for an operation."

Klein also suggested that money could have been headed for terrorists planning to infiltrate the United States.

> Klein refused to say how much money Aziz was transporting or where it came from. In recent months federal investigators have suggested that a large source of financing of terrorists has come from illegal activities within the United States. For example, the FBI linked an Arizona drug operation last year to a terrorist financing network.
>
> Federal sources also told the Times last year that it was believed that desolate areas of Mexico might be the location of terrorist training camps linked to Al Qaeda. Klein refused to comment yesterday on the possibility that Aziz might have been headed to such a camp.

I sat there staring at the screen for a long moment, wondering if I had just stumbled onto something more significant than a way to take a jab at the feds. I wondered if what I had just read could in some way be connected to my own investigation. Could the agents on the ninth floor in Westwood have connected the movie money to this terrorist?

My thoughts were broken by a loudspeaker announcement that the library was closing in fifteen minutes. I clicked on the PRINT button for the story and went back to the story list. I scrolled through the headlines, looking for follow-ups to the Aziz arrest. I found only one, which was published two days after the first story. I called it up and found it to be only a short. It said that an arraignment for Aziz was postponed indefinitely while he was continuing to be debriefed by federal agents. The tone of the article indicated that Aziz was cooperating with investigators, though it did not specifically or clearly say that. The story said that changes in federal laws enacted after the September 11 attacks gave federal authorities wide leeway in holding suspected terrorists as enemy combatants. The rest of the story was background information already contained in the first story.

I went back to the list and continued to scroll through the headlines. It took nearly ten minutes but I never found another story about Mousouwa Aziz.

The loudspeaker announced that the library was closing. I looked around and saw Mrs. Molloy back at the front desk. She was putting things away in the drawers, getting ready to go home. I decided that I now didn't want Parenting Today to know what I had been looking up on the computer. At least not right away. So I stayed in the cubicle until after the next announcement that the library was closed. I stayed until Mrs. Molloy came to the cubicle and told me I had to leave. She had my printouts. I paid her then folded the printouts and put them in my coat pocket with my notebook. I thanked her and left the reference room.

On my way out I pretended that I was studying the mosaics and architecture of the building, turning several times in complete circles in the rotunda as I watched for the tail man. I never saw him and began to wonder if I was being overly paranoid.

It looked like I was the last to leave through the public exit. I thought about finding the employee exit and waiting for Mrs. Molloy to come out so I could ask her if she had been questioned about me and my research requests. But I thought maybe I would only end up scaring her and let it go.

Alone as I walked through the third level of the garage toward my car, I felt the faint chill of fear move down my spine. Whether I was being tailed or not, I had successfully spooked myself. I picked up my pace and was almost trotting by the time I got to the door of the Mercedes.

18

Paranoia is not always a bad thing. It can help you keep an edge and sometimes an edge is the difference. From the library I headed over to Broadway and then toward the Civic Center. It might seem normal enough, an ex-cop heading toward the police department. Nothing unusual about that. But as I got to the *Los Angeles Times* complex I yanked the wheel hard left without using the brakes or a turn signal and sliced through oncoming traffic into the Third Street tunnel. I pinned the accelerator and the Mercedes responded, the front end rising like a boat as it picked up speed and roared through the three-block tunnel.

As often as I could I checked the rearview mirror for a follower. The tiles on the rounded walls of the tunnel carried headlights like halos. Filmmakers rent it from the city all the time for that reason. Any car trying to keep pace with me would be advertising, unless the lights were turned off, and that would be just as obvious in the mirror.

I was smiling. I'm not sure why. Having a possible FBI tail isn't necessarily something to be happy about. And the FBI is generally humorless about it as well. But I felt all at once that I had made the right move with the Mercedes. The car was flying. I was up high — higher than in any police car I had ever been in — so I had a good view in the mirror. It was as if I had planned for this and the plan was working. And that brought the smile.

As I came out of the tunnel I hit the brakes and took a hard right. The thick tires held the pavement, and when I was clear of the mouth of the tunnel I stopped completely. I waited, my eyes on the mirror. Of the cars that came out of the tunnel none turned right behind me and none even braked as they went through the intersection. If I had a tail I had either lost it or the follower was proficient enough at the game to be willing to lose the target in order to avoid obvious exposure. The latter didn't fit with the way Parenting Today had been so obvious in the library.

The third possibility I had to now consider was electronic surveillance. The bureau could have easily tricked my car at almost any point during the day. In the garage at the library a tech could have slid under and wired it. The same tech could have been waiting for me to show up at the federal building as well. This of course would mean that they already knew of my ride about town with Roy Lindell. I was tempted to call the agent and warn him but decided that I shouldn't use my cell phone to contact him.

I shook my head. Maybe paranoia was not such a good thing after all. It can help you keep an edge but it can also paralyze you. I pulled back into traffic and worked my way over to the Hollywood Freeway. I kept my eyes off the rear view as much as possible.

The freeway is elevated as it cuts through Hollywood and into the Cahuenga Pass. It offers a good view of the place where I spent the most significant part of my time as a cop. With just glancing looks I could pick out some of the buildings where I had worked cases. The Capitol Records building, designed to resemble a stack of records. The Usher Hotel, now being renovated as luxury apartments as part of the Hollywood core–area redesign and development. I could see the lighted homes rising up on the dark hillsides in Beechwood Canyon and Whitley Heights. I could see the ten-story image of a local basketball legend on the side of an otherwise nondescript office building. Smaller in stature but still covering the side of a building was a Marlboro Man with a drooping cigarette in his mouth, his steely coolness replaced by a symbol of impotence.

Hollywood was always best viewed at night. It could only hold its mystique in darkness. In sunlight the curtain comes up and the intrigue is gone, replaced by a sense of hidden danger. It was a place of takers and users, of broken sidewalks and dreams. You build a city in the desert, water it with false hopes and false idols, and eventually this is what happens. The desert reclaims it, turns it arid, leaves it barren. Human tumbleweeds drift across its streets, predators hide in the rocks.

I took the Mulholland exit and crossed over the freeway, then at the split took Woodrow Wilson on up the side of the mountain. My house was dark. The only light I saw when I came through the carport door was the red glow from the answering machine on the kitchen counter. I hit a light switch and then pushed the PLAYBACK button on the phone.

There were two messages. The first was from Kiz Rider and she had already told me about that. The second was from Lawton Cross. He had held back on me once again. He said he had something, his voice croaking into the phone like static. I pictured his wife holding the phone to his mouth.

The message had been left two hours before. It was getting late but I called back. The man lived in a chair. What was late to him? I had no idea.

Danny Cross answered. She must have had caller ID on the phone because her hello was clipped and carried an edge of malice in it. Or was I reading too much into it?

"Danny, it's Harry. I'm returning your husband's call."

"He's asleep."

"Can you wake him, please? It sounded important."

"I can tell you what he wanted to tell you."

"Okay."

"He wanted to tell you that when he was working he used to keep copies of his active files. He kept them here in the home office."

I didn't recall seeing an office in the house.

"Full copies?"

"I don't know. He had a filing cabinet and it was full."

"Had?"

"His sitting room is where the office was. I had to move everything out. It's all in the garage now."

I realized I needed to stop the flow of information from her. Too much had already been said on the phone. Paranoia was raising its ugly head again.

"I'm coming out tonight," I said.

"No, it's too late. I'm going to bed soon."

"I'll be there in half an hour, Danny. Wait up for me."

I hung the phone up before she could further dispute my intentions. Without having gone further into the house than the kitchen I turned and left, this time leaving the light on.

A light rain had begun to fall in the Valley. Oil beaded on the freeway and slowed everybody down. I used all of the half hour and more to get to the house on Melba and shortly after I pulled into the driveway the garage door started to go up. Danny Cross had been watching for me. I got out of the Mercedes and entered the garage.

It was a two-car garage and it was cluttered with stacked boxes and furniture. There was an old Chevy Malibu with its hood sprung like somebody had been working on the engine and had just lowered the lid without latching it while taking a break. I think I remembered something about Lawton Cross driving a '60s muscle car as a private vehicle. But there was a thick layer of dust on the car and boxes stacked on its roof. One thing for sure was that he was never going to work on it or drive it again.

A door that connected to the house opened and Danny stood there in a long bathrobe with a belt knotted tightly around her thin waist. She had the same look of disapproval she always had on her face and that I had become quite used to. It was too bad. She was a beautiful woman. Or had been, at least.

"Danny," I said, nodding. "I won't be long. If you can just point me in —"

"It's all over there next to the washing machine. The file cabinets."

She pointed to a spot in front of the Malibu where there was a laundry alcove. I walked around the car and found two double-drawer file cabinets standing next to the stacked washer and dryer. They were key-lock cabinets but the locks had been punched out on each. Lawton had probably picked them up used at a yard sale.

There was no exterior labeling on the four drawers that could help me with my search so I bent down and opened the first drawer on the left. It contained no files. Rather, it held what looked like the contents of a top of a desk. There was a Rolodex file, its phone cards yellowed, a stand-up photo frame featuring Danny and Lawton Cross at some happier moment, and double-decked in and out trays. The only thing in the tray marked "IN" was a folded map of Griffith Park.

The next drawer contained Cross's files. I thumbed through the tabs looking at the names and hoping for connections to what I was working. Nothing. I went to the top drawer of the second cabinet and found more files. Finally, I found a file marked "Eidolon Productions." I pulled it and put it on top of the cabinet. I went back to thumbing through the files, knowing that often cases expanded into many folders.

I came across a file marked "Antonio Markwell" and remembered the case because it had played hotly in the media about five or six years earlier. Markwell was a nine-year-old boy who disappeared from his backyard in Chatsworth. RHD worked the case with the FBI. It lasted a week, until they found a suspect — a pedophile with a motor home. He led Lawton Cross and his partner, Jack Dorsey, to the boy's body in Griffith Park. It had been buried up near the caves in Bronson Canyon. They would have never found it if they hadn't turned the killer. There were too many places to hide a body in those hills.

It had been a big case, the kind that made your name in the department. I imagined that both Cross and Dorsey thought that they were golden after that. They had no idea what the future was holding for them.

I closed the drawer. There were no other files that seemed connected to my investigation. The bottom drawer, the last one, was empty. I took the file I had pulled over to the Malibu. I put the file down on the hood and opened it. I should have just put it under my arm and left with it. But I was excited. I was anticipating something. A new lead maybe, a break. I wanted to see what Lawton Cross had kept in the file.

As soon as I opened it I knew the file was incomplete. Cross had copied some of the working documents of the case for use at home or on the road. The basic case reports were missing. There were no reports that specifically related to the investigation of the murder of Angella Benton. The file mostly contained reports relating to the movie set robbery and shoot-out. There were witness reports — including my own — and forensic reports. There was a DNA comparison between the blood found in the stolen movie van and the semen found on Angella Benton's body; no match. There were interview summaries and a time and location spread sheet — a document on which the locations of various players in the case are charted at different times important to the case. These T&L reports were also known as alibi sheets. It was a way of sifting through multiple players in a case and possibly coming up with a suspect.

I quickly went through the pages of this report and determined that Cross and Dorsey had been charting eleven different people and not all of the names were familiar to me. The T&L report was a good find. I put the document to the side because I would put it at the top of the stack in the file when I was finished my review.

I moved on and had just picked up a copy of the currency report, which contained the serial numbers taken at random from the stolen money, when I heard Danny's voice behind me. She had remained in the doorway to the house watching me and I hadn't realized it.

"Find what you were looking for?"

I turned and looked back at her. The first thing I noticed was that the belt of her robe was untied and the robe had fallen open to reveal the light blue nightgown beneath.

"Uh, yes, it's here. I was just taking a quick look. I can go now if you want."

"What's your hurry? Lawton is still asleep. He won't wake up until the morning."

She held my eyes as she said the last line. I was trying to read what was said and what was meant. Before I could respond, the moment was broken by the sound and the lights of a car pulling quickly into the driveway.

I turned and saw a standard government car — a Crown Victoria — pulling into the light from the open garage. Two men were in the car and I recognized the one in the passenger seat. With as little noticeable movement as I could manage I lowered the currency report onto the T&L report. I then picked them both up and slid them into the crack between the Malibu's hood and fender. I heard the pages fall through the slot into the engine compartment. I then stepped back from the car, leaving the rest of the file open on the hood, and around into the open bay of the garage.

A second Crown Vic pulled into the driveway. The two men from the first car were already out and entering the garage.

"FBI," said the man I recognized as Parenting Today.

He held up an ID case with a badge affixed to it. He just as quickly closed it and put it away.

"How are the kids?" I asked.

He seemed confused for a moment and it put a pause in his step. But then he pressed on and took a position in front of me while his partner, who had not shown a badge, stood a few feet to my right.

"Mr. Bosch, we are going to need you to come with us," said Parenting Today.

"Well, I'm kind of busy at the moment. I'm trying to get this garage in shape."

The agent looked over my shoulder at Danny Cross.

"Ma'am, could you return inside and close the door? We'll be out of your hair in a few moments."

"This is my garage, my house," Danny responded.

I knew her protest was useless but I liked that she'd made it just the same.

"Ma'am, this is FBI business. It does not concern you. Please step inside."

"If it is in my garage it concerns me."

"Ma'am, I won't ask you again."

There was a pause. I kept my eyes on the agent. I heard the door close behind me and knew my witness was gone. In the same moment the agent to my right made his move. He raised both hands and charged me, pushing me into the side of the Malibu. My elbow slid across the roof and hit a box, sending it over the other side of the car and crashing to the floor. It sounded like it had glassware in it.

The agent was well practiced and I offered no resistance. I knew that would be a mistake. That would be what he wanted. He roughly pushed my chest against the car and pulled my arms behind my back. I felt the handcuffs cinch tightly around my wrists, then his hands patted me down for weapons and invaded my pockets in a routine search.

"What are you doing? What is going on?"

It was Danny. She had heard the crash.

"Ma'am," Parenting Today said sternly, "go back inside and close the door."

The other agent twirled me away from the car and pushed me out of the garage toward the second car. I looked back at Danny Cross just as she was closing the door. The look of disapproval I was so used to was gone. There was a look of concern on her face now. I also saw that her bathrobe had been retied.

The silent agent opened the back door of the second car and started pushing me in.

"Watch your head," he said just as he put his hand on my neck and pushed my head sharply into the door frame. I went sprawling across the backseat. He slammed the door, narrowly missing my ankle with it. I could almost hear a groan of disappointment from him through the glass.

He knocked his fist on the roof of the car and the driver dropped the transmission into reverse and hit the gas. The car jerked backwards and the sudden motion threw me off the seat onto the floor. I was unable to break my fall and the side of my face hit hard on the sticky floor. With my hands behind me I struggled to push myself back onto the seat. But I did it quickly, my struggle fueled by my anger and embarrassment. I sat up as the car jerked forward and I was thrown back into the seat. The car sped away from the house and through the rear window I saw Parenting Today standing in the garage and staring back at me. He held Lawton Cross's file down at his side.

I breathed heavily and watched the agent grow small in the window. I could feel crud from the floor mat on my face and could do nothing about it. My face burned. Not with pain and no longer with anger and embarrassment. It was pure helplessness that burned me now.

19

Halfway to Westwood I stopped talking to them. It was useless and I knew it but I had spent twenty minutes hitting them with questions, then veiled threats, and no matter what I said there was no response. When we finally got to the federal building the bureau car was driven down into a subterranean garage and I was pulled out and shoved into an elevator marked "Security Transport Only." One of the agents put a card key into a slot on the control panel and punched the 9 button. As the stainless steel cube rose I thought about how far I had fallen from the badge. I had no juice with these men. They were agents and I was nothing. They could do with me what they wanted and we all knew it.

"I can't feel my fingers," I said. "The cuffs are too tight."

"That's nice," one of the agents said, his first words of the evening to me.

The doors opened and each one of them took an arm and pushed me into the hallway. We came to a door one of them opened with the card key, then we went down a hallway to another door, this one with a combination lock.

"Turn away," an agent said.

"What?"

"Turn away from the door."

I followed instructions and was turned away when the other agent tapped in the combination. We then went through and I was led into a dimly lit hallway of doors with small square windows head high. At first I thought they were interview rooms but then I realized there were too many. These were cells. I turned my head to look through some of the windows as we passed and through two of them I saw men looking back out at me. They were dark skinned and of Middle Eastern descent. They wore unkempt beards. Through a third window I saw a short man looking out, his eyes barely at the bottom level of the small window. He had bleached blond hair that had a quarter inch of black at its roots. I recognized him from the photo I had seen on the computer at the library. Mousouwa Aziz.

We stopped in front of a door marked "29," and it was popped open electronically by some unseen hand. One of the agents stepped behind me and I heard him working a key into the handcuffs. I was beyond being able to feel it. Soon my wrists were free and I brought my hands around so that I could rub them and get the circulation going again. They were as white as soap, and a deep red welt ran around the circumference of each wrist. I had always believed that cuffing a suspect too tightly was a bullshit thing to do. Same with hitting a custody's head on the frame of the car door. Easy to do, easy to get away with. But always a bullshit move. A bully's move. The kind of thing a boy who enjoyed teasing the younger kids in the schoolyard would grow up to do.

As the tingling feeling started to work its way into my hands a burning sense of anger started building behind my eyes, edging my vision with a velvet blackness. In that darkness was a voice urging me to retaliate. I managed to ignore it. It's all about power and when to use it. These guys didn't know that yet.

A hand pushed me toward the cell and I involuntarily braced myself. I didn't want to go in there. Then a sharp kick hit me behind my left knee and my leg buckled and I was hurled forward with a stiff-arm shove from behind. I crossed the small square cell to the opposite wall and put my hands up to stop my forward momentum.

"Make yourself at home, asshole," the agent said to my back.

The door was slammed before I could get back to it. I stood there looking at the square of glass, realizing that the other prisoners I had seen in the hallway had been looking at themselves. The glass was mirrored.

Instinctively I knew the agent that had kicked and shoved me was on the other side looking at me. I nodded to him, sending the message that I would not forget him. He was probably on the other side laughing back at me.

The light in the room stayed on. I eventually stepped away from the door and looked around. There was a one-inch-thick mattress on a shelflike outcropping from the wall. Built into the opposite wall was a sink-and-toilet combination. There was nothing else except a steel box in one of the upper corners with a two-inch-square window behind which I could see a camera lens. I was being watched. Even if I used the toilet I was being watched.

I checked my watch but there was no watch. They had somehow taken it, probably when they took off the cuffs and my wrists were so numb I could not feel the theft.

I spent what I thought was the first hour of my incarceration pacing in the small space and trying to keep my anger sharp but controlled. I walked without pattern other than that I used the entire space, and when I came to the corner where the camera was located I raised the middle finger of my left hand to the lens. Every time.

In the second hour I sat on the mattress, determined not to exhaust myself with the pacing and trying to keep track of time. On occasion I still gave the camera my finger, usually without even bothering to look up while I delivered it. I started thinking about interview room stories to pass the time. I remembered one about a guy we had brought in as a suspect in a double bagger involving a drug rip-off. Our plan was to sweat him a little before we went into the room and tried to break him down. But soon after being placed in the room he took his pants off, tied the legs around his neck and tried to hang himself from the overhead light fixture. They got to him in time and the man was saved. He protested that he would rather kill himself than spend another hour in the room. He had only been in there twenty minutes.

I started laughing to myself and then remembered another story, one that wasn't so funny. A man who was a peripheral witness to a strong-arm robbery was brought into the box and questioned about what he saw. It was late on a Friday. He was an illegal and he was scared shitless, but he wasn't a suspect and it would mean too many phone calls and too much paperwork to send him back to Mexico. All that the detective wanted was his information. But before he got it the detective was called out of the interview room. He told the man to sit tight, that he'd be back. Only he never came back. Breaking events on the case took him out into the field and soon he forgot about the witness. On Sunday morning another detective who had come in to try to catch up on his paperwork heard a knocking sound and opened the interview room door to find the witness still there. He had taken empty coffee cups out of the trash can and filled them with urine during the weekend. But as instructed he had never left the unlocked interview room.

Remembering that one made me feel morose. After a while I took off my jacket and lay back on the mattress. I put the jacket over my face to try to block out the light. I tried to give the impression I was sleeping, that I didn't care what they were doing to me. But I wasn't sleeping and they probably knew it. I'd seen it all before when I had been on the other side of the glass.

Finally, I tried to concentrate on the case, running all of the latest occurrences through my head, trying to see how they fit. Why had the bureau stepped in? Because I was getting a copy of Lawton Cross's file? It seemed unlikely. I decided that I had struck the nerve in the library when I had looked up the reports on Mousouwa Aziz. They had talked to the librarian or checked the computer — new laws allowed them to. That was what brought them out. That was what they wanted to know about.

After what I estimated to be about four hours in the cube the door snapped open with an electronic release. I pulled the jacket off my face and sat up just as an agent I had not seen before stepped in. He was carrying a file and a cup of coffee. The agent I knew as Parenting Today stood behind him with a steel chair.

"Don't get up," the first agent said.

I stood up anyway.

"What the hell is —"

"I said don't get up. You sit back down or I'm out of here and we'll try again tomorrow."

I hesitated a moment, holding my pose as an angry man and then sat down on the mattress. Parenting Today put the chair down just inside the door and then stepped out of the cell and closed the door. The remaining agent sat down and lowered his steaming coffee to the floor. The smell of it filled the room.

"I'm Special Agent John Peoples with the Federal Bureau of Investigation."

"Good for you. What am I doing here?"

"You are here because you do not listen."

He brought his eyes to mine to make sure I was doing what he just said I do not do. He was my age, maybe a little older. He had all of his hair and it was a little too long for the bureau. I guessed that it wasn't a style choice. He was just too busy to get it properly cut.

His eyes were the thing. Every face has a magnetic feature, the thing that draws you in. A nose, a scar, a cleft chin. With Peoples everything was drawn to the eyes. They were deeply set and dark. They were worried. They carried a secret burden.

"You were told to stand down, Mr. Bosch," he said. "You were told rather explicitly to leave things alone and yet here we are."

"Can you answer a question?"

"I can try. If it's not classified."

"Is my watch classified? Where's my watch? It was given to me when I retired and I want it back."

"Mr. Bosch, forget about your watch for now. I am trying to get something through that thick skull of yours but you don't want it to get through, do you?"

He reached down for his coffee and took a sip. He grimaced as he burned his mouth. He put the cup back down on the floor.

"More important things are at work here than your private investigation and your hundred-dollar retirement watch."

I put a look of surprise on my face.

"You really think that's all they spent on me after all those years?"

Peoples frowned and shook his head.

"You are not helping yourself here, Mr. Bosch. You are compromising an investigation that is vitally significant to this country and here all you want to do is show how clever you are."

"This is the national security rap, right? It is, isn't it? Well, Special Agent Peoples, you can hang on to it for next time. I don't consider a murder investigation to be unimportant. There are no compromises when it comes to murder."

Peoples stood up and stepped toward me until he was looking directly down at me. He leaned over the bed, putting his hand against the wall for support.

"*Hieronymus Bosch,*" he yelled, actually pronouncing it correctly. "You are trespassing! You are driving the wrong way down a one-way street! Do you understand!"

He then turned and went back to his chair. I almost laughed at the theatrics and for a moment thought that he did not realize that I had spent twenty-five years working in rooms like these.

"Am I getting through to you at all?" Peoples said, his voice calm once again. "You are not a cop. You carry no badge. You have no provenance, no case. You have no standing."

"It used to be a free country. That used to be enough standing."

"It's not the same country it used to be. Things have changed."

He proffered the file held in his hand.

"The murder of this woman is important. Of course it is. But there are other things at play here. More important matters. You must step back from it, Mr. Bosch. This is the final warning. *Stand down.* Or we will stand you down. And you won't like it."

"I bet I'll end up back here? Right? With Mouse and the others? The other enemy combatants. Isn't that what you call them? Does anyone even know about this place, Agent Peoples? Anyone outside your own little BAM squad?"

He seemed momentarily taken aback by my knowledge and use of the term.

"I recognized Mouse when they brought me in. I was window shopping."

"And from that you think you know what goes on here?"

"You're working the guy. It's obvious and that's fine. But what if he's the one who killed Angella Benton? What if he killed the bank security man? And what if he killed an FBI agent, too? Don't you care about what happened to Martha Gessler? She was one of your own. Has the world changed that much? Is a special agent no longer special under these new rules of yours? Or does the line change according to convenience? Am I an enemy combatant, Agent Peoples?"

I could see it hurt. My words opened an old wound if not an old debate. But then a resolve came across his face. He opened the file in his hands and took out the printout I had made at the library. I could see the mugshot of Aziz.

"How did you know about this? How did you make this connection?"

"You people."

"What are you talking about? No one here would tell you —"

"They didn't have to. I saw your man tailing me in the library. Make a note of that — he's not that good. Tell him to try *Sports Illustrated* next time. I knew something was up so I ran a search through the newspaper files and came up with that. I printed it out because I knew it might flush you people out. And it did. Your kind are very predictable.

"Anyway, then I saw Mouse when they were walking me down the hall and I sort of put things together. Money from my robbery was under the seat of his car when you arrested him. But you don't care about that or the two and maybe three murders attached to it. You just want to know where that money was going. And you don't want a little thing like justice for the dead to get in the way of that."

Peoples slowly slid the printout back into the file. I could see his face changing, growing darker around the eyes. I had stuck my words directly into a nerve.

"You have no idea what the world is like out there or what we are doing about it in here," he said. "You can sit here and be smug and talk about your ideas of justice. But you have no fucking idea what is out there."

My response to that was a smile. My words came readily.

"You can save that speech for the politicians who change the rules for you until there are no rules anymore. Until something like justice for a murdered and violated woman adds up to nothing in the equation. That's what's going on out there."

Peoples leaned forward. He was about to spill and he wanted to make damn sure I got it.

"Do you know where Aziz was going with that money? We don't know but I can tell you where I think he was going with it. To a training camp. A terrorist training camp. And I'm not talking about in Afghanistan. I'm talking about within a hundred miles of our border. A place where they train people to kill us. In our buildings, in our planes. In our sleep. To come across that line and kill us with blind disregard for who we are and what we believe. Are you going to tell me that I'm wrong, that we should not do everything we can to find such a place if it exists? That we should not take whatever measures are necessary with that man to get the information we need from him?"

I leaned back across the mattress until my back was against the wall. If I'd had a cup of coffee I wouldn't have ignored it the way he was ignoring his.

"I'm not telling you anything," I said. "Everybody's got to do what they've got to do."

"Wonderful," he said sarcastically. "Words of wisdom. I'm going to get a wall plaque for my office and put that right on it."

"You know, I was in a trial once and the lawyer on the other side said something I always try to remember. She quoted a philosopher whose name I don't recall offhand — I've got it written down at the house. But this guy said that whoever is out there fighting the monsters of our society should make damn sure that they don't become monsters themselves. See, because then all is lost. Then we don't have a society. I always thought that was a good line."

"Nietzsche. And you almost got the quote right."

"Getting the quote right isn't what matters. It's remembering what it means."

Peoples reached into the pocket of his coat. He pulled out my watch. He threw it to me and I started putting it on. I looked at the face. The hands of the clock were set against a gold detective's badge with the city hall on it. I noted the time and saw that I had been in the cube longer than I had thought. It was almost dawn.

"Get out of here, Bosch," he said. "If you cross our field of vision on this again you will find yourself back here faster than you'd think was possible. And no one will know you are here."

The threat was obvious.

"I'll be among the disappeared then, huh?"

"Whatever you want to call it."

Peoples raised his hand over his head so the camera would see it. He twirled a finger in the air and the electronic lock on the door clacked and the door opened a few inches. I stood up.

"Go," Peoples said. "Somebody will see you out. I'm cutting you a break here, Bosch. Remember that."

I headed toward the door but hesitated when I was passing him. I looked down at him and the file he still clutched.

"I assume you cleaned me out, took my files. Lawton Cross's too."

"You won't be getting it back."

"Right, I understand. National security. What I was going to say is look through the photos. Find one of the photos of Angella on the tile. Look at her hands, man."

I headed toward the open door.

"What about her hands?" he called after me.

"Just look at her hands. The way we found them. You'll know what I'm talking about then."

In the hallway Parenting Today was waiting for me.

"This way," he said curtly and I could tell he was disappointed that I was being cut loose.

On the way up the hallway I looked for Mousouwa Aziz in one of the square windows but didn't see him. I wondered if by chance I had looked into the face of the killer I was looking for and that it would be my only glimpse, that I would get no closer. I knew that as long as he was in here I would never get to him, literally or legally. He was gone from me. He was among the disappeared. The ultimate dead end.

We went out through two electronic doors and then I was delivered to an elevator alcove. There was no button for me to push. Parenting Today looked up at a camera in the corner of the ceiling and rolled an extended finger in the air. I heard the elevator start coming.

When the doors opened he escorted me on. We went down to the basement but not to a car. He walked me up the ramp after yelling to a garage man to open the roll-up door. As the door went up I was hit with sunlight and had to squint.

"I take it you aren't giving me a ride back to my car."

"You can take it any way you want to. Have a good day."

He left me there at the top of the ramp and turned around to get under the door before it reclosed on him. I watched him disappear as the steel curtain dropped. I tried to think of a clever line to throw at him but I was too damn tired and let it go.

20

The bureau had been in my house. That was expected. But the agents had been subtle about it. The place hadn't been torn apart and left for me to put back together. It had been methodically searched and most things had been left exactly in place. The dining room table, where I had left the spread of files relating to Angella Benton's murder, had been cleared. It looked like they might have even polished the empty surface with Pledge when they were through. I had been left nothing. My notes, my files, my reports were all gone and so it seemed was the case. I didn't dwell on it. I looked at my murky reflection in the polished surface of the table for a few moments and decided I needed to sleep before making my next move.

I grabbed a bottle of water out of the refrigerator and went out through the slider to the back deck to watch the sun come up over the hills. The cushion on the lounge chair had morning dew on it so I flipped it over and sat down. I put my legs up and leaned back into the soft comfort. There was a slight chill in the air but I still had my jacket on. I put the water bottle on the arm of the chair and tucked my hands into the pockets of the jacket. It felt good to be home after the night in the cube.

The sun was just cresting the hills on the other side of the Cahuenga Pass. The sky was filled with diffused light as its rays refracted off the billions of microscopic particles that hung in the air. Soon I would need sunglasses but I was too dug in to get up to get them. I closed my eyes instead and soon fell asleep. I dreamt of Angella Benton, of her hands, of a woman I never knew in life but who came alive in my dreams and reached out to me.

I woke up a couple hours later with the sun burning through my eyelids. Soon I realized that the pounding I had thought was in my head was actually coming from the front door. I got up, knocking the unopened water bottle off the arm of the lounge chair. I made a grab for it but missed. It rolled off the deck and down into the brush below. I walked to the rail and looked down. Steel pylons held my house cantilevered over the canyon. I could not see the bottle down there.

Whoever it was out front knocked again and then I heard a muffled version of my name. I went in off the deck and crossed the living room to the front hallway. He was pounding on the door again when I finally opened it. It was Roy Lindell and he wasn't smiling.

"Rise and shine, Bosch."

He started to push by me into the house but I put my hand on his chest and pushed him backwards. I shook my head and he picked up the vibe. He pointed in the house and put a question mark in his eyes. I nodded and stepped out through the door, pulling it closed behind me.

"Let's take my car," he said in a low voice.

"Good. 'Cause mine's in Woodland Hills."

His bureau car was parked illegally at the front curb.

We got in and headed up Woodrow Wilson to the curve that took it around toward Mulholland. I didn't think he was taking me anywhere. We were just driving.

"What happened to you?" he asked. "I heard through the grapevine you got picked up last night."

"That's right. By your BAM squad. They put the bam on me, you could say."

Lindell looked over at me and then back at the road.

"You don't look the worse for wear. You even got some color in your cheeks."

"Thanks for noticing, Roy. Now what do you want?"

"You think they've got your house bugged?"

"Prob'ly. I haven't had time to check. What do you want? Where are we going?"

Though I guessed I knew. Mulholland wound around the hill to an overlook with views, depending on the smog ratio, from the Santa Monica Bay to the spires of downtown.

As expected, Lindell pulled into the small parking lot and stopped next to a Volkswagen van three decades out of place. The smog was heavy. For the most part the view dropped off just past the Capital Records building.

"Get to the point, huh?" Lindell said, turning in his seat toward me. "Okay, I'll get to it. What's going on with the investigation?"

I looked at him for a long moment, trying to gauge whether he had turned up because of Marty Gessler or as a follow-up from Special Agent Peoples. As a test to determine if I was out of it. Sure Lindell and Peoples were different animals from different floors of the federal building. But they both carried the same badge. And there was no telling what kind of pressure had been brought to bear on Lindell.

"What's going on is that there is no investigation."

"What? Are you fucking me?"

"No, I'm not fucking you. You could say I see the light. I was made to see it."

"Then what are you going to do, just drop it?"

"That's right. I'm going to get my car and go on vacation. Vegas, I think. I got a start on the sunburn this morning. I might as well go lose my money, too."

Lindell smiled like he was clever.

"Fuck you," he said. "I know what you're doing. You think I've been sent out to test you, huh? Well, fuck you."

"That's nice, Roy. Can you take me back now? I need to pack a bag."

"Not until you tell me what is really going on."

I cracked the door.

"Okay, I can walk. I need the exercise."

I got out and started walking toward Mulholland. Lindell threw open his door, hitting the side of the old van. He came hurrying after me.

"Listen, Bosch, listen to me."

He caught up to me and stood in front of me, very close, forcing me to stop. He put his hands into fists and held them up in front of his chest as if he was trying to break apart a chain that was binding him.

"Harry, I'm here for me. Nobody sent me, okay? Do not drop this. Those guys down there, they were probably just throwing you a scare, that's all."

"Tell that to the people they've been holding in there. I don't feel like disappearing, Roy. You know what I mean?"

"Bullshit. You've never been the kind of guy who would —"

"Hey! Asshole!"

I turned around at the sound of the voice and saw two men piling out of the sliding door of the Volkswagen van. They were bearded longhairs who looked like they belonged on Harleys, not in a hippie van.

"You dented the shit out of the door," the second one yelled.

"How the fuck can you tell?" Lindell shot back.

Here we go, I thought. I looked past the approaching behemoths and could see a four-inch crease in the front passenger door of the Volkswagen. Lindell's door was still open and in contact with it, the obvious culprit.

"You think it's a joke?" said the first heavy. "How about if we put a dent in your face?"

Lindell reached behind his back and in one swift move his hand came out from under his jacket with a pistol. With his free hand he reached forward and grabbed the first heavy by the front of his shirt and pulled him forward, taking a handful of beard in the process. The gun came up and the barrel was pressed into the taller man's throat.

"How 'bout you and David Crosby get back in that piece of shit and flower power your way the fuck out of here?"

"Roy," I said. "Easy."

The smell of marijuana was just now reaching us from the van. There was a long moment of silence while Lindell held eyes with the first heavy. The second stood nearby watching but unable to make a move because of the gun.

"Okay, man," the first one finally said. "Everything's cool. We'll just back on out of here."

Lindell shoved him away and dropped the gun down to his side.

"Yeah, you do that, Tiny. Back on out. Go smoke the peace pipe somewhere else."

We watched silently while they went back to the van, the second man angrily slamming Lindell's door so he could get into the front passenger seat of the van. The engine started and the van backed out and pulled out onto Mulholland. The requisite hand gestures were offered from both driver and passenger and then they were gone. I thought about myself just a few hours earlier giving the same salute to the camera in the cube. I knew how helpless the two men in the van felt.

Lindell turned his attention back to me.

"That was good, Roy," I said to him. "With skills like that I'm surprised they didn't tap you for a ninth-floor gig."

"Fuck those guys."

"Yeah, that's the way I was feeling a few hours ago."

"So then what's it going to be, Bosch?"

He had just pulled a gun on two strangers in a near-violent collision of high-testosterone levels and already the tide had subsided. The surface was calm. The incident was off his radar screen after only one sweep. It was a trait that in the past I had most often seen in psychopaths. I wanted to give Lindell the benefit of the doubt so I chalked it up to the sort of federal arrogance I had also seen before as a genetic trait in bureau men.

"You staying or running?" he asked.

That made me angry but I tried not to show it. I cracked a smile.

"Neither," I said. "I'm walking."

I turned and left him there. I started walking up Mulholland toward Woodrow Wilson and home. He threw a barrage of curses at my back but that didn't slow me down.

21

The garage door was open at Lawton Cross's house and it looked as though it might have been left that way through the night. I had the cab drop me off in the street next to my Mercedes. It didn't look like the car had been moved, though I had to assume it had been searched. I had left it unlocked and it still was. I put the small bag I had packed and brought with me into the backseat. I then got behind the wheel, started the engine and pulled the car into the open bay of the garage.

After I got out I went to the house's door and pushed a button that would either ring a bell inside or close the garage door. It closed the door. I went over to the Chevy, slid my hands beneath the hood and felt for the release latch. The steel springs yawned loudly as I raised the hood. I looked down at a dusty but clean engine with a chrome air filter cowling and fan highlighting a painted red block. Lawton had obviously babied the car and had appreciated its internal as well as exterior beauty.

The documents from the investigative file that I had slipped beneath the hood the night before had survived the

FBI search. They had fallen and been cradled by the web of spark plug wires on the left side of the block. As I gathered them I noticed that the car's battery had been disconnected and I wondered when this had been done. It was a smart thing to do with a car that was not going to be used for a while. Lawton probably would have thought of doing it but would not have been able to actually do it. Maybe he had talked Danny through the procedure.

"What's going on? What are you doing, Harry?"

I turned. Danny Cross was in the doorway to the house.

"Hello, Danny. I just came back for some things I forgot. I also need to use some of Law's tools. I think something's wrong with my car."

I gestured toward the workbench and Peg-Board that lined the wall next to the Malibu. An array of tools and automotive equipment was on display. She shook her head like I had forgotten to explain the obvious.

"What about last night? They took you. I saw the handcuffs. The agents who stayed said you wouldn't be coming back."

"Scare tactics, Danny. That's all that was. As you can see, I'm back."

I closed the hood with one hand, leaving it partially sprung in the way I had found it. I walked to the Mercedes and reached the documents in through the open window to the passenger seat. I then thought better about that and opened the door, raised the floor mat and put them under it. It wasn't a great hiding place but it would do for the moment. I closed the door and looked at Danny.

"How is Law?"

"Not good."

"What's wrong?"

"They were in there with him last night. They wouldn't let me in and then they turned off the monitor so I couldn't exactly hear everything. But they scared him. And they scared me. I want you to go, Harry. I want you to go and not come back."

"How'd they scare you? What did they say?"

She hesitated and I knew that was part of the scare.

"They told you not to talk about it, right? Not to talk to me?"

"That's right."

"Okay, Danny, I don't want to get you in trouble. What about Law? Can I talk to him?"

"He said he doesn't want to see you anymore. That it's caused too much trouble."

I nodded and looked over at the workbench.

"Then let me just get to my car and I'll get out of here."

"Did they hurt you, Harry?"

I looked at her. I think she really cared about the answer.

"No, I'm all right."

"Okay."

"Uh, Danny, I need to get something from Law's sitting room. Should I go in or can you get it for me? What would be better?"

"What is it?"

"The clock."

"The clock? Why? You gave it to him."

"I know. But I need it back."

A look of annoyance came across her face. I thought maybe the clock had been a point of argument between them, and now I was taking it back.

"I'll get it but I'm telling him you're the one taking it off the wall."

I nodded. She went inside the house and I went around the Malibu and found a dolly leaning against the workbench. I took a pair of pliers and a screwdriver off the Peg-Board and went back to the Mercedes.

After throwing my jacket into the car I got down on the dolly and slid under the car. It took me less than a minute to find the black box. A satellite tracker about the size of a hardback book was held to the gas tank with two industrial-size strip magnets. There was a twist to the setup I hadn't seen before. A wire extended from the box to the exhaust pipe where it was connected to a heat sensor. When the pipe heated up, the sensor switched on the tracker, conserving the unit's battery when the vehicle wasn't moving. The boys on the ninth floor got the good stuff.

I decided then to leave the box in place and slid out from underneath the car. Danny was standing there, holding the clock. She had taken the back off, exposing the camera.

"I thought it was too heavy for just a wall clock," she said.

I started getting up.

"Look, Danny . . ."

"You were spying on us. You didn't believe me, did you?"

"Danny, that's not what I want it for. Those men that came here last —"

"But it *is* what you put it on that wall for. Where's the tape?"

"What?"

"The tape. Where did you watch this?"

"I didn't. It's digital. It's all right there in the clock."

That was a mistake. As I reached for the clock she raised it up over her head and then threw it down to the concrete floor. The glass shattered and the camera broke loose from the clock shell and skittered under the Mercedes.

"Goddamnit, Danny. It isn't mine."

"I don't care whose it is. You had no right to do that."

"Look, Law told me you weren't treating him right. What was I supposed to do? Just take your word for it?"

I got down on the floor and looked under the car. The camera was within reach and I pulled it out. The casing was badly scratched but I could not make any judgment about its interior mechanisms. I ejected the memory card the way Andre Biggar had taught me and it looked okay to me. I stood up and held it up for Danny to see.

"This might be the only thing that keeps those men from coming back. You better hope it's not damaged."

"I don't carc. And I hope you really enjoy what you see on it. I hope you're very proud of yourself when you watch it."

I had no response for that.

"Don't come back here ever again."

She turned and went into the house, her hand slapping the wall button, which brought the garage door up behind me. She closed the house's door without looking back at me. I waited a moment to see if she would reappear and throw another verbal attack at me. But she didn't. I pocketed the memory card and then squatted down to gather the pieces of the broken clock.

22

At Burbank Airport I parked in the long-term lot, got my bag out and took the tram to the terminal. At the Southwest counter I used a credit card to buy a round-trip ticket to Las Vegas on a flight leaving in less than an hour. I kept the return open. I then proceeded through the security checkpoint, waiting in line like everybody else. I put my bag on the conveyor and dropped my watch, car keys and the camera's memory card into a plastic bowl so I would not set off the metal detector. I realized I had left my cell in the Mercedes and then thought, just as well, they might use it to triangulate my location.

Near the departure gate I stopped and bought a ten-dollar phone card and took it to a nearby bank of pay phones. I read the instructions on the phone card twice. Not because they were complicated but because I was hesitant. Finally, I picked up the receiver and called long distance. It was a number I knew by heart but had not called in almost a year.

She answered after only two rings but I could tell I had woken her up. I almost hung up, knowing that even if she had caller ID she would not be able to tell it had been me. But after her second hello I finally spoke.

"Eleanor, it's me, Harry. Did I wake you up?"

"It's okay. Are you all right?"

"Yeah, I'm fine. Were you playing late?"

"Till about five and then we went for breakfast. I feel like I just got to bed. What time is it?"

I told her it was after ten and she groaned. I felt the confidence go out of my plan. I also got stuck wondering who the 'we' she referred to was but didn't ask. I was supposed to be long past that.

"Harry, what is it?" she said into the silence. "Are you sure you're all right?"

"Yeah, I'm fine. I didn't get to sleep till about the same time, too."

More silence slipped into the wire. I noticed that they were boarding my flight.

"Is that why you called me? To tell me your sleeping habits?"

"No, I, uh . . . well, I sort of need some help. Over there in Vegas."

"Help? What do you mean? You mean like on a case? You told me you retired."

"I did. I am. But there's this thing I'm working on. . . . Anyway, I was wondering if you could meet me at the airport in about an hour. I'm flying in."

There was silence while she registered this request and all that it might mean. As I waited my chest felt heavy and tight. I was thinking about the single-bullet theory when she finally spoke.

"I can be there. Where am I taking you?"

I realized I had been holding my breath. I exhaled. Deep down in the velvet folds I knew that would be her answer but hearing it spoken out loud, the confirmation of it, filled me immediately with my own confirmation of the feelings I still carried. I tried to picture her on the other end of the line. She was in bed, the phone on the bed table, her hair messy in a way I always found to be a turn-on, that made me want to stay in bed with her. Then I remembered that this was a cell number. She didn't have a landline, at least one that I had the number for. And then that "we" thing came up again, intruding like a telephone solicitor. Whose bed was she in?

"Harry, you still there?"

"Yeah, I'm here. Uh, just to a car-rental place. Avis, I guess. They try harder. Supposedly."

"Harry, they have buses that come by the airport every five minutes for that. What do you need me for? What's going on?"

"Look, I'll explain when I get there. My flight's boarding. Can you be there, Eleanor?"

"I said I'll be there," she said in a tone I was too familiar with, as if she was relenting and reluctant at the same time.

I didn't dwell on it. I had what I needed. I left it at that.

"Thank you. How about right outside Southwest? Is it still the Taurus you had before?"

"No, Harry, it's a silver Lexus now. Four-door. And I'll have my lights on. I'll flick them if I see you first."

"Okay, I'll see you then. Thanks, Eleanor."

I hung up and headed for the gate. A Lexus, I thought as I moved. I had priced them before buying the used Mercedes. They weren't outrageous but they weren't cheap. Things must be changing for her. I was pretty sure I was happy about that.

By the time I got on the plane there was no room in the overhead compartments for my bag and only middle seats left for me. I squeezed in between a man in a Hawaiian shirt and thick gold neck chain and a woman so pale I thought she might detonate like a match the moment she was hit by the Nevada sun. I zoned out, kept my elbows to myself, though the Hawaiian shirt guy didn't, and managed to close my eyes and almost sleep for most of the short flight. I knew there was a lot to think about and the memory card was almost burning a hole in my pocket as I wondered about its contents, but I also instinctively knew that I needed to grab rest while I could. I wasn't expecting to get too much of it once I got back to L.A.

Less than an hour after takeoff I walked out through the terminal's automatic doors at McCarran and was hit with the oven-dry blast of heat that signaled arrival in Las Vegas. It didn't faze me. My eyes intently searched the vehicles stacked in the pickup lanes until they held on a silver car with its lights on. The sunroof was open and the driver's hand was reaching through it and waving. She was flicking the brights at me, too. It was Eleanor. I waved and trotted to the car. I opened the door, threw my bag over the seat into the back and got in.

"Hi," I said. "Thanks."

After a moment's hesitation we both leaned to the middle and kissed. It was brief but good. I had not seen her in a long time and I was suddenly shocked by the realization of how fast time could slip between two people. Though we talked every year on birthdays and Christmas, it had been almost three years since I had actually seen her, touched her, been with her. And immediately it was intoxicating and depressing at the same time. For I had to go. This would be quicker than any of those birthday calls we made each year.

"Your hair's different," I said. "It looks good."

It was the shortest I had ever seen it, cut cleanly at the midpoint of her neck. But it wasn't a false compliment. She looked good. But then again she would have looked good to me with hair to her ankles or even shorter than mine.

She turned from me to check traffic over her left shoulder. I could see the nape of her neck. She pulled into the through lane and we headed out. As she drove she reached up and held her finger on the button that closed the sunroof.

"Thank you, Harry. You don't look that different. But you still look good."

I thanked her and tried not to smile too much as I got my wallet out.

"So," she said, "what's this big mystery that you couldn't tell me about on the phone?"

"No mystery. I just want some people to think I'm in Las Vegas."

"You are in Las Vegas."

"But not for long. As soon as I pick up the car I'm heading back."

Eleanor nodded like she understood. I pulled my ATM and American Express cards out of my wallet. I kept my Visa card for the car rental and anything else that might come up.

"I want you to take these cards and use them over the next couple of days. The ATM code is oh-six-thirteen. Should be easy enough to remember."

It had been our wedding day.

"Funny," she said. "You know, this year it falls on a Friday. I checked. That's bad luck, Harry."

Friday the thirteenth somehow seemed appropriate. For a moment I wondered what it meant that she was checking on when future anniversaries of a failed marriage landed on the calendar. I dropped it and came back to the present.

"So just use them over the next few days. You know, go have dinner or something. If I were here I'd probably buy you a present for letting me stay with you. So go to the ATM and get some money and buy something you like. The AmEx still has my full name on it. You shouldn't have a problem."

Most people don't know what gender my given name Hieronymus is. When we had been married Eleanor regularly used my credit cards without a problem. The only difficulty that would arise now would occur if an ID was requested at point of purchase. This rarely happens in restaurants anywhere and especially not in Las Vegas, a place that takes your money first and asks questions later.

I handed her the cards but she didn't take them.

"Harry, what is this? What's going on with you?"

"I told you. I want some people to think I am over here in Vegas."

"And these are people who can monitor credit-card purchases and ATM usage?"

"If they want to. I don't know if they will. This is just a pre—"

"Then you're talking about the cops or the bureau. Which is it?"

I laughed quietly.

"Well, it might be both. But as far as I know it's the bureau that's most interested."

"Oh, Harry . . ."

She said it with a here-we-go-again tone in her voice. I thought about telling her that it involved Marty Gessler but decided I shouldn't involve her any further than I already had.

"Look, it's no big deal. I'm just working on one of my old cases and it's got an agent's nose out of joint. I want him to think he scared me off. For just a few days. Okay, Eleanor? Can you do this, please?"

I held the cards out again. After a long moment she reached up and took them without a word. We were on an airport road where all the rent-a-car complexes were lined up in a row. I wanted to say something else. Something about us and about how I wanted to come back over when all of this nastiness was finished. If she wanted me to. But she pulled into the Avis lot and put her window down to tell a security man that she was just there to drop me off.

The interruption ruined the flow of the conversation, if it even was a conversation. I lost my momentum and dropped any thought of saying anything further about us.

She pulled up to the Avis pickup office and it was time for me to get out. But I didn't. I sat there and looked at her until she finally turned and looked at me.

"Thank you for doing this, Eleanor."

"It's not a problem. You'll get the bill."

I smiled.

"Do you ever go back to L.A.? You know, to the card rooms or anything?"

She shook her head.

"Not in a long time. I don't like to travel anymore."

I nodded. There didn't seem like there was anything else to say. I leaned over and kissed her, this time just on the cheek.

"I'll call you tomorrow or the next day, okay?"

"Okay, Harry. Be careful. Good-bye."

"I will. Good-bye, Eleanor."

I got out and watched her drive off. I wished I had been able to spend more time with her and wondered if she would have let me if I'd had the time. I then put those thoughts away and went inside. I showed my driver's license and credit card and picked up the key to my rental. It was a Ford Taurus and I had to get used to being low to the ground again. On my way out of rent-a-car row I saw a sign with an arrow pointing the way to Paradise Road. I thought that everybody needed a sign like that. I wished that it was that easy.

23

Four hours and a nonstop drive across the desert later I was in the tech lab at Biggar & Biggar. I took the memory card from my pocket and handed it to Andre. He held it up and looked at it and then looked at me as though I had just put used gum in his hand.

"Where's the case?"

"The case? You mean the clock? It's still on the wall."

I hadn't figured out yet how to tell him that the clock was broken and probably the camera as well.

"No, the plastic case for the card. You put the spare card I gave you into the clock when you took this one out, right?"

I nodded.

"Right."

"Well, you should have put this one into the spare card's case. This is a delicate instrument. Carrying it around with your pocket change and lint is not the proper way of—"

"Andre," Burnett Biggar interrupted, "let's just see if it's going to work. It was my mistake for not schooling Harry on the finer points of care and maintenance. I forgot he's such a throwback."

Andre shook his head and walked over to a workbench with a computer set up on it. I looked at Burnett and nodded my thanks for the rescue. He winked at me and we followed Andre.

The son used a pneumatic air gun that looked like it was from a dentist's office to blast dust and debris off the memory card I had mishandled and then plugged it into a receptacle that was attached to the computer. He typed in a few commands and soon the images from Lawton Cross's sitting room were playing on the computer screen.

"Remember," Andre said, "we were using the motion sensor so it's going to be a bit jerky. Watch the clock in the corner and you'll be able to keep track."

The first image on the screen was my own face. I was staring right at the camera as I adjusted the time on the clock. I then backed away, revealing Lawton Cross in his chair behind me.

"Oh, man," Burnett said, seeing his former colleague's condition and situation. "I don't know if I want to see this."

"It gets worse," I said, confident in what I thought was ahead on the surveillance.

Cross's voice croaked from the computer's speakers.

"Harry?"

"What?" I heard myself ask.

"Did you bring me some?"

"A little."

On the screen I flipped open the toolbox to get the flask.

In the lab I said, "Can you fast-forward this?"

Andre nodded and used the computer's mouse to click a FAST-FORWARD button on the screen. The screen blinked black for a moment, indicating the camera had gone off for lack of movement. It then came back on as Danny Cross entered the room. Andre switched the playback to real time. I checked the time and saw this was just a few minutes after I had left the room. Danny stood with her arms crossed in front of her and stared at her invalid husband as though he was a misbehaving child. She started speaking and it was hard to hear because of the television noise.

"This is amateur hour here," Andre said. "Why'd you put it next to the TV?"

He was right. I hadn't thought about that. The camera's microphone was picking up the voices from the television better than those in the room.

"Andre," Burnett said, quieting his son's complaint. "Just see if you can clean it up some."

Andre used the mouse again to manipulate the sound. He backed the image up and played it again. The television noise was still intrusive but at least the conversation in the room was audible.

Danny Cross spoke with a sharp tone in her voice.

"I don't want him coming back here," she said. "He's not good for you."

"Yes, he is. He's fine. He cares."

"He's using you. He pours booze into you so he gets the information he needs."

"So what's wrong with that? I think it's a good trade."

"Yes, until the morning, when the pain comes."

"Danny, if one of my friends comes here, you let him in."

"What did you tell him this time, that I'm starving you? That I abandon you at night? Which lie this time?"

"I don't want to talk now."

"Fine. Don't talk."

"I want to dream."

"Be my guest. At least one of us still can."

She turned and left the room and the picture held on Lawton's motionless body. Soon his eyes closed.

"There's a sixty-second cutoff," Andre explained. "The camera stays on for a minute after motion ceases."

"Fast-forward," I said.

We spent the next ten minutes fast-forwarding and then stopping to watch mundane yet heart-ripping scenes of Lawton being fed and cleaned by Danny. At the end of the first night he was wheeled out by his wife and the camera went dark for nearly eight hours before he was wheeled back into the room. A new round of feedings and cleanings began.

It was horrible to look at, made more so because the clock was positioned just to the left of the television. Lawton Cross spent his time looking at the TV but the angle was so close it almost looked like he was staring up at the camera, looking right at us.

"This is pathetic," Andre finally said. "And there's nothing here. She treats him fine. Better than I would."

"You want to see it through, Harry?" Burnett asked.

I nodded.

"I think you're right. She's clean. But there's something coming up. He had visitors last night. I want to see that. You can fast-forward if you want. It was near midnight."

Andre worked the toggle and sure enough at 12:10 A.M. on the surveillance clock two men entered the room. I recognized Parenting Today and his partner. The first thing Parenting Today did was walk behind Lawton to turn off the baby monitor on the bureau. He then signaled his partner to close the door. Lawton's eyes were open and alert. He'd been awake before they had come into the room and the camera had activated. His eyes moved about in their sunken sockets as he tried to track the agent moving behind him.

"Mr. Cross, we need to have a little talk," Parenting Today said.

He moved forward past Cross's chair and reached up and turned off the television.

"Thank God for that," Andre said.

"Who are you people?" Cross rasped from the screen.

Parenting Today turned and looked at him.

"We're the FBI, Mr. Cross. Who the fuck are you?"

"What do you mean? I don't —"

"I mean who the fuck do you think you are, compromising our investigation?"

"I don't — what is this?"

"What did you tell Bosch that put the fire under his ass?"

"I don't know what you're talking about. He came to me, I didn't go to him."

"Doesn't look like you can go anywhere now, does it?"

There was a short silence and I could see Lawton's eyes working. The man couldn't move a single limb but his eyes showed all the body language necessary.

"You're not FBI," he said gallantly. "Let me see badges and IDs."

Parenting Today moved two steps toward Cross, his back blocking our view of the man in the chair.

"Badges?" he said in his best Mexican accent. "We don't need no *steenking* badges."

"Get out of here," Cross said, his voice the clearest and strongest I had heard since I first visited him. "When I tell Harry Bosch about this, you better watch your ass."

Parenting Today turned in profile to smile at his partner.

"Harry Bosch? Don't worry about Harry Bosch. We're taking care of him. Worry about yourself, Mr. Cross."

He leaned down now, putting his face close to Cross's. We now could see Lawton's eyes as they looked into the agent's.

"Because you are in harm's way. You are trespassing on a federal case. That is federal with a capital F. You understand?"

"Fuck you. And that is fuck you with a capital F. You understand?"

I had to smile. Lawton was doing his best to stand up to him. The bullet had taken away his body but not his spine and not his balls.

On the screen Parenting Today moved away from the chair and to the left. The camera caught his face and I could see the anger in his eyes. He leaned against the bureau, just out of the reach of Cross's view.

"Your hero, Harry Bosch, is gone and he might not be coming back," he said. "The question is, do you want to go where he's gone? A guy like you, in your condition, I don't know. You know what they do to guys like you in lockup? They wheel them into the corner and make them give blow jobs all day. Nothing they can do about it but sit there and take it. You into that, Cross? That what you want?"

Cross closed his eyes for a moment but then came back strong.

"You think you can pull that off, then take your best shot, Big Man."

"Yeah?"

Parenting Today came off the bureau and up behind Cross. He leaned over his right shoulder as if to whisper in his ear. But he didn't.

"What if I take my shot here? Huh? How would that be?"

The agent brought his hands up on both sides of Cross's face. He took hold of the plastic breathing tubes that were attached to Cross's nostrils. With his fingers he crimped the tubes closed, cutting off the air supply.

"Hey, Milton . . . ," the other agent said.

"Shut up, Carney. This guy thinks he's smart. Thinks he doesn't have to cooperate with the federal government."

Cross's eyes grew wide and he opened his mouth to gulp for air. He wasn't getting any.

"Motherfucker," Burnett Biggar said. "Who is this guy?"

I said nothing. I watched silently, the anger rising in me. Biggar had it right, though. In the lexicon of cop talk "motherfucker" was the ultimate expletive, the one reserved for the worst offender, the worst enemy. I felt like saying it but my voice wouldn't come. I was too consumed by what I saw on the screen. What they had done to me was nothing compared to the humiliation and scarring they were putting on Lawton Cross.

On the screen Cross was trying to speak but couldn't get the words out with no air in his lungs. There was a sneer on the face of the agent I now knew was named Milton.

"What?" he asked. "What's that? You want to talk to me?"

Cross tried again to talk but couldn't.

"Nod your head if you want to tell me something. Oh, that's right, you can't nod your head, can you?"

He finally let go of the tubes and Cross began to pull in air like a man coming up out of the water from fifty feet down. His chest heaved and his nostrils flared as he tried to recover.

Milton came around in front of the chair. He looked down upon his victim and nodded.

"You see? That's how easy it is. You want to cooperate now?"

"What do you want?"

"What did you tell Bosch?"

Cross's eyes flicked up toward the camera for a moment and then back to Milton. In that moment I didn't think he was checking the time. I suddenly thought that maybe Lawton knew about the camera. He'd been a good cop. Maybe he knew what I had been doing all along.

"I told him about the case. That's all. He came to me and I told him what I knew. I don't remember it all. I got hurt, you know. I got hurt and my memory isn't so good. Things are just starting to come back to me. I —"

"Why did he come here tonight?"

"Because I forgot I had some files. My wife called for me and I left him a message. He came for the files."

"What else?"

"Nothing else. What do you want?"

"What do you know about the money that was taken?"

"Nothing. We never got that far."

Milton reached forward and held the breathing tubes again. He didn't crimp them this time. The threat was enough.

"I'm telling you the truth," Cross protested.

"You better be."

The agent let go of the tubes.

"You are finished talking to Bosch, is that understood?"

"Yes."

"Yes, what?"

"Yes, I'm finished talking to Bosch."

"Thank you for your cooperation."

When Milton moved away from the chair I saw Cross's eyes were downcast. As the agents were leaving, one of them — probably Milton — hit the wall switch and the room and screen dropped into darkness.

We stood there staring at the screen and in the minute before the camera cut off we could hear but not see Lawton Cross crying. They were the deep sobs of a wounded and helpless animal. I did not look at the two men with me and they didn't look at me. We just watched the dark screen and listened.

The camera finally — thankfully — cut off at the end of the minute but then the screen came alive again when the room's light was flicked back on and Danny entered the room. I checked the time on the screen and saw this was only three minutes after the agents had left the room. Her husband's face was streaked with tears. Tears he could do nothing to hide.

She crossed the room to him. Without a word she climbed onto the chair in front of him, her knees alongside his thin thighs. She lowered her hips onto his lap. She opened her bathrobe and pulled his face forward to her breasts. She held him there and he cried again. No words were spoken at first. She quietly and tenderly shushed him. And then she started to sing to him.

The song I knew and she sang it well. Her voice was as soft as a breeze, whereas the song's original voice carried the rasp of all the world's anguish in it. I didn't think anybody could ever touch Louis Armstrong but Danny Cross certainly did.

I see skies of blue
And clouds of white
The bright blessed day
The dark sacred night
And I think to myself
What a wonderful world

And that was the hardest part of the surveillance to watch. That was the part that made me feel the most like an intruder, as if I had crossed some line of decency within myself.

"Turn it off now," I finally said.

24

The defining moment for me as a police officer did not occur on the street or while I worked a case. It occurred on March 5, 1991. It was during the afternoon and I was in the squad room in Hollywood Division ostensibly doing paperwork. But like everybody else in the squad I was waiting. When everybody started leaving their desks to gather at the televisions I got up, too. There was one in the lieutenant's office and one was mounted overhead on the wall by the burglary table. I didn't get along with the lieutenant at the time so I moved to the burglary pen to watch. We had already heard about it but few of us had actually seen the tape yet. And there it was. Grainy black-and-white but still clear enough to see and to know that things would change. Four uniform cops gathered around a man flopping on the ground. Rodney King, ex-con and now speeding scofflaw. Two of the cops were wailing on him with batons. A third kicked him while the fourth controlled the juice for the Taser gun. A second larger ring of uniforms stood around and watched. A lot of jaws dropped in the squad room as we looked up at the screen. A lot of hearts fell. We felt betrayed in some way. To a man and woman we all knew that the department would not withstand the tape. It would change. Police work in Los Angeles would change.

Of course we didn't know how or whether it would be for better or for worse. We didn't know then that political motives and racial emotions would rise up over the department like a tidal wave, that there would later be a deadly riot and complete tearing of the city's social fabric. But as we watched that grainy video we all knew something was coming. All because of that one moment of anger and frustration acted out under a streetlight in the San Fernando Valley.

As I sat in the waiting room of a downtown law office I thought about that moment. I remembered the anger I felt and I realized it had come back to me across time. The recording I had of Lawton Cross being abused was no Rodney King tape. It would not set back law enforcement and community relations decades. It would not change the way people viewed police and decided whether to back them or cooperate with them. But it had a clear kinship in its sickeningly pure depiction of the abuse of power. It didn't have the juice to change a city but it could change a bureaucracy like the Federal Bureau of Investigation. If I wanted it to.

But I didn't. What I wanted was something else and I was going to use the recording to get it. In the short run at least. I wasn't thinking yet about what might happen with it or with me further down the road.

The law library I sat in an hour after leaving Biggar & Biggar was lined with cherry wood paneling and bookshelves full of leather-bound volumes of law books. In the few open spaces on the walls there were lighted oil paintings depicting the law firm's partners. I stood in front of one of the paintings studying the fine brushwork. It showed a handsome man standing tall with brown hair and piercing green eyes set off by a deep tan. The gold plate on the top of the mahogany frame said his name was James Foreman. He looked like everything a successful man should be.

"Mr. Bosch?"

I turned. The matronly woman who had escorted me to the library now beckoned to me at the door. I went to her and she led me down a hall thickly carpeted in a soft green that whispered *money* with every step I took. She led me to an office where a woman I didn't recognize was waiting behind a desk. She stood up and offered her hand.

"Hello, Mr. Bosch, I'm Roxanne, Ms. Langwiser's assistant. Would you like a bottle of water or coffee or anything?"

"Uh, no, I'm fine."

"You can go on in, then. She's waiting."

She pointed me toward a closed door to the side of her desk and I walked to it, knocked once on it, and went in. I was carrying a briefcase I had borrowed from Burnett Biggar.

Janis Langwiser was sitting behind a desk that reminded me of a two-car garage. She also had the twelve-foot ceiling and the cherry wood paneling and shelves. She wasn't a small woman. Rather, she was tall and slim. But the office made her look diminutive. She smiled when she saw me and I did likewise.

"They never asked me if I wanted bottled water or coffee when I came to see you at the DA's office."

"I know, Harry. Times have certainly changed."

She stood up and reached her hand across the desk. She had to lean forward to make it. We shook hands. I met her when she was a rookie filing deputy in downtown criminal courts. I watched her grow up and handle some of the biggest and toughest cases. She was a good prosecutor. Now she was trying to be a good criminal defense attorney. Rare was the prosecutor who made a whole career of it. The money was too good at the other table. Judging by the office I was in, Janis Langwiser was sitting pretty at that other table.

"Have a seat," she said. "You know I've been meaning to track you down and call you. You just turning up like this today is great."

I was confused.

"Track me down for what? You're not repping anybody I put in the clink, are you?"

"No, no, nothing like that. I wanted to talk to you about a job."

I raised my eyebrows. She smiled like she was offering me the keys to the city.

"I don't know what you know about us, Harry."

"I know you were pretty hard to find. You're not listed in the phone book. I had to call a friend of mine at the DA's office and he got me the number."

She nodded.

"That's right. We're not listed. We don't need to be. We have very few clients and we handle every legal detail that crops up in their lives."

"And you handle the criminal details."

She hesitated. She was trying to judge where I was coming from.

"That's right. I'm the firm's criminal expert. That's why I was meaning to call you. When I heard you retired I thought this would be perfect. Not full-time, but sometimes — depending on the case — it gets hot and heavy. We could really use somebody with your skills, Harry."

I took a moment to compose my answer. I didn't want to offend her. I wanted to hire her. So I decided not to tell her that what she was suggesting was impossible. That I could never move to the other table, no matter what the money was. It wasn't in me. Retired or not, I had a mission in life. Working for a defense attorney wasn't part of it.

"Janis," I said, "I'm not looking for a job. I sort of already have one. The reason I'm here is because I want to hire you."

She giggled.

"You're kidding," she said. "Are you in trouble?"

"Probably. But that's not why I want to hire you. I need a lawyer I can trust to hold something for me and take the appropriate actions with it if necessary."

She leaned forward in her desk. She still was at least six feet away from me.

"Harry, this is getting mysterious. What is going on?"

"First off, what is your normal retainer? Let's get the client thing out of the way first."

"Harry, our minimum retainer is twenty-five thousand dollars. So forget about that. I owe you for all of those air-tight cases you brought me. Consider yourself a client."

I pushed the surprise off my face.

"Really? Twenty-five grand just to open a file?"

"That's right."

"Well, they got the right person for it."

"Thank you, Harry. Now what is this thing you want me to do?"

I opened the briefcase Burnett Biggar had given me to carry the second round of equipment I borrowed from him along with the memory card and the three CDs containing copies of the clock surveillance. Andre had made the copies. I put the card and the CDs on her desk.

"This is a surveillance I took. I want you to hold the original — the memory card — in a safe place. I want you to hold an envelope with one of the CDs and a letter from me. I want your private office number. I'm going to call it every night by midnight and tell you I am okay. In the morning you come in and if the message is there, then everything is all right. If you come in and there is no message from me, then you deliver the envelope to a reporter at the *Times* named Josh Meyer."

"Josh Meyer. That name is familiar. Is he on courts?"

"I think he used to cover local crime stuff. Now he's on terrorism. I think he works out of D.C. now."

"Terrorism, Harry?"

"It's a long story."

She checked her watch.

"I've got time. I've also got a computer."

I first took fifteen minutes to tell her about my private investigation and everything that had happened since Lawton Cross had called me out of the blue and I had pulled down the box of old cases off the closet shelf. Then I let her put the CD in her computer and watch the surveillance video. She didn't recognize Lawton Cross until I told her who he was. She reacted with appropriate outrage when she viewed the section with Agents Milton and Carney. I had her turn it off before Danny Cross came into the room and comforted her husband.

"First question, were they real agents?" she asked after the computer kicked the disk out.

"Yeah, they're part of the anti-terrorism squad working out of Westwood."

She shook her head in disgust.

"If this ever gets to the *Times* and then onto TV, then —"

"I don't want it to get there. Right now, that is the worst-case scenario."

"Why not, Harry? Those are rogue agents. At least that one Milton is. And the other is just as guilty for standing there and letting him do it."

She gestured toward her computer, where the surveillance video had been replaced by a screensaver that showed a bucolic scene of a house on a cliff overlooking the ocean, the waves rolling endlessly to shore.

"Do you think this is what the attorney general and the Congress of the United States wanted when they enacted legislation that changed and streamlined the bureau's rules and tools after September eleventh?"

"No, I don't," I answered. "But they should have known what could happen. What's the saying, absolute power corrupts absolutely? Something like that. Anyway, it's a given that this sort of thing would happen. They should have known. The difference here is that that isn't some Middle Eastern bag man on there. That's an American citizen. He's a former cop and he's a goddamn quadriplegic because he took a bullet in the line of duty."

Langwiser nodded somberly.

"That is exactly why you should get this out. It has to be see—"

"Janis, are you working for me or should I gather all this up and just find somebody else?"

She threw her hands up in surrender.

"Yes, I'm working for you, Harry. I'm just saying that this should not be allowed to just go by."

"I'm not talking about letting it go by. I just don't want it out yet. I need to use it as leverage first. I need to get what I want out of it first."

"Which is what?"

"I was going to get to that but you started in like Ralph Nader."

"Okay, I'm sorry. I'm all calmed down now. Tell me your plan, Harry."

And so I did.

25

Kate Mantilini's on Wilshire Boulevard had a row of high-backed booths that afforded their inhabitants more interior privacy than the lap dance cubicles in the back rooms of any of the strip clubs in town. That was why I chose the restaurant for the meeting. It was very private yet very public. I was there fifteen minutes before the appointed time, got a booth with a window fronting Wilshire and waited. Special Agent Peoples got there a little early, too. He had to walk along the row of booths and look into each one to find me. He then slipped silently and morosely into the space across from me.

"Agent Peoples, glad you could make it."

"I didn't feel like I had much choice."

"I guess you didn't."

He flipped open one of the menus that were on the table.

"Never been here before. Food any good?"

"It's not bad. Good chicken pot pie on Thursdays."

"It's not Thursday."

"And you're not here to eat."

He looked up from the menu and gave me his best dead-eye stare but he didn't have the juice this time. We both knew I was holding the high card this time. I looked out the window and glanced up and down Wilshire.

"You have your people out there, Agent Peoples? Are they waiting for me?"

"I came alone as instructed by your attorney."

"Well, just so you're clear. If your people grab me again or make any move against my attorney, then the consequences are that the surveillance recording you were e-mailed will go to the media and out across the Internet. There are people who will know if I disappear. They'll put it out, no hesitation."

Peoples shook his head.

"You keep saying that. 'Disappear.' This isn't South America, Bosch. And we're not Nazis."

I nodded in agreement.

"Sitting in this nice restaurant it sure doesn't seem so. But when I was sitting in that cube on the ninth floor and nobody knew I was there, that was a different story. Mouse Aziz and those other guys you've got up there probably don't know the difference between California and Chile right now either."

"And you are defending them now, is that it? The men who would like to see this country burn to the ground."

"I'm not de—"

I stopped when the waitress came to the booth. She said her name was Kathy and asked if we were ready to order. Peoples ordered coffee and I ordered coffee and an ice cream sundae with no whipped cream. After Kathy left, Peoples looked at me funny.

"I'm retired. I can have a sundae."

"Some retirement."

"They make good sundaes here and they're open late. That's a good combination."

"I'll remember that."

"Did you ever see the movie *Heat*? This is the place where Pacino the cop meets De Niro the burglar. It's where they both tell each other they won't hesitate to put the other down if it comes to that."

Peoples nodded and we held each other's eyes for a long moment. Message delivered. I decided to get down to the business at hand.

"So what did you think of my clock camera?"

The façade dropped and Peoples suddenly looked wounded. He looked as though he had been thrown to the lions. He knew what the future held for him if that recording got out. Milton worked for him; therefore he'd take the fall, too. The Rodney King tape cut a swath through the LAPD that went all the way to the top. Peoples was smart enough to know he would get trampled if he didn't contain this problem.

"I was disgusted by what I saw. First off, I apologize to you and my plan is to go out to see that man, Lawton Cross, and apologize as well."

"That's nice of you."

"Don't think for a moment that that is how we operate. That it is the status quo. That I condone it. Agent Milton is gone. He's out. I knew that the moment I saw the recording. I'm not promising you he will be prosecuted, but he won't be carrying a badge for very long. Not an FBI badge. I'll see to that."

I nodded.

"Right, you'll see to that."

I said it with high-octane sarcasm and I could see it put some color in his cheeks. The color of anger.

"You called the meeting, Bosch. What do you want?"

There it was. The question I was waiting for.

"You know what I want. I want you people off my back. I want my files and my notes back. I want Lawton Cross's file back. I want a copy of the LAPD murder book — which I know you must have — and I want access to Aziz and what you have on him."

"What we have on him is classified. It's a national security matter. We can't —"

"Declassify it. I want to know how strong the connection is to my movie heist. I want to know what you have on his whereabouts on two nights. All that federal intelligence has got to be good for something and I want it. And then I want to talk to him."

"Who? Aziz? That's not going to happen."

I leaned across the table.

"Yes, it is. Because the alternative to that is that everybody who has a TV or America Online is going to see what your boy Milton did to a helpless man in a wheelchair. Make that a highly decorated retired cop who had the use of his limbs and fucking life taken from him while in the line of duty. You think the Rodney King tape did some damage to the LAPD? You wait and see what happens with this one. I guarantee you that Milton and you and your whole little ninth-floor BAM squad will be cut loose by the bureau and the attorney general and everybody else faster than you can say civil rights indictment. You understand, *Special* Agent Peoples?"

I gave him a moment to respond but he didn't. His eyes were fixed and staring out through the window to Wilshire.

"And if you think for one minute I won't pull the trigger on this, then you haven't done your homework on me."

This time I waited him out and eventually his eyes came back through the window and to me. The waitress came and put down our coffees and told me my sundae was on the way. Neither Peoples nor I said thank you.

"Believe me," Peoples said, "I know you will pull the trigger. You are that kind of guy, Bosch. I know your kind. You will put yourself and your own interests ahead of the greater good."

"Don't give me that 'greater good' bullshit. This isn't about that. You give me what I want and you get rid of Milton, then you get to cruise along like nothing ever happened. The recording is never seen. How's that for greater good?"

Peoples leaned forward to sip his coffee. As he had done in the cube on the ninth floor he burned his mouth and grimaced. He pushed the cup and saucer away on the table and then slid to the edge of the booth before looking back at me.

"I'll be in touch."

"Twenty-four hours. I hear from you by this time tomorrow night or all bets are off. I go public with it."

He stood up and remained next to the booth looking at me and still holding a napkin. He nodded his agreement.

"Let me ask you something," he said. "If you're here, who used your credit card tonight to buy dinner at Commander's Palace in Vegas?"

I smiled. They had been tracking me.

"A friend. Is that a nice place, Commander's Palace?"

He nodded.

"One of the best. I've been there. The shrimp in the gumbo is as soft as marshmallow."

"That's great, I guess."

"Expensive too. Your friend put over a hundred bucks on your AmEx. Dinner for two it looked like."

He tossed his napkin onto the table.

"I'll be in touch."

A moment after he was gone the waitress brought my sundae. I asked her for the check and she said she'd bring it right away.

I poked a spoon into the fudge and ice cream but I didn't taste it. I sat there thinking about what Peoples had just said. I wasn't sure if there was an implied threat in his telling me he knew somebody was using my credit card. Maybe he even knew who. But the thing I thought about the most was what he had said about it being dinner for two at Commander's Palace. That "we" thing again. Just as with Eleanor, I couldn't let it go.

26

Since the Las Vegas ruse was no longer in play I drove out to Burbank Airport, turned in my rental and took the tram out to the long-term lot to collect my car. I had borrowed Lawton Cross's dolly and it was in the back of the Mercedes. Before driving off I got it out and slid underneath the car. I detached the satellite tracker and the heat sensor and slid under the pickup truck parked in the next space. I attached the equipment to the pickup's underside and then got into the Mercedes. As I backed out I saw that the pickup had an Arizona plate. I figured if Peoples didn't dispatch somebody soon to collect the bureau's equipment, then they'd have to chase it to the next state. That left me smiling to myself when I pulled up to the parking booth to pay.

"You must have had a nice flight," said the woman who took my ticket.

"Yeah, I guess you could say that. I made it back alive."

I went home and called Janis Langwiser on her cell phone as soon as I got in the door. She had changed my plan a little bit. She didn't want me leaving a message on her office line every night. She insisted I call her directly on her cell.

"How did it go?"

"Well, it went. Now I just have to wait. I gave him until tomorrow night. I guess we'll know by then."

"And how did he take it?"

"About what we expected. Not well. But I think by the end he saw the light. I think he'll call tomorrow."

"I hope so."

"Everything set on your end?"

"I think so. The memory card's in the office safe and I'll wait to hear from you. If I don't, then I'll know what to do."

"Good, Janis. Thanks."

"Good night, Harry."

I hung up and thought about things. Everything seemed to be in place. It was Peoples who would have to make the next move. I lifted the phone again and called Eleanor. She answered immediately, no sleep in her voice.

"Sorry, it's Harry. Are you playing?"

"Yes and no. I'm playing but I'm not doing well so I took a break. I'm standing outside the Bellagio watching the fountains."

I nodded. I could picture her there at the railing, the dancing fountains lit up in front of her. I could hear the music and the splash of water over the phone.

"How was Commander's Palace?"

"How did you know about that?"

"Had a visit from the bureau tonight."

"That was quick."

"Yeah. I heard that's a good restaurant. Shrimp like marshmallow. Did you like it?"

"It's nice. I like the one in New Orleans better. The food's the same but the original is the original, you know?"

"Yeah. Plus it's probably not so great eating by yourself."

I almost cursed out loud at how lame and transparent that was.

"I wasn't alone. I took a friend that I play with. One of the girls. You didn't tell me there was a spending limit, Harry."

"No, I know. There wasn't."

I needed to steer away from this. We both knew what I had been asking about and it was getting embarrassing, especially considering there might be other ears listening.

"You didn't notice anybody watching you, did you?"

There was a pause.

"No. And I hope you didn't get me into any kind of trouble, Harry."

"No, you're fine. I'm just calling to let you know the scam is over. The bureau knows I'm still here."

"Damn, I never got the chance to go shopping and get myself that present you promised."

I smiled. She was kidding and I could tell.

"That's okay, you can still do that."

"Is everything okay, Harry?"

"Yeah, fine."

"You want to talk about it?"

Not on this line, I thought but didn't say.

"Maybe when I see you next time. I'm too tired right now."

"Okay, then I'll let you go. What should I do with your cards? And you know you left your bag on my backseat."

She said it like she knew I had done it on purpose.

"Um, why don't you just hold on to that stuff for now

and maybe when I get past this thing I'm working on I'll come back out and get it from you."

It was a long time before she answered.

"Just give me a little more notice than you did today," she finally said. "So I'm ready."

"Sure, no problem. I will."

"Okay, Harry, I'm going to go back in. Maybe talking to you will have changed my luck."

"I hope so, Eleanor. Thanks for doing this for me."

"No problem. Good night."

"Good night."

She disconnected.

"And good luck," I said into the dead line.

I hung the phone up again and tried to think about the conversation and what she had meant. *Just give me a little more notice than you did today. So I'm ready.* It was like she wanted a warning before I came out. So she could do what? What did she have to get ready for?

I realized that I could drive myself nuts thinking and worrying about it. I put Eleanor and all of that aside and grabbed a beer out of the refrigerator and took it out to the back deck. It was a cool and clear night and the lights of the freeway far below seemed to sparkle like a diamond necklace. I could hear a woman's laughter carrying up the hillside from somewhere down below. I started thinking about Danny Cross and the song she had gently sung to her husband. In love and in loss the night is always sacred. It's only a wonderful world if you can make it that way. There are no street signs pointing to Paradise Road.

I decided that when all of this was over I would go to Vegas and not turn back. I would throw the dice. I would go see Eleanor and take my chances.

27

The next morning I spread the documents I had rescued from the engine compartment of Lawton Cross's muscle car across the table. I went into the kitchen to brew a pot of coffee but found out I was out of coffee. I could go down the hill to the store but I didn't want to leave the phone. I was expecting Janis Langwiser to call early. So I sat down at the table with a bottle of water and started in on the reports Cross had copied and taken home almost four years before.

What I had was a copy of the currency report prepared by the bank which had loaned the cash to the movie company, and the time and location sheets that Lawton Cross and Jack Dorsey had been working on before their schedule became crowded with other cases.

The currency report was four pages of typed serial numbers taken from randomly selected one-hundred-dollar bills contained in the shipment to the movie set. The report was prepared by two people listed as Linus Simonson and Jocelyn Jones. It was then signed off on by a bank vice president named Gordon Scaggs.

Simonson was a name I knew. He had been one of the bank employees at the movie set on the day of the heist. He had been wounded during the shoot-out. Now I knew why he was there; he had helped prepare the money shipment and was most likely there to baby-sit it through the day of filming.

Scaggs was also a name that was familiar to me. It was among the names given to me by Alexander Taylor when I had asked the film producer who specifically knew about the cash delivery to the movie set. I no longer had the list of nine names I had collected from Taylor. The FBI had taken that during the search of my home. But I remembered the name Scaggs.

Committed to studying everything about the case I could get my hands on, I scanned the listings of currency numbers, thinking maybe something would stick out. But nothing grabbed me. The numbers were like an unbreakable code locking away the secret to the case. It was simply four pages of numbers in no particular sequence.

Finally, I put the currency report aside and took up the alibi sheets. I first checked for the names Scaggs, Simonson and Jones and saw that Dorsey and Cross had indeed run out T&L checks on all three of the bank employees. Cross had taken Scaggs and Jones while Dorsey ran down Simonson. Their locations were checked against key times in the murder of Angella Benton and the subsequent movie set heist.

All three were cleared by alibi of physical involvement in the crimes. Simonson, of course, was at the scene of the heist, but he was there as a representative of the bank. His being shot by one of the robbers also tended to add weight to his clearance. This did not, of course, clear them of ancillary involvement. Any one of them could have been the mastermind behind the heist who had stayed in the background as the plan was carried out. Or, at the very least, any one of them could have simply been the source of information on the delivery of money to the movie set.

The same went for the other eight names in the T&L report. All were cleared by alibi of active involvement in the crimes. But I had no other files or reports to indicate what had been done to determine if they had a background connection to the crime.

I realized I was spinning my wheels. I was trying to play solitaire without a full deck. The aces were gone and there was no way I could win. I had to get all the cards. I took a swig of water and wished it was coffee. I started thinking about how important the play with Peoples was. If it didn't work, I was done. Angella Benton's outstretched hands might haunt me for the rest of my life but there wasn't anything I was going to be able to do about it.

As if on cue the telephone rang. I went into the kitchen and picked up. It was Janis Langwiser, though she didn't identify herself.

"It's me," she said. "We have to talk."

"Okay, I'm in the middle of something. I'll call you right back."

"Good."

She hung up without a protest. I took that as a sign that she now believed what I had told her about my house and phone being bugged. I also took it as a sign that Peoples was acting in the way I had hoped he would. I grabbed my keys off the counter and went out the door.

I drove down the hill. At the place where Mulholland wraps around the other side of the hill and meets Woodrow Wilson at Cahuenga I saw a vintage yellow Corvette waiting at the light across from me. I knew the driver, sort of. Every now and then I'd see him jogging or driving the 'vette past my house. And I'd seen and spoken to him in the police station on occasion, too. He was a private eye who lived on the other side of the ridge from me. I put my arm out the window and gave him the sweeping palm-down salute. He did likewise back to me. Smooth sailing, my brother. I was going to need it. The light changed and he went south on Cahuenga while I went north.

I bought a cup of coffee in a convenience store and used a pay phone next to the Poquito Mas to call Langwiser back on her cell. She answered right away.

"They came in last night," she said. "Just like you predicted."

"Did you get it on the camera?"

"Yes! It's perfect. Clear as day. It was the same guy in the first surveillance. Milton."

I nodded to myself. The call to my house the night before in which Janis said she'd locked the memory card in her office safe had been the bait and Milton had taken it. Before leaving her office I had set up another one of Biggar & Biggar's cameras — the radio — on her desk and trained it toward the bookcase which hid the safe.

"He stumbled around looking for a while but then he found it. He took the whole safe out of the wall. It's gone."

She had emptied everything from the safe the night before. I had put in a folded piece of paper. It said, "Fuck you, with a capital F." I imagined Milton unfolding it and reading it — if he had managed to get the safe open.

"Anything else hit in the offices?"

"A couple drawers pulled out here and there. The quarter jar in the coffee room. All just cover to make it look like a regular burglary."

"Anybody call the police to report it?"

"Yes, but nobody's shown up yet. Typical."

"Keep the surveillance out of it. For now."

"I know. Like we said. What should I do now?"

"You still have Peoples's e-mail address?"

"Sure do."

The night before, she had gotten the e-mail address rather easily from a former colleague who worked at the U.S. Attorney's office.

"Okay, send Peoples another e-mail. Attach the latest surveillance and tell him I've changed the deadline to noon today. I hear from him by then or he can start watching CNN for the results. Send it as soon as you can."

"I'm on-line now."

"Good."

I sipped coffee while listening to her type. Andre Biggar had included in the briefcase I borrowed the computer attachment Langwiser would need to view the memory card taken from the radio camera. She could now attach a file containing the surveillance recording to an e-mail.

"It's away," she finally said. "Good luck, Harry."

"I'll probably need it."

"Remember, call me tonight by midnight or I'll follow the instructions."

"Gotcha."

I hung up and went back to the convenience store for a second cup of coffee. I was already wired from Langwiser's report but I figured I might be needing the spare caffeine before the day was finished.

When I got back to the house the phone was ringing. I got the door unlocked and got inside just in time to grab the phone off the kitchen counter.

"Yeah?"

"Mr. Bosch? John Peoples here."

"Good morning."

"Not really. When can you come in?"

"I'm on my way."

28

Special Agent Peoples was waiting for me in the first-floor lobby of the federal building in Westwood. He was standing when I got there. Maybe he'd been standing there the whole time since he'd made the call.

"Follow me," he said. "We're going to make this quick."

"Whatever works."

After giving a uniformed guard the nod he led me through a security door using a card key and then he used it again to access the elevator I was already familiar with.

"You guys got your own elevator and everything," I said. "Pretty cool."

Peoples wasn't impressed. He turned so he was looking right at me.

"I'm doing this because I have no choice. I've decided to agree to this extortion because I believe in the greater good of what I'm trying to accomplish here."

"Is that why you sent Milton into my lawyer's office last night? Was that all part of the greater good you're talking about?"

He didn't answer.

"Look, you can hate me and that's fine. That's your option. But let's not bullshit each other. Don't hide behind that stuff, because we both know what's going on here. Your guy crossed the line and got caught. Now it's just time to pay the price. That's what this is about. It's that simple."

"And meantime an investigation is compromised and lives may be at stake."

"We'll see about that, won't we?"

The elevator opened on the ninth floor. He led me out without answering. The ever handy card key got us through another door and into a squad room where several agents were working at desks. As we passed through, most of them stopped what they were doing to look at me. I assumed that they had either been briefed on who I was and what I was doing or just the occurrence of a non-agent in the inner sanctum was worth noting.

When I was halfway across the room I spotted Milton sitting at a desk near the back. He was leaning back in his chair giving me his best show of being relaxed. But I could sense the anger pulsing beneath the façade. I winked at him and turned my attention away.

Peoples led me into a small room with a desk and two chairs. On the desk was a cardboard box. I looked into it and recognized my own notebook and the file I had kept on Angella Benton. There was also the file from Lawton Cross's garage and a black binder full of documents two inches thick. I assumed it was the copy of the LAPD's murder book. I got excited just looking at it. It was the full deck of cards I had been looking for.

"Where's the rest?" I asked.

Peoples walked around behind the desk and opened the

middle drawer. He removed a file and dropped it on the top of the desk.

"In there you will find subject location reports covering the two dates you requested. I don't think they will help you but it's what you wanted. You can look at them here but you cannot take them with you. They will not leave this office. Do you understand that?"

I nodded, deciding not to push it.

"What about Aziz?"

"When you are ready I will put you in a room with him. But he won't talk to you. You'll be wasting your time."

"Well, it's mine to waste."

"Then, before you leave here, you will call your attorney and instruct her to turn over to me the original and all copies of the surveillance recordings you have from last night and the night before."

I shook my head.

"Sorry, that's not the deal."

"It certainly is."

"No, I never said I would turn over the recordings. What I said was that I would not go public with them. There's a difference. I'm not going to turn over the only leverage I've got. I'm not stupid, John."

"We had a deal," he said, his cheeks beginning to quiver with anger.

"And I'm keeping the deal. Exactly as offered."

I reached into my pocket and pulled out a cassette tape. I held it out to him.

"If you don't believe me you can listen for yourself. I was wearing a wire last night in the booth."

I watched his eyes register that I now even had him directly tied in.

"Take it, John. Call it a goodwill gesture. It's the original. No copies were made."

He slowly reached up and took the tape. I moved around behind the desk.

"Why don't I take a look at what you've got in the file while you go do whatever you have to do to get Aziz ready?"

Peoples pocketed the tape and nodded.

"I'll be back in ten minutes," he said. "If anyone comes in here and asks what you are doing, close that file and tell them to see me."

"One last thing. What about the money?"

"What about it?"

"How much money from the movie set heist did Aziz have under his car seat?"

I thought I saw a small smile start to play on Peoples's face, but then it went away.

"He had a hundred bucks. One bill traced to the heist."

He stayed long enough to see the disappointment on my face, then turned to the door.

After he left the room I sat down at the desk and opened the file. It contained two pages that had security stamps on them and had words in the middle of paragraphs and then whole paragraphs blocked out with black ink. Peoples clearly wasn't going to let me see anything I had not bargained for — or extorted from him, as he had put it.

The pages were taken from what I assumed was a larger file. There was a coding in small print at the top left corner. I reached into the cardboard box and opened my file. I took out one of the loose sheets of note paper and wrote the code number from each page down. I then read what Peoples was allowing me to read.

The first page had two dated paragraphs.

5-11-99 — SUBJECT confirmed in Hamburg at in company with and . SUBJECT seen in restaurant by approximately 20:00 until 23:30 hours. No further detail.

7-1-99 — SUBJECT passport scan at Heathrow at 14:40 hours. Follow up determination arrival on Lufthansa Flight 698 from Frankfurt. No further detail.

The paragraphs before and after these two were completely blacked out. What I was looking at was the log in which tabs on Aziz had been kept over the years by the feds. He was on the watch list. This is what it amounted to. Sightings by informants or agents and airport passport checks.

The two dates on the page were on either side of the murder of Angella Benton and the movie set heist. It by no means cleared Aziz of active or background involvement in the crimes. Yet, if I believed the document in front of me, he was in Europe both before and after the occurrence of the crimes I was investigating. But it was no alibi. Aziz was known, according to the *Times* article I had read, to travel with false identification. It was possible he had slipped into this country to commit the crimes and then slipped out.

I went on to the next page. This one had only one paragraph that was not blacked out. But the date was a direct hit.

3-19-00 — SUBJECT passport scan at LAX-CA. Arrival on Qantas Flight 88 from Manilla at 18:11 hrs. Security check and search. Questioned by , Los Angeles field office. See transcript #00-44969. Released at 21:15 hrs.

Aziz had what appeared to be a perfect alibi for the night Agent Martha Gessler disappeared. He was being questioned by an FBI agent at Los Angeles International Airport until 9:15 P.M., which put him in federal custody at the same time Gessler disappeared while on her way home from work.

I put the two sheets back in the file and put it back in the drawer. I wrote no further notes — there was nothing to write — on the page from my file. I put it back inside the file and lifted out the murder book. I was just about to start into it when the door to the room opened and there was Milton. I said nothing. I waited for him to make the first move. He stepped in and looked around the room as though it was the size of a warehouse. He finally spoke without looking at me.

"You have some balls on you, Bosch. Doing what you're doing and thinking you're going to just walk away from it. Away from me."

"I guess I could say the same thing about you."

"If it was me I would have called your bluff."

"Then you would have called it wrong."

He leaned down and put both hands on the table and looked right at me.

"You are a has-been, Bosch. The world's passed you by, but here you are, grabbing at straws, fucking with people who are trying to protect the future."

I was unimpressed and hoped I showed it. I leaned back and looked up at him.

"Why don't you relax, man? You've got nothing to worry about as far as I can tell. You've got a boss who's more interested in a cover-up than a cleanup. You'll do okay on this, Milton. I think he's mad because you got caught, not because of what you did."

He pointed a finger at me.

"Don't fucking go there. Don't. The day I want career advice from you is the day I turn in my badge."

"Fine. Then what do you want?"

"I want to give you a warning. Watch out for me, Bosch. 'Cause I'm coming."

"Then I'll be ready."

He turned and walked out, leaving the door open. A few seconds later Peoples was back.

"You ready?"

"Been ready."

"Where's the file I gave you?"

"It's back in the drawer."

He leaned over the desk and slid open the drawer to make sure. He even opened the file to make sure I hadn't pulled a fast one.

"Okay, let's go. Bring your box."

I followed him through a couple security doors and I was once again in the hallway of cells. But before we got close to the doors with the mirrored windows he used his card key to open a door and he ushered me into an interview room. There was a table and two chairs. Mousouwa Aziz was already sitting in one of them. An agent I had not seen before was leaning against the corner to the left of the door. Peoples moved into the other corner.

"Have a seat," he said. "You've got fifteen minutes."

I put the box I carried down on the floor, pulled out the remaining chair and sat down across the table from Aziz. He looked weak and thin. A line of dark hair had grown in below the blond dye job. His hooded eyes were bloodshot and I wondered if they ever turned the light out in his cell. Things had certainly changed in his world. Two years ago his arrival and identification at LAX had brought a custody hold for a few hours while an agent attempted to interview him. Now a border stop got him an interminable hold in the FBI's inner sanctum.

I wasn't expecting much from the interview but felt I needed the face-to-face before proceeding or disposing of Aziz as a suspect. After viewing the intelligence reports a few minutes earlier, I was leaning toward the latter. All I had that connected the diminutive would-be terrorist to Angella Benton was the money. At the time of his arrest at the border he'd had in his possession one of the hundred-dollar bills that had come from the movie set heist. Only one. There were probably a lot of explanations for this and I was beginning to think that his involvement in the murder and heist was not one of them.

Reaching down to the cardboard box I pulled up my file on Angella Benton and opened it on my lap, where Aziz could not see it. I took out the photo of Angella that had been provided by her family. It showed her in a studio portrait taken at the time of her graduation from Ohio State, less than two years before her death. I looked up at Aziz.

"My name is Harry Bosch. I am investigating the death of Angella Benton four years ago. Does she look familiar to you?"

I slid the photo across the table and studied his face and eyes for any tell, any giveaway. His eyes moved over the photograph but I saw nothing in the way of a reaction. He said nothing.

"Did you know her?"

He didn't answer.

"She worked for a movie company that was robbed. You ended up with some of the money. How?"

Nothing.

"Where did the money come from?"

He raised his eyes from the photo to mine. He said nothing.

"Did these agents tell you not to talk to me?"

Nothing.

"Did they? Look, if you didn't know her, then tell me."

Aziz dropped his sad eyes to the table again. He appeared to be looking at the photo again but I could tell he wasn't. He was looking at something far away. I knew it was useless, just as I had probably known before sitting down.

I got up and turned to Peoples.

"You can keep the rest of the fifteen minutes."

He pushed off the wall and looked up at an overhead camera. He made the little swirling motion with a finger and the door's electronic lock snapped open. Without thinking I moved toward the door and pushed it open. Almost immediately I heard a banshee cry from behind me and Aziz was up and over the table. He hit me in the upper back with all his weight — maybe 130 pounds tops — and I went through the door and into the hallway.

Aziz was still on me and as I started to go down I felt his arms and legs flailing for purchase. He then jumped off and started running down the hall. Peoples and the other agent were quickly down the hall after him. As I got up I saw them corner Aziz at a dead end. Peoples held back while the other agent moved in and roughly wrestled the smaller man to the ground.

Once Aziz was controlled Peoples turned and came back to me.

"Bosch, are you all right?"

"I'm fine."

I stood up and made a show of straightening my clothes. I was embarrassed. I had been taken by surprise by Aziz and I knew it would probably be the talk of the squad room at the other end of the hall.

"I wasn't ready for that. I guess being out of the life so long, I got rusty."

"Yes. You never can turn your back on them."

"My box. I forgot it."

I went back into the interview room and got the photo off the table and the box. Just as I came back out Aziz was being walked by, his wrists cuffed behind his back.

I watched him go by and then Peoples and I followed at a safe distance.

"And so," Peoples said, "all of this was for naught."

"Probably."

"And it all could have been avoided if . . ."

He didn't finish so I did.

"Your agent hadn't committed those crimes on camera. Yeah."

Peoples stopped in the hallway and I did, too. He waited for the other agent and Aziz to go through the door.

"I'm not comfortable with this arrangement," he said. "I have no guarantees. You could walk out of here and get hit by a truck. Does that mean those recordings will end up on the news?"

I thought for a moment, then nodded.

"Yeah, it does. You better hope that truck misses me."

"I don't want to live and work under the weight of that."

"I don't blame you. What are you going to do about Milton?"

"What I told you. He's out. He just doesn't know it yet."

"Well, let me know when that happens. Then we can talk about the weight again."

He looked like he was about to say something more but then thought better of it and started walking again. He led me through the security doors to the elevator. He used his card key to summon it and then to push the button for the lobby. He held his hand on the door's bumper.

"I'm not going down with you," he said. "I think we've said enough."

I nodded and he stepped back through the door. He stood there and watched, maybe to make sure I didn't sneak off the elevator and try to spring the incarcerated terrorists.

Just as the door started closing I hit the bumper with the side of my hand and it slowly reopened.

"Remember, Agent Peoples, my lawyer has taken steps to secure herself and the recordings. If something happens to her it's the same as it happening to me."

"Don't worry, Mr. Bosch. I will make no move against her or you."

"It's not you I'm worried about."

The door closed as we were holding each other's eyes in a pointed stare.

"I understand," I heard him say through the doors.

29

My dance with the *federales* was not totally for naught as I had led Peoples to believe. Yes, my chasing down of the tiny terrorist may have been a false lead but in any case there are always false leads. It is part of the mission. At the end of the day what I had was the full record of the investigation and I was happy with that. I was playing with a full deck — the murder book — and it allowed me to write off in my mind all that had occurred in the two days leading up to the point I got it, including my hours in lockdown. For I knew that if I was to find Angella Benton's killer, the answer, or at least the key that would turn the case, would likely be sitting somewhere in the middle of that black plastic binder.

I got home from the federal building and came into the house like a man who thinks he may have won the lottery but needs to check the numbers in the newspaper to be sure. I went directly to the dining room table with my cardboard box and spread out everything I carried in it. Front and center was the murder book. The Holy Grail. I sat down and started reading from page one. I didn't get up for coffee, water or beer. I didn't turn on music. I concentrated fully on the pages I was turning. On occasion I jotted notes down on my notepad. But for the most part I just read and absorbed. I got in the car with Lawton Cross and Jack Dorsey and I rode through their investigation.

Four hours later I turned the last page in the binder. I had carefully read and studied every document. Nothing struck me as the key, the obvious strand to pursue, but I wasn't discouraged. I still believed it was in there. It always was. I would just have to sift it from a different angle.

The one thing that struck me from the intense immersion into the documented part of the case was the difference in personalities of Cross and Dorsey. Dorsey was a good ten years older than Cross and had been the mentor in the relationship. But in their writing and handling of reports I sensed strong differences in their personalities. Cross was more descriptive and interpretive in his reports. Dorsey was the opposite. If three words summed up an interview or a lab report, then he went with the three words. Cross was more likely to put down the three words and then add another ten sentences of interpretation of what the lab report or the witness's demeanor meant. I preferred Cross's method. It had always been my philosophy to put everything in the book. Because sometimes cases go months and even years long and nuances can be lost in time if not set down as part of the record.

It also made me conclude that maybe the two partners had not been close. They were close now, inextricably linked in department mythology as keepers of the ultimate bad luck. But maybe if they had been close that moment in the bar, things would have been different.

Thinking about what could have been made me remember Danny Cross singing to her husband. I finally got up and went to the CD player and put in a disc of the collected works of Louis Armstrong. It had been put out in unison with the Ken Burns documentary on jazz. Most of it was the very early stuff but I knew it ended with "What a Wonderful World," his last hit.

Back at the table I looked at my notepad. I had written down only three things during my first read-through.

$100K
Sandor Szatmari
The money, stupid

The company that had insured the money on the movie set, Global Underwriters, had put up a $100,000 reward for an arrest and conviction in the case. I hadn't known about the reward and was surprised that Lawton Cross hadn't told me. I guessed that it was just another detail that had escaped from his mind due to trauma and the passage of time.

The fact that there was a reward was of little personal consequence to me. I assumed that since I was a former cop who at one time was involved in the case, albeit before the heist that spawned the reward, I would not be eligible for it if my efforts resulted in an arrest and conviction. I also knew that it was likely that the small print on the reward proclamation said that full recovery of the $2 million was required for collection of the hundred thousand, with the amount prorated according to the amount of recovery. And four years after the crime the chances of there being anything left to recover were small. Still, the reward was good to know about. It might be useful as a tool of leverage or coercion. I might not be eligible but I might encounter someone useful who would be. I was glad I found out about it.

Next on the notepad was the name Sandor Szatmari. He or she — I didn't know which — was listed as the case investigator for Global Underwriters. He or she was someone I needed to talk to. I opened the murder book to the first page, where investigators usually kept a page of most often called phone numbers. There was no listing for Szatmari but there was for Global. I went into the kitchen to get the phone, turned down Louis Armstrong on the CD player and made the call. I was transferred twice before I finally got a woman who answered with "Investigations."

I had trouble with Szatmari's name and she corrected me and then told me to hold. In less than a minute Szatmari picked up. The name belonged to a he. I explained my situation and asked if we could meet. He seemed skeptical, but that might have just been because he had an accent from Eastern Europe that made him hard to read. He declined to discuss the case over the phone with a stranger but ultimately agreed to meet me in person at ten o'clock the next morning at his office in Santa Monica. I told him I'd be there and hung up.

I looked at the last line I had written on the notepad. It was just a reminder of an old adage good for almost any investigation. Follow the money, stupid. It always leads to the truth. In this case the money was gone and the trail — other than blips on the radar in Phoenix and involving Mousouwa Aziz and Martha Gessler — had gone cold. I knew that left me one alternative. To go backwards. Trace the money backwards and see what came up.

To do that I needed to start at the bank. I checked the phone number page in the murder book again and called Gordon Scaggs, the vice president at BankLA who had arranged the one-day loan of $2 million to Alexander Taylor's film company.

Scaggs was a busy man, he told me. He wanted to put off meeting with me until the following week. But I was persistent and got him to squeeze me in for fifteen minutes the next afternoon at three. He asked me for a callback number so his secretary could confirm in the morning. I made up a number and gave it to him. I wasn't going to give him the opportunity to have the secretary call me back and tell me the meeting had been canceled.

I hung up and weighed my options. It was late afternoon and at the moment I was clear until ten the following morning. I wanted to take another run at the murder book but knew I didn't need to be sitting in the house to do that. I could just as easily be sitting on a plane.

I called Southwest Airlines and reserved a flight from Burbank to Las Vegas, arriving at 7:15, and a return flight leaving early the next morning and arriving at 8:30 back at Burbank.

Eleanor answered her cell phone on the second ring and seemed to be whispering.

"It's Harry. Is something wrong?"

"No."

"Why are you whispering?"

She spoke up.

"Sorry, I didn't realize I was. What's going on?"

"I'm thinking about coming over there tonight to get my bag and my credit cards."

When she did not respond right away, I asked, "Are you going to be around?"

"Well, I was going to play tonight. Later."

"My plane gets in at seven-fifteen. I could come by around eight. Maybe we could have dinner before you go to play."

I waited and again it seemed like she was taking too long to respond.

"Dinner would be nice. Are you staying overnight?"

"Yeah, I've got an early flight out. I have some things to do over here in the morning."

"Where are you going to stay?"

There was as clear a signal as any.

"I don't know. I didn't reserve anything yet."

"Harry, I don't think it would be good for you to stay here."

"Right."

The line was as silent as the three hundred miles of desert between us.

"I know, I can get you comped at the Bellagio. They'll do it for me."

"You sure?"

"Yes."

"Thanks, Eleanor. You want me to come to your place after I get in?"

"No, I'll come pick you up. Are you checking luggage?"

"No. You already have my bag."

"Then I'll be parked out in front of the terminal at seven-fifteen. I'll see you then."

I noticed she was whispering again but I didn't say anything about it this time.

"Thanks, Eleanor."

"Okay, Harry, I need to juggle some things to get free tonight. So I'm going to go. I'll see you at the airport. Seven-fifteen. Bye."

I said good-bye but she had already hung up. It sounded as though there was another voice in the background just as she disconnected the call.

As I thought about this, Louis Armstrong started singing "What a Wonderful World" and I turned it up.

30

At 7:15 that night Eleanor and I repeated the same airport scene. Right down to the kiss when I got into the car. Afterward, I turned awkwardly and lifted the heavy murder book I'd been carrying over the front seats to the back. I dropped it on the backseat next to my suitcase which was on the seat behind Eleanor.

"That looks like a murder book, Harry."

"It is. I thought I might be able to go through it on the flight."

"And?"

"I had a screaming baby in the seat behind me. Couldn't concentrate. Why would anybody bring a kid to Vegas anyway?"

"It's actually not a bad place to raise a kid. Supposedly."

"I'm not talking about raising. I mean, why take a little kid like that on a vacation to Sin City? Take him to Disneyland or something."

"I think you need a drink."

"And some food. Where do you want to eat?"

"Well, remember when we were still . . . in L.A. and we'd go to Valentino on special occasions?"

"Don't tell me."

She laughed and just being able to look at her again thrilled me. I really liked the way her hair accented her lovely neck.

"Yep, they have one here. I made a reservation."

"They must have one of everything in Las Vegas."

"Except you. There's absolutely no duplicating Harry Bosch."

The smile stayed on her face as she said it and I liked that, too. We soon dropped into a silence probably as comfortable as it can get with two formerly married people. She expertly maneuvered through traffic that looked like it could easily rival anything found on Los Angeles' clogged streets and freeways.

It had been about three years since I'd been on the strip but Vegas was a place that taught that time was relative. In three years it had all seemed to change again. I saw new resorts and attractions, taxicabs with electronic ad placards on their roofs, monorails connecting the casinos.

The Las Vegas version of Valentino was in the Venetian, one of the newest jewels in the crown of high-end casinos on the strip. It was a place that didn't even exist the last time I had been in town. When Eleanor pulled into the valet parking circle I told her to pop the trunk so I could put my suitcase and the murder book in it.

"I can't. It's full."

"I don't want to leave this stuff out, especially the murder book."

"Well, put it in the bag and put it on the floor. It will be all right."

"Don't you have room back there for just the book?"

"No, everything is jam-packed in there and if I open it, then it will all spill out. I don't want that to happen here."

"What is in it?"

"Just clothes and things. Stuff I want to take to the Salvation Army but haven't had the time."

Two valets opened our doors simultaneously and welcomed us to the resort. I got out, opened the back door and leaned in to open the carry-on bag and put the murder book inside it. After closing the bag I slid it down to the floor behind Eleanor's seat.

"You coming, Harry?" Eleanor asked from behind me.

"Yeah, I'm coming."

As the valet was driving the car away I looked at the trunk and back end. It didn't seem particularly heavy. I looked at the license plate and silently read it three times to myself.

Valentino was Valentino. As far as I could tell, the L.A. restaurant had been perfectly cloned. It was like trying to tell the difference between one McDonald's and another — on a much different culinary level.

I didn't force the conversation while we ate. I was comfortable and happy just being with her. At first the conversation, though spare, was focused on me and my retirement or lack thereof. I told her about the case I was working, including the connection to her old friend and colleague Marty Gessler. In another lifetime Eleanor had been an FBI agent and she still had the analytical mind of an investigator. When we were together in L.A. she had often been a sounding board for me and on more than one occasion had helped with a suggestion or idea.

This time she had only one piece of advice and that was to stay clear of Peoples and Milton and even Lindell. Not that she knew them personally. She just knew the FBI culture and knew their kind. Of course, her advice came too late for me.

"I'm doing my best to do just that," I told her. "It would be fine with me if I never see any of them ever again."

"But not very likely."

I suddenly thought of something.

"You don't have your cell phone on you, do you?"

"Yes, but I don't think they like you using cells in a place like this."

"I know. I'll go outside. I just remembered I have to make a call or the shit's going to hit the fan."

She got her phone out of her purse and gave it to me. I left the restaurant and stood in an indoor shopping mall that had been built to look like a Venetian canal complete with gondolas. The concrete sky was painted blue with wisps of white clouds. It was phony but at least it was air-conditioned. I called Janis Langwiser's cell number and told her the coast was clear.

"I was beginning to worry because I hadn't heard from you. I've called your house twice."

"Everything's fine. I'm in Vegas and will be back tomorrow."

"How do I know you're not under duress? You know, being held and forced to say that."

"You got caller ID?"

"Oh, that's right. I saw it was a seven-oh-two number. All right, Harry. Don't forget, call me tomorrow. And don't lose too much money over there."

"I won't."

When I got back to the table Eleanor wasn't there. I sat down and was anxious about it but she came back from the rest room in a few minutes. As I watched her approach

I felt she was different but I couldn't place how. It was more than the hair and the deeper tan. It was like she carried more confidence than I remembered. Maybe she had found what she needed on the blue-felt poker tables on the strip.

I gave her back the phone and she dropped it into her purse.

"So how has it been here?" I asked. "We've been talking about my case. Let's talk about your case for a while."

"I don't have a case."

"You know what I mean."

She shrugged.

"Things are going well this year. I won a satellite and took a button. I get to play in the series."

I knew she was talking about winning a qualifying tournament for the World Series of poker. The last time we talked about poker she had told me that her secret goal was to be the first woman to ever win the series. The winner of a qualifying tournament can take the cash prize or a so-called button, which is an entry into the series.

"This will be your first time in the series, right?"

She nodded and smiled and I could tell she was proud and excited.

"It starts pretty soon."

"Well, good luck. Maybe I'll come over and watch."

"Bring me luck."

"It still must be hard, Eleanor, making a living on the turn of the cards."

"I'm good at it, Harry. Besides, I've got backers now. It spreads the risks."

"What do you mean?"

"That's how it works these days. I have backers. I use their money when I play. They get seventy-five percent of what I win. If I lose, they take the loss. But I don't lose too often, Harry."

I nodded.

"Who are these people? Are they . . . you know?"

"Legitimate? Yes, Harry, very. They're businessmen. Microsoft men. From Seattle. I met them when they were out here playing. So far I've made them money. With the way the stock market's been, they'd rather invest in me. They're happy and so am I."

"Good."

I thought about the money Alex Taylor had offered me. And then there was the reward offered on the heist case. If I solved it, got back some of the money and somehow qualified for the reward, I could be her backer. It was a pipe dream. I wondered if she would even take my money.

"What are you thinking about?" she asked. "You look so concerned."

"Nothing. I was just thinking about the case for a second. Something I want to ask the insurance investigator tomorrow."

The waiter brought the check and I paid after getting my AmEx card back from Eleanor. We left and got the car and I checked to make sure the suitcase was still in the back. We drove over to the Bellagio, a short distance that took a long time because of the traffic. I grew nervous as we got closer because I didn't know what was going to happen when we got there. I checked my watch. It was almost ten.

"What time do you play?"

"I like to start around midnight."

"Why do you like to play through the night? What's wrong with the day?"

"The real players come out at night. The tourists go to bed. There's more money on the table."

We rode in silence for a little bit and she eventually continued as though there had been no pause.

"Plus, I like coming out at the end of the night and seeing the sun coming up. Something about it, like you're just happy you survived another day or something."

Inside the Bellagio we went to the VIP desk and picked up a card key that had been left under Eleanor's name. It was that simple. She led me to the elevator like she had been in it a hundred times and we went up to a suite on the twelfth floor. It was the nicest hotel room I had ever seen, with a living room and a bedroom and a view that looked down on the signature lighted fountains in the front pond.

"This is nice. You must know some people."

"I'm getting a rep. I play here three or four nights a week and it's starting to draw people. High rollers who want to play me. They know that here, and they don't want me to play anywhere else."

I nodded and turned to her.

"I guess things are really going well for you."

"I'm not complaining."

"I guess . . ."

I didn't finish. She walked over to me and stood in front of me.

"You guess what?"

"I don't know what I was going to ask. I guess I wanted to know what was missing. Are you with somebody now, Eleanor?"

She drew closer. I could feel her breath.

"You mean am I in love with somebody? No, Harry, I'm not."

I nodded and she spoke again before I could.

"Do you still believe in that thing you told me? About the single-bullet theory."

I nodded without hesitation and looked into her eyes. She leaned forward, her head against my chin.

"What about you?" I asked. "Do you still believe what that poet said, that there is no end of things in the heart?"

"Yes, I believe it. Always."

I raised her chin with my hand and kissed her. Soon our arms were around each other and her hand was on the back of my neck pulling me toward her. I knew we were going to make love. And I knew for a moment what it meant to be the luckiest man in Las Vegas. I pulled away from her lips and just hugged her to my chest.

"All I want in this world is you," I whispered.

"I know," she whispered back.

31

On the flight back to Los Angeles I tried to refocus on the case. But it was a fruitless effort. I had spent a good part of the night watching Eleanor win several thousand dollars from five men at a table down in the Bellagio poker room. I had never watched her play at any length before. It is fair to say she embarrassed the other players, cleaning out all but one of them, and even he was left with only a single stack of chips by the time she cashed out five racks of her own. She was a cold, hard player who was as impressive as she was mysterious and beautiful. I spent my life learning to read people. But I never read anything off of her while she was playing. There was not a tell anywhere in her game as far as I could see.

But when she was finished with those men she was also finished with me. Outside the poker room she told me she was tired and had to go. She said I couldn't go with her. She didn't even offer me a ride to the airport. It was a short good-bye. We parted with a kiss as lacking in passion as our moments in the suite above had seemingly been full of it. We parted without promises of rejoining or of even calling each other again. We just said good-bye and I watched her walk away through the casino.

I got to the airport on my own. But once on the plane I couldn't let it go. I tried opening the murder book but it did me no good. I kept thinking about the mysteries. Not the good moments, the smiles and the memories and the making love. I thought about our abrupt departure and how she had skillfully avoided the question when I'd asked if she was with somebody. She'd said she wasn't in love but that didn't really answer the question. I thought about why she had wanted me to stay in a hotel room and why she wouldn't open her car's trunk. On the front page of the murder book I wrote down her license plate number from memory. After doing it I felt like I had in some way betrayed her and I then crossed it out. But even as I did this I knew I could not cross it out in my memory.

32

The investigative offices of Global Underwriters were in a six-story black box on Colorado about six blocks from the ocean. When I got there the secretary who guarded entrance to the office of Sandor Szatmari looked at me as though I had just ridden the elevator down from the moon.

"Didn't you get the message?"

"What message?"

"I left a message for you after getting your number from Mr. Scaggs's office. Mr. Szatmari had to cancel your appointment this morning."

"What happened, somebody die?"

She looked slightly insulted by my brashness. Her voice took on a tone of impatience.

"No, in reviewing his schedule for the day he decided he did not have the time to fit you in."

"So he's here?"

"He cannot see you. I'm sorry you didn't get the message. I thought there was something wrong with the number I got, but I *did* leave a message."

"Please tell him I'm here. Tell him I didn't get the message because I was out of town. I flew in for this meeting. I'd still like to see him. It's important."

Now she looked annoyed. She lifted the phone to make the call but then thought better of it and hung up. She got up and walked down a hallway off to the side of the waiting room so she could deliver the message in person. A few minutes later she came back and sat down. She took her time in delivering the news to me.

"I talked to Mr. Szatmari," she said. "He'll try to get you in as soon as he can."

"Thank you. That's nice of him and nice of you."

There was a couch and a coffee table with a spread of outdated magazines on it. I had brought the murder book with me, mostly as a prop, so I could impress Szatmari with it and the access it showed I had. I sat down on the couch and spent the time waiting by leafing through it and rereading some of the reports. Nothing new hit me but I was becoming well versed in the facts of the case. This was important because I knew it would help when I sifted through new information to not have to check the murder book every time.

A half hour went by and then the secretary's phone buzzed and she got the word to send me in.

Szatmari was a solidly built man in his midfifties. He looked more like a salesman than an investigator but the walls of his office were hung with commendations and handshake photos testifying to his success as one. He pointed me to a chair in front of his cluttered desk and spoke as he wrote something down on a report.

"I'm busy, Mr. Bosch. What can I do for you?"

"Well, like I told you yesterday on the phone, I'm working one of your cases. I thought maybe we could share some information, see if one of us has gonc down a road the other hasn't."

"Why should I share with you?"

Something was wrong. He was predisposed not to like me before I had even set foot in his office. I wondered if somehow Peoples had talked to him about me. Maybe Szatmari had called the LAPD or the bureau to check me out and got the word not to cooperate. Maybe that was why the appointment had been canceled.

"I don't get this," I said. "Is something wrong? It's called solving the case, that's why maybe we should share information."

"And how about you? Would you share with me? How much of the reward do you give to me?"

I nodded. Now I got it. The reward.

"Mr. Szatmari, you have it wrong. You have me wrong."

"Sure. Have reward, will travel. I see your kind all the time. Come in here, wanting information, maybe make some big bucks."

His accent became more pronounced as he got worked up. I flipped open the murder book and found the black-and-white photocopies of the murder scene photos. I tore the page with Angella Benton's hands on it out of the book and slapped it down on his desk.

"That's why I'm doing this. Not the money. Her. I was there that day. I was a cop. I'm retired now but I was on this case until they took me off it. That probably cuts me out of any reward, okay?"

Szatmari studied the grainy copy of the photo. He then looked at the binder on my lap. He then finally looked at me.

"I remember you now. Your name. You were the one who hit one of the robbers with a round."

I nodded.

"I was there that day, but since we never found the robbers it's not known for sure who hit who."

"Come on, eight rent-a-cops and an LAPD veteran. It was you."

"I think so."

"You know, I tried to talk to you back then. Interview you. But the department stonewalled me."

"How come?"

"They'd do anything they could to keep other investigations and investigators out of the picture. They're like that over there."

"I know. I remember."

He smiled and leaned back in his seat.

"And now here you are, wanting cooperation from me. Ironic, eh?"

"Very."

"Is that the investigative file? Let me see it, please."

I handed the heavy binder across his desk. He put it down and flipped back to the front section and started leafing through the reports until he came to the original offense report. The homicide. He worked a finger down the page until he came to my name in the block marked "I/O" for investigating officer. He then closed the murder book but didn't hand it back.

"Why now? Why do you investigate this?"

"Because I just retired and it's one of the ones that won't let go."

He nodded that he understood.

"Our investigation, you understand, was in regard to the money, not the woman."

"It's all the same thing, you ask me."

"Our investigation is no longer active. The money is gone by now. Split up, spent. Without the possibility of recovery. There are other cases."

"The money's been written off," I said, "but she hasn't been. Not by me, not by those who knew her."

"*Did* you know her?"

"I met her that day."

He nodded again, seeming to understand what that meant. He straightened the corners on a stack of files on his desk.

"Did it ever go anywhere?" I asked. "Did you get close to anything?"

He took a long time answering.

"No, not really. Only dead ends on this one."

"When did you put it aside?"

"I don't remember. It was a long time ago."

"Where's your file on it?"

"I cannot give you my file. It is against company policy."

"Because of the reward thing, right? The company doesn't allow you to cooperate with unofficial investigations if there's a reward."

"It can lead to collusion," he said, nodding. "Also, there is the legal jeopardy. I don't have the luxury of the protections the police have. If my investigative notes and summaries were to become public, I'd be left open to possible lawsuits."

I tried to think for a minute about how to play this. Szatmari seemed to be holding something back and whatever it was might be in the file. I think he wanted to give it to me but wasn't sure how.

"Take a look at the photocopy again," I said. "Look at her hands. Are you a religious man, Mr. Szatmari?"

Szatmari looked at the photo of Angella Benton's hands again.

"Sometimes I am religious," he said. "Are you?"

"Not really. I mean, what is religion? I don't go to church, if that's what it is. But I think about religion and I think I have something like it inside. A code is like religion. You have to believe it. You have to practice it. The thing is, look at her hands, Mr. Szatmari. I remember when I saw her down on the tile and saw how her hands were . . . I sort of took it as a sign."

"A sign of what?"

"I don't know. A sign of something. Like religion. That's why this is one of the cases that didn't go away."

"I understand."

"Then pull out the file and put it on your desk," I said as if giving instruction to someone in a hypnotic trance. "Then go get a cup of coffee or have a smoke. And take your time. I'll wait for you right here."

Szatmari looked at me for a long moment and then reached down to what I guess was a file drawer in the desk. He finally took his eyes off me so he could pull the right file. He brought it up — it was a thick one — and put it down on the desk. He then pushed back his chair and got up.

"I'm going to grab a cup of coffee," he said. "You want something?"

"I think I'll be fine. But thanks."

He nodded and went out, closing the door behind him. The moment it clicked I was up out of my seat and moving behind the desk. I sat down and dove into the file.

For the most part, Szatmari's file was filled with documents I had already seen before. There were also copies of contracts and directives between Global and its client BankLA that were new, as well as summaries of interviews with several bank and film company employees. Szatmari had conducted interviews with every one of the security transport men who had been on the scene the day of the shoot-out and heist.

But there was no interview with me. As usual the LAPD had put up a wall. Szatmari's request to interview me never even got to me. Not that I would have accepted the request if I had seen it. I had an arrogance then that I hoped I had now lost.

I scanned the interviews and summaries as fast as I could, paying particular attention to the reports pertaining to the three bank employees I hoped to talk to later in the day, Gordon Scaggs, Linus Simonson and Jocelyn Jones. The subjects did not give Szatmari much. Scaggs was the one who handled everything and he was very specific as to the steps he had taken and the planning of the one-day loan of $2 million in cash. The interviews with Simonson and Jones depicted them as worker bees who did what they were told. They could have just as easily been putting labels on cans as counting twenty thousand hundred-dollar bills and writing down eight hundred serial numbers while they were at it.

My curiosity meter jumped when I came across documents pertaining to the financial backgrounds of Jack Dorsey, Lawton Cross and myself. Szatmari had pulled TRW reports on all of us. He had apparently called our banks and credit-card companies. He wrote short summaries on each of us, my record coming out cleanest, while Cross and Dorsey did not fare as well. According to Szatmari, both men carried huge credit-card debt, with Dorsey in the most difficult financial position because he was divorced but still supporting four children, two of whom were in college.

The door to the office opened and the secretary looked in, just about to say something to Szatmari when she saw it was me behind his desk.

"What are you doing?"

"Waiting for Mr. Szatmari. He went to get a coffee."

She put her hands on her ample hips, the international sign of indignation.

"Did he tell you to go behind his desk and start reading that file?"

It was incumbent upon me not to leave Szatmari in a potential jam.

"He told me to wait. I'm waiting."

"Well, you get right back around to the other side of that desk. I'll be informing Mr. Szatmari about what I saw."

I closed the file, got up and came around the desk as instructed.

"You know, I'd really appreciate it if you didn't do that," I said.

"I don't care what you'd appreciate, I'm telling him."

She then disappeared, leaving the door open in her wake. A few minutes went by and Szatmari stormed in and closed the door sharply. He then lost his anger as he turned to face me. He was carrying a coffee mug with steam rising out of it.

"Thanks for playing it that way," he said. "I just hope you got whatever you needed because now to make good on the little fit I had out there I have to throw you out."

"No problem," I said, standing up. "I've got one question, though."

"Go ahead."

"Was that just routine to do the background financials on the cops on the case? Me, Jack Dorsey and Lawton Cross."

Szatmari folded his brow as he tried to remember the reason for the financial checks. Then he shrugged.

"I forgot about that. I think I just thought that with the money that was at stake I should check everybody out. Especially you, Bosch, with the coincidence of you being there at the set at the right moment."

I nodded. It sounded like a solid investigative move.

"Are you angry about it?"

"Me? No, not mad. I was just curious about where it came from, that's all."

"Anything else helpful?"

"Maybe, you never know."

"Good luck then. If you don't mind, keep me informed of any progress."

"I will. I'll let you know."

We shook hands. On my way out I passed by the indignant secretary and told her to have a nice day. She didn't respond.

33

The interview with Gordon Scaggs went quickly and smoothly. He met me at the agreed-upon time at the BankLA tower in downtown. His forty-second-floor office faced east and had one of the best views of the city's smog I had ever seen. His recounting of his involvement in the ill-fated $2 million loan to Eidolon Productions deviated in no noticeable way from his statement in the murder book. He negotiated a $50,000 fee for the bank, the costs of security included. The money was to go out in the morning on the day of filming and come back before 6 P.M. closing time.

"I knew there was a risk," Scaggs told me. "But I saw a nice, quick profit for the bank. I guess you could say that clouded my vision."

Scaggs turned the money transport issues over to Ray Vaughn, head of bank security, while he turned his attention to the chores of insuring the one-day operation through Global Underwriters and then gathering together the $2 million in cash. It would have been highly unusual for a single bank — even the downtown flagship — to have that much money in cash available on one day. So in thc days before the loan took place Scaggs had to arrange for cash shipments from various BankLA branches to the downtown location. On the day of the loan the money was loaded into an armored vehicle and driven from downtown to the movie set in Hollywood. Ray Vaughn rode in a lead car. He was in constant radio contact with the driver of the armored truck and led him on a meandering course through Hollywood in an effort to determine if they were being followed.

When they arrived at the set location they were met by more armed security and Linus Simonson, one of the assistants who had helped Scaggs pull the cash together and had created the list of serial numbers the insurance company had demanded.

And, of course, the bank entourage was met by the hooded and heavily armed robbers as well.

One thing new I got from Scaggs during the initial part of the interview was that bank policy had changed since the heist. BankLA no longer engaged in what he called boutique cash loans to the movie industry.

"What is that saying?" he asked. "Once burned is an education. Twice burned is just plain stupidity. Well, we're not stupid here, Mr. Bosch. We're not going to get burned by those people again."

I nodded in agreement.

"So you feel confident it was 'those people' where this came from? The heist originated over there and not here within the bank?"

Scaggs looked indignant at the very thought of anything else.

"I should say so. Look at the poor girl who was murdered. She worked for them, not me."

"True. But her murder could have been part of the plan. To throw suspicion on the movie production instead of the bank."

"Impossible. The police have been over this place with a fine-tooth comb. Same with the insurance company. We received a clean bill of health from everyone involved. We are absolutely one-hundred-percent clean on this."

I nodded again.

"Then I guess you won't mind if I talk to your employees, too. I'd like to speak to Linus Simonson and Jocelyn Jones."

Scaggs realized he'd been cornered. How could he not let me speak to employees after that ringing endorsement of honesty and innocence on the bank's behalf?

"The answer is yes and no," he said. "Jocelyn is still with us. She's an assistant branch manager now in West Hollywood. I don't think there will be a problem talking to her.

"And Linus Simonson?"

"Linus never came back to us after that awful day. I guess you know he got shot up by those bastards. Him and Ray. Ray didn't make it but Linus did. He was in the hospital and then he was on sick leave and then he didn't want to come back at all and I can't see as I blame him."

"He quit?"

"That's right."

I had not seen mention of this in the murder book or even in Szatmari's records. I knew the investigation was most intense in the days and weeks after the heist. This was probably when Simonson was still recovering and still technically an employee. The investigative records generated at this time would have no reason to mention his leaving employment at the bank.

"Do you know where he went from here?"

"I used to. I don't now. But to lay it all out there for you, Linus went and got himself a lawyer who started making liability claims. You know, that the bank put Linus in harm's way and all of this nonsense. None of the claims mentioned that he volunteered to be out there that day."

"He wanted to be there?"

"Sure. He was a young guy. He grew up in town and probably had Hollywood aspirations at one time or another. Everybody does. He thought spending the day on the set, being the guy in charge of the money, would be a good deal. He volunteered and I said fine, go. I wanted somebody from my office there anyway. Besides Ray Vaughn, I mean."

"So did Simonson actually sue the bank or just make noise with his lawyer?"

"He made noise. But he made enough noise that legal settled him out. They gave him a chunk of cash and he went away. I heard he used it to buy a nightclub."

"How much they give him?"

"I don't know. One time I asked our attorney, Jim Foreman, what the kid got and he wouldn't tell me. He said terms of the settlement were confidential. But from what I understand, this club he bought, it was a nice one. One of those Hollywood-type places."

I thought of the portrait I had looked at in the legal library while waiting to see Janis Langwiser.

"Your lawyer is James Foreman?"

"Not my lawyer. The bank's lawyer. Outside counsel. They decided not to keep it in-house because of the possible conflict."

I nodded.

"Do you know the name of the club he bought?"

"No, I don't."

I sat there looking past Scaggs at the smog through the window behind him. I was seeing but not seeing. I had gone inside where I was feeling the first stirrings of instinct and excitement, of the state of grace that comes with my religion.

"Mr. Bosch?" Scaggs said. "Don't disappear on me. I've got an officers' meeting in five minutes."

I came out of it and looked at him.

"Sorry, sir. I'm done here. For now. But before your meeting can you call Jocelyn Jones and tell her I'm coming out to see her? I need to know where the branch is, too."

"That will be no problem."

34

On the way to the West Hollywood branch of BankLA to see Jocelyn Jones I had some time to kill so I drove west on Hollywood Boulevard. I had not been down there much since my retirement and I wanted to see the old beat. According to the newspaper it was changing and I wanted to see this for myself.

The asphalt on the boulevard still glittered in the sunlight but the storefronts and office buildings near Vine still slumbered beneath the patina of a half century of smog. No difference there. But once past Cahuenga and onto Highland I saw where the new Hollywood was springing to life. New hotels — and I'm not talking about the type with hourly rates — and theaters, people centers with popular up-style restaurant franchises anchoring them. The streets and sidewalks were crowded, the brass stars imbedded in the sidewalks were polished. It was safer and cleaner but less genuine. Still, the word that popped into my head was *hope.* There was a sense of hope and vigor. There was a definite vibe coming off the street and I guess I liked it. The idea, I knew, was that the vibe would spread from this core area and move down the boulevard like an earthquake wave, leaving renovation and reinvention in its wake. A few years ago I would have been first to say the plan had no chance. But maybe I was wrong.

Still feeling lucky from Vegas I decided to let the vibe ride and dropped down Fairfax to Third and pulled into the farmer's market to grab something to eat.

The market was another remake job I had stayed away from. There was a new parking garage and open-air people center built next to the old clapboard market with its comforting combination of good, cheap food and kitsch. I think I liked it better when you could just pull into a parking space next to the newsstand but I had to admit they had done it right. It was the old and new sitting side by side and getting along. I walked through the new section, past the department stores and the biggest bookstore I had ever seen and into the old. Bob's Donuts was still there and every other place that I remembered. It was crowded. People were happy. It was too late in the day for a doughnut so I picked up a BLT and change for a dollar at the Kokomo Café and ate the sandwich in one of the old-time phone booths that they had left in place next to the Dupar's. I called Roy Lindell first and caught him eating at his desk.

"What do you have?"

"Tuna on rye with pickles."

"That's sick."

"Yeah, what do you have?"

"BLT. Double-smoked bacon from Kokomo's."

"Well, that beats me all to hell. What do you want, Bosch? Last time I saw you, you wanted nothing to do with me. In fact, I thought you went to Vegas."

"I did go but I'm back. And things are smoothing out now. You could say I've come to an understanding with your pals on the ninth floor. You want back in on this thing or you want to pout about it?"

"You got something?"

"Maybe. Not much more than a feeling at the moment."

"What do you want from me?"

I shoved my sandwich wrapper off the murder book and opened it to get the information I needed.

"See what you can come up with on a guy named Linus Simonson. Thirty-one-year-old white male. He owns a club in town."

"What's it called?"

"I don't know yet."

"That's great. You want me to pick up your dry cleaning while I'm at it?"

"Just run the name. You'll get a hit or you won't."

I gave him Simonson's birthdate and the address listed in the murder book, although I had a feeling it was old.

"Who is he?"

I told him about Simonson's former work at BankLA and about him being shot during the movie set heist.

"The guy was a victim. You think he set it up and told his guys to shoot him in the ass?"

"I don't know."

"And what's he got to do with Marty Gessler?"

"I don't know. Maybe nothing. *Probably* nothing. But I just want to check him out. Something doesn't seem right to me."

"Okay, you keep having the hunches and I'll do the legwork, Bosch. Anything else?"

"Look, if you don't want to do it, just say so. I'll get somebody else to —"

"Look, I said I'll do it, and I will. Anything else?"

I hesitated but not for too long.

"Yeah, one other thing. Can you run a plate for me?"

"Give it to me."

I gave him the number I had gotten off the car Eleanor had been driving. It was still in my memory and I figured it would stay there until I checked it out.

"Nevada?" Lindell asked, suspicion obvious in his voice. "This have to do with your trip to Vegas or this thing over here?"

I should have known. Lindell was a lot of things but stupid wasn't one of them. I had already opened the door. I had to step inside.

"I don't know," I lied. "But could you just get me the registration on it?"

If the car, as I suspected, was registered in someone other than Eleanor's name, I could make up a story about thinking I had been followed and Lindell would never know the difference.

"All right," the FBI agent said. "I gotta go. Call me later."

I hung up and that was that. Guilt washed around me like the waves hitting the pylons under the pier. I might be able to fool Lindell with the request but not myself. I was running a check on my former wife. I wondered if I was capable of doing anything lower.

Trying not to dwell on it, I picked up the receiver and dumped more change into the phone. I called Janis Langwiser and realized as I waited for her to answer that I might be about to answer the question I had just posed to myself.

Langwiser's secretary said she was on a phone call and she would have to call me back. I said I wasn't reachable but would call back in fifteen minutes. I hung up and walked around the market, spending the most time in a small store that sold only hot sauce, hundreds of different brands of it. I wasn't sure when I would use it because I rarely cooked at home anymore, but I bought a bottle of Gator Squeezins because I liked the place and I needed more change for the call back.

Next stop was the bakery. Not to buy, just to look. When I was a kid and my mother was still around, she used to take me to the farmer's market on Saturday mornings. What I remember most was watching through the bakery window when the cakemaker would dress the cakes people ordered for birthdays and holidays and weddings. He would make grand designs on the top of each cake, squeezing the icing through a funnel, his thick forearms covered in flour and sugar.

My mother usually had to hold me up at the window so I could see the top of the cake being decorated. Sometimes she would think I was watching the cakemaker but I was really watching her in the reflection of the window, trying to figure out what was wrong.

When she would grow tired of holding me up she'd go grab a chair from the nearby restaurant seating area — what they now call a food court in the malls — and I would stand on that. I used to look at the cakes and imagine what parties they would go to and how many people were going to be there. It seemed like those cakes could only go to happy places. But I could tell that when the baker was icing a wedding cake, it made my mother sad.

The bakery and the cakemaker's window were still there. I stood in front of the glass with my bag of hot sauce, but there was no baker there. I knew it was too late in the day. The cakes were made early each day so they would be ready for pickup or delivery for birthday parties and weddings and anniversaries and things like that. On the rack next to the window I looked at the selection of stainless steel funnel tips the baker could use to make various designs and flowers out of icing.

"No use waiting. He's done for the day."

I didn't need to turn. In the reflection of the window, I saw an old lady walking by behind me. It made me think of my mother again.

"Yeah," I said. "I think you are right."

The second time I went into the phone booth and called Langwiser she was available and picked up right away.

"Is everything okay?"

"Yeah, fine."

"Good, you scared me."

"What are you talking about?"

"You told Roxanne that you couldn't be reached. I thought maybe you were in a cell or something."

"Oh, sorry. I didn't think about that. I'm just not using the cell phone still."

"You think they are still listening?"

"I don't know. Just precautions."

"So is this just your daily check-in?"

"Sort of. I've got a question, too."

"I'm listening."

Maybe it was because of the way I hadn't told Lindell the whole truth or because of the way checking out Eleanor made me feel, but I decided not to run a play on Langwiser. I decided to simply play the cards I had.

"A few years ago your firm handled a case. The attorney was James Foreman and the client was BankLA."

"Yes, the bank's a client. What was the case? I wasn't here a few years ago."

I closed the door to the phone booth even though I knew it would quickly get hot in the tiny cubicle.

"I don't know what it was called but the other party's

name was Linus Simonson. He worked for the bank as an assistant to the vice president. He took a bullet in the shootout during the movie set heist."

"Okay. I remember somebody was wounded and somebody was killed but I don't remember the names."

"He was the wounded. The dead guy was Ray Vaughn, chief of security for the bank. Simonson lived. In fact, he only took a round in the ass. Probably a ricochet, if I remember the way the shooting team worked it out."

"So he then sued the bank?"

"I'm not sure if it went that far. The point is he was out on medical for a while and then decided he didn't want to come back. He got a lawyer and started making noise about the bank being liable for putting him in a position where he was in harm's way."

"Sounds reasonable."

"Even though he volunteered to be there. He had helped put the money together and then volunteered to baby-sit it during the movie shoot."

"Well, it still was probably actionable. He could make a case for volunteering under duress or —"

"Yeah, I know all of that. I'm not worried about whether he had a case or not. He apparently did, because the bank settled and James Foreman handled it."

"Okay, so where is this going? What is your question?"

I reopened the door of the booth so I could get some fresh air.

"I want to know what he settled for. How much did he get?"

"I'll call Jim Foreman right now. You want to hold?"

"Uh, it's not that simple. I think there was a confidentiality agreement."

There was silence from her and I actually smiled while I waited. It had felt good to just come out with what I wanted.

"I see," Langwiser finally said. "So you want me to violate that by finding out what he got."

"Well, when you put it that way . . ."

"What other way is there to put it?"

"I'm working this thing and he's come up. Simonson. And it would just help me a lot if I knew how big a chunk of cash the bank gave him. It would help me a lot, Janis."

Again my words were met with a long silence.

"I'm not going to go snooping through files in my own firm," she finally said. "I'm not going to do anything that could get me in the shit. The best thing I can do is just go to Jim and ask him and see what he says."

"Okay."

It was better than I thought I would get.

"The wedge I have is that BankLA remains a client. If you are saying that this guy Simonson might have been part of this heist which lost the bank two million and its chief of security, then he might be inclined."

"Hey, that's good."

I had thought of that angle but wanted her to come to it. I started to get jazzed. I thought maybe she'd be able to get what I needed from Foreman.

"Don't get excited, Harry. Not yet."

"Okay."

"I'll see what I can do and then I'll call you. And don't worry, if I have to leave a message on your home number it will be in code."

"Okay, Janis, thanks."

I hung up and left the booth. On the way back through the market in the direction of the parking garage I passed the cake window and was surprised to see that the baker was there. I stopped for a minute and watched. It must have been a last-minute order because it looked like the cake had been taken out of one of the inside display cabinets. It was already iced. The man behind the window was just putting on flowers and lettering.

I waited until he wrote the message. It was pink writing on a field of chocolate. It said, *Happy Birthday, Callie!* I hoped it was another cake going to a happy place.

35

Jocelyn Jones worked in a branch bank on Santa Monica at San Vicente. In a county for decades known as the bank robbery capital of the world she was in about as safe a location as was possible. Her branch was right across the street from the sheriff's department's West Hollywood station.

The branch was a two-story art deco job with a curving façade with large round windows along its second level. Inside, the tellers' counter and new-accounts desks were on the first floor and the executive offices upstairs. I found Jones up there in an office with a porthole that looked over the sheriff's compound to the Pacific Design Center, known locally as the Blue Whale because from some angles its blue-sheathed façade looked like the tail of a humpback protruding from the ocean.

Jones smiled and invited me to sit down.

"Mr. Scaggs told me you would be coming by and that it was all right to talk to you. He said you were working on the robbery."

"That's right."

"I'm glad it hasn't been forgotten about."

"Well, I'm glad to hear you say that."

"What can I do for you?"

"I'm not sure. I'm sort of retracing a lot of steps that were taken before. So it might be repetitive but I'd just like to hear you talk about your part in it. I'll ask questions if I come up with any."

"Well, there isn't a whole lot for me to tell. I mean, I wasn't there like Linus and poor Mr. Vaughn were. I was mostly around the money before it was transported. I was an assistant at that time to Mr. Scaggs. He's been my mentor with the company."

I nodded and smiled like I thought it was all nice. I was moving slowly, the plan being to gradually steer her in the direction I wanted to go.

"So you worked on the money. You counted it, packaged it, got it ready. Where was that?"

"At the downtown center. We were in a vault the whole time. The money came in to us from the branches and we did everything right there without ever leaving. Except, you know, at the end of the day. It took about three, three and a half days to get everything ready. Mostly waiting for it to come in from the branches."

"When you say 'us,' you mean Linus . . ."

I opened the murder book on my lap as if to check a name I didn't recall.

"Simonson," she said for me.

"Right, Linus Simonson. You worked on this together, correct?"

"That's right."

"Was Mr. Scaggs his mentor, too?"

She shook her head and slightly blushed, I think, but it was hard to tell because she was very dark-skinned.

"No, the mentoring program is a minority program. I

should say 'was.' They suspended it a year ago. Anyway, Linus is white. He grew up in Beverly Hills. His father owned a bunch of restaurants and I don't think he needed a mentor."

I nodded.

"Okay, so you and Linus were in there for three days putting all of this money together. You also had to record serial numbers off the bills, right?"

"Yes, we did that, too."

"How was that done?"

She didn't answer for a moment as she tried to remember. She swiveled slowly back and forth in her chair. I watched a sheriff's helicopter land on the roof of the station across Santa Monica.

"What I remember is that it was supposed to be random," she said. "So we just took bills out of the bricks at random. I think we had to get about a thousand numbers and record them. That took a long time, too."

I leafed through the murder book until I found a copy of the currency report she and Simonson had put together. I unsnapped the binder's rings and removed the report.

"According to this you recorded eight hundred of the bills."

"Oh, okay. Eight hundred, then."

"Is this the report?"

I handed it to her and she studied it, looking at each page and her signature at the bottom of the last page.

"It looks like it but it's been four years."

"Yes, I know. That was the last time you saw it — when you signed it?"

"No, after the robbery I saw it. When I was questioned by the detectives. They asked if that was the report."

"And you said it was?"

"Yes."

"Okay, going back to when you and Linus made this report, how did that go?"

She shrugged.

"Linus and I just took turns typing the numbers into his laptop."

"Isn't there some sort of computer scanner or copier that could have recorded the serial numbers much more easily?"

"There is but it wouldn't work for what we had to do. We had to randomly select and record bills from every pack but keep each recorded bill in its original pack. That way if the money was stolen and split up, there would be a chance of tracing every pack."

I nodded.

"Who told you to do it that way?"

"Well, I guess it came down from Mr. Skaggs or maybe Mr. Vaughn. Mr. Vaughn was the one who dealt with security and the instructions from the insurance company."

"Okay, so you are in the vault with Linus. How exactly did you record the money?"

"Oh, Linus thought it would take forever if we wrote down the numbers and then had to type them into a computer. So he brought his laptop in and we entered them directly. One of us would read off the number while the other typed."

"Which one of you did which?"

"We both did. We switched. You might think sitting at a table with two million dollars in cash on it is a real thrill but it actually was boring. So we switched around. Sometimes I read and he typed, and then I'd type while he read out the numbers."

I thought about this, trying to see how it could have worked. It might appear that having two employees put the list together would provide a double-checking system, but it didn't. Whether Simonson was reading off numbers or entering them on the laptop computer, he was controlling the data. He could have made up numbers in either position and Jones would not have known it unless she looked at either the bill or the computer screen.

"Okay," I said. "Then when you were finished you printed out the computer file and signed the report, right?"

"Right. I mean, I think so. It was a while back."

"Is that your signature on there?"

She flipped to the last page of the document and checked. She nodded.

"That's it."

I held out my hand and she gave me the document back.

"Who took the report to Mr. Scaggs?"

"Probably Linus. He printed it out. Why are all of these details so important?"

Her first suspicion of where I was going. I didn't answer. I flipped the report she had been studying to the back page and looked at the signatures myself. Her signature was below Simonson's and above Scaggs's scrawl. It had been the order of signing. Simonson, then her, then it was taken to Scaggs for final sign-off.

As I held the report up to the light from the porthole, I thought I saw something I hadn't noticed before. It was only a photocopy of the original or maybe even a copy of a copy, but even still, there were gradations in the ink in Jocelyn Jones's signature. It was something I had seen before on another case.

"What is it?" Jones asked.

I looked at her while putting the document back into the murder book.

"Excuse me?"

"You looked like you saw something important."

"Oh, nothing. I'm just looking at everything. I have just a few more questions."

"Good. I should get downstairs. We're closing soon."

"I'll get out of your hair, then. Mr. Vaughn, was he part of this process in which the money was prepared and the serial numbers documented?"

She shook her head once.

"Not really. He sort of supervised us and came in a lot, especially when the money came in from the branches or the Federal Reserve. He was in charge of that, I guess."

"Did he come in when you guys were dictating the numbers and typing them into the computer?"

"I don't remember. I think he did. Like I said, he came in a lot. I think he liked Linus so he came in a lot."

"What do you mean, he 'liked' Linus?"

"Well, you know."

"You mean Mr. Vaughn was gay?"

She shrugged.

"I think he was, but not in an open way. It was a secret, I guess. It was no big deal."

"What about Linus?"

"No, he's not gay. That's why I don't think he liked Mr. Vaughn coming in so much."

"Did he say that to you or was that just your take on it?"

"No, he sort of said something about it one day. Like he joked, saying he was going to have a sexual harassment suit if this keeps up. Something like that."

I nodded. I didn't know if this meant anything to the case or not.

"You didn't answer my question before."

"What was that?"

"About why you are focusing so much on all of this. The currency numbers, I mean. And Linus and Mr. Vaughn."

"I'm not really. It just seems that way to you because that is the part of this you are familiar with. But I'm trying to be thorough about all aspects of this. Do you ever hear from Linus anymore?"

She seemed surprised by the question.

"Me? No. I visited him in the hospital once, right after the shooting. He never came back to work, so I never saw him again. We worked together but we weren't really friends. Different sides of the tracks, I guess. I always thought that was why Mr. Scaggs picked us."

"What do you mean?"

"Well, we weren't really friends and Linus was, you know, Linus. I think Mr. Scaggs picked two people that were different and weren't friends so we wouldn't get any ideas. About the money."

I nodded and didn't say anything. She seemed to go off into a thought and then she shook her head in a self-deprecating way.

"What?"

"Nothing. It's just that I was thinking about going to see him at one of the clubs but thought they probably wouldn't even let me in. And if I said I knew him, it might be embarrassing, you know, if they called him and he acted like he didn't remember or something."

"Clubs? There is more than one?"

She closed her eyes to suspicious slits.

"You told me you were being thorough. But you really don't even know who he is now, do you?"

I shrugged.

"Who is he now?"

"He's Linus. Like he only uses his first name now. He's famous. He and his partners own the top clubs in Hollywood now. It's like where all the celebrities go to see and be seen. Lines out the door and velvet ropes."

"How many clubs?"

"I think at least four or five now. I don't really keep track. They started with the one and then they kept adding."

"How many partners are there?"

"I don't know. There was a magazine story — wait a second, I think I saved it."

She bent down and opened a drawer at the bottom of her desk. I heard her shuffling its contents around and then she came out with a copy of *Los Angeles Magazine,* the coffee-table monthly. She started turning its pages. It was a glossy magazine that listed restaurants in the back and usually ran two or three long feature articles on living and dying in L.A. Behind the gloss was a bite, though. Twice over the years writers from the magazine had done stories on my cases. I always thought they had come closest of any media reports to the truth of a crime in terms of its effects on a family or neighborhood. The ripple effect.

"I don't know why I was holding on to this," Jones said, a bit embarrassed after just saying she didn't keep track of her former coworker. "I guess because I knew him. Yeah, here."

She turned the magazine around. There was a two-page opening spread on the story under a headline that said, "The Night Kings." There was an accompanying photo of four young men posed side by side behind a dark mahogany bar. Behind them were shelves of colored bottles lit from beneath.

"Can I see that?"

She closed it and handed it across the desk to me.

"You can have it. Like I said, I don't think I'll ever be seeing Linus again. He has no time for me. He did what he said he was going to do and that's that."

I looked up from the magazine to her.

"What do you mean? What did he tell you he was going to do?"

"When I saw him in the hospital. He told me the bank owed him a lot of money for getting shot in the . . . uh, you know. He said he was going to get it, quit his job and open up a bar. He said he wouldn't make the mistakes his dad made."

"His dad?"

"I didn't know what that meant. I didn't ask. But for some reason, opening that bar was Linus's life ambition. To be king of the night, I guess. Well, he got there."

Her voice had a mixture of longing and jealousy in it. It didn't work well with her and I wished I could tell her what I thought of her hero. But I didn't. I didn't have everything I needed yet.

Thinking I had taken the interview about as far as I could, I stood up and held up the magazine.

"Thanks for your time. Are you sure you don't mind me taking this?"

She waved me off.

"No, go ahead. I've looked at it enough. One of these nights I ought to just put on my black jeans and black T-shirt and go on down and see if I can catch Linus for a minute. We could talk about the good old days but he probably doesn't want to hear about them."

"Nobody does, Jocelyn. Because the old days weren't that good."

I got up. I wanted to offer her some words of encouragement. I wanted to tell her not to be jealous, that what she had and what she'd accomplished were things to be proud of. But the sheriff's helicopter took off and banked across the street and over the bank. The place shook like an earthquake and took my words with it. I left Jocelyn Jones sitting there thinking about the other side of the tracks.

36

The magazine had been published seven months earlier. The story on Linus Simonson and his partners was not a cover story but it was hyped on the cover with a line that said, "Hollywood's After Hours Entrepreneurs." The story was hooked to the impending opening of a sixth club in the foursome's lineup of all-star late-night establishments. The article referred to Simonson as the king of the night crawlers, the one who parlayed the whole empire out of one hole-in-the-wall bar he had bought with a legal settlement. He had taken that first club, in an alley off of Hollywood and Cahuenga, renovated it, cut the lighting in half and brought in female bartenders who were prized more for their looks and tattoos than their skills at mixing drinks and adding bar tabs. He played the music loud, charged a $20 cover and didn't let anyone in wearing a tie or a white shirt. The club had no name on the wall outside and no listing in the phone book. A flashing neon blue arrow over the front door was the only indication of a commercial venture. But soon the arrow was no longer needed and was removed because there was always a line of clubbers stretching from the door down the alley.

The article stated that Linus — he was referred to by first name through most of the article — then partnered up with three buddies from his days at Beverly Hills High School and started opening new clubs at a rate of one every six months. The entrepreneurs primarily followed the pattern that worked with the first club. Buy a rundown establishment, renovate and reopen, put the word into the pipeline and wait for it to spread through the ranks of the Hollywood cool. After the nameless bar, the lounges the group opened tended in style and name to follow a literary or musical theme.

The second bar the group bought, closed and then reopened was Nat's Day of the Locusts, a nod to Nathanael West and his classic Hollywood novel. It wasn't their name. The place had been known as simply Nat's for decades and most patrons probably believed it was named for Nat King Cole. Either way the name was cool and the group kept it.

Nat's was also the same place Dorsey and Cross had gotten shot up in. The article reported that the murder had acted to depress the sales price of the place. In fact, it was a steal. But once the bar was reopened — without a name change — and marketed to the night crawlers, the place's history only added to its mystique. It was another immediate and huge success for the high school pals who called their burgeoning company Four Kings Incorporated.

For a long time in my life I did not believe in coincidence. I now know better. But there are coincidences and there are coincidences. Kiz Rider coming to my house and laying the high jingo on me as Art Pepper was playing it — that was coincidence. But as I sat in the Mercedes and read the magazine article, I wasn't accepting the happenstance of Linus Simonson buying the bar in which two detectives who investigated the heist of $2 million he counted and prepared for shipment were shot. I didn't think it was coincidence for a moment. I thought it was pure arrogance.

Besides the nameless bar and Nat's, the foursome also opened places called Kings' Crossing, Chet's and Cozy's Last Stand, named, according to the article, after a friend who had disappeared. The place which had occasioned the magazine story and was due to open was to be called Doghouse Reilly's, after an alias used by private eye Philip Marlowe in a Raymond Chandler novel.

The story didn't delve deeply into the financing behind the four-man operation. It was more interested in the glitz than the underpinnings of the supposed success story. It was taken and reported as a given that the first establishments supported the group's expansion in a continuing cycle. Profits from the first bar financed the second and so on.

But the picture wasn't purely positive. The article's writer ended the story with a suggestion that the four kings might become victims of their own success. The theory espoused was that the population of black-clad night crawlers was finite in Hollywood, and that opening and operating six lounges did not convincingly expand the client base. It only spread it out. The article noted that there were also many pretenders to the throne, a raft of inferior, uncool bars and lounges that had opened in recent years.

The story ended by noting that on a recent Friday night at midnight, there was no line of night crawlers waiting to get into the nameless club. It cynically suggested that it might be time to put up the blue arrow again.

I dropped the magazine into the binder and sat there thinking about things. I had the sense that things were coming together. I felt anxious because I knew instinctively I was close. I didn't have all the answers but experience told me that they would come. What I had was the direction. It had been more than four years since I had looked down on Angella Benton's body and I finally had a solid suspect.

I opened the center console and got out the cell phone. I figured there would be no harm in calling my own home number. I checked messages and found I had two. The first was from Janis Langwiser. It was short and sweet.

"It's me. Call me but use all precautions."

I knew that meant a pay phone. The next message was from Roy Lindell. He also followed the standard of brevity.

"All right, asshole, I've got something for you. Call me."

I looked around. I was parked in front of a post office on San Vicente. My meter was up and I was out of change for both the parking and the calls I needed to make. But I figured there would be a phone inside the post office and a machine for getting change to buy stamps from other machines. I got out and went in.

The main post office was closed but in an outer room that was open after hours I found the machine and pay phone I was looking for. I called Langwiser first because I figured that I had already moved the investigation past the information I had asked Lindell to get for me.

I got Langwiser on her cell but she was still in her office.

"What did you get from Foreman?" I asked, getting right to the point.

"This has to remain highly confidential, Harry. I did talk to Jim and when I explained the circumstances he didn't mind talking to me about it. The caveat being that this information goes into no reports and you never reveal its source."

"No problem. I don't write reports anymore, anyway."

"Don't be so quick and cavalier about it. You're not a cop anymore and you're no lawyer. You have no legal shield."

"I have a private eye ticket."

"Like I said, you have no shield. If a judge ever ordered you to reveal your source you would have to do it or face contempt. That would mean possibly going to jail. Ex-cops in jail don't do so well."

"Tell me about it."

"I just did."

"Okay, I understand. It's still no problem."

The truth was, I couldn't see how this would ever come up in a court and with a judge. I wasn't worried about the possibility of jail.

"Okay, as long as we're clear. Jim told me that Simonson settled for fifty thousand dollars."

"That's all?"

"That's it and it really isn't that much. He was represented by a thirty-five percenter. He also had to pay filing costs."

He'd had a lawyer who took a 35 percent cut of any settlement in exchange for working the case without hourly billing. It meant that Simonson probably cleared a little over thirty grand. It wasn't a lot when it came to quitting your day job and starting a late-night lounge empire.

The sense of anxiety I had been feeling ticked into a higher gear. I had suspected that the settlement would be low but not that low. I was beginning to convince myself.

"Did Foreman say anything else about the case?"

"Just one other thing. He said that it was Simonson who insisted on the confidentiality agreement and that the agreement itself was unusual. It required that there be not only no public announcement about the settlement but no public record of it."

"Well, it never went to court anyway."

"I know, but BankLA is a publicly held corporation. So what the confidentiality agreement entailed was that Simonson be carried under a pseudonym on all financial records related to the payout. He's carried, again at his request, as Mr. King."

I didn't respond as I thought about this.

"So how did I do, Harry?"

"You did real good, Janis. Which reminds me, you've been doing a hell of a lot of work on this. Are you sure you don't want to bill me?"

"Yes, I'm sure. I still owe you."

"Well, now I'll owe you. I want you to do one last thing for me. I just decided that tomorrow I'm going to give what I've got to the powers that be. It might be good if you were there. You know, to sort of make sure I don't step across any lines with these people."

"I'm there. Where?"

"You want to check your calendar first?"

"I already know I have the morning free. You want to do it here or are you going into the police station?"

"No, I've got butting jurisdictions. I'd like to do it at your place. You have a room we can put about six or seven people in?"

"I'll book the conference room. What time?"

"How about nine o'clock?"

"Fine. I'll be here early if you want to come in and talk first and go over everything."

"That would be good. I'll see you about eight-thirty."

"I'll be here. Do you think you have it?"

I knew what she meant. Did I have the story, if not the actual evidence that would push the LAPD and FBI into running with the case again.

"It's coming together. There's maybe one more thing I can do and then I've got to give it to somebody who can get warrants and knock down doors."

"I get it. I'll see you tomorrow. And I'm glad you made it through on this. I really am."

"Yeah, me too. Thanks, Janis."

After hanging up I realized I had forgotten about the parking meter. I went out to feed it but it was too late. West Hollywood Parking Enforcement had beat me there. I left the ticket on the windshield and went back inside. I got Lindell in his office just before he was leaving for the day.

"What do you got?"

"Herpes simplex five. What do you got?"

"Come on, man."

"You're an asshole, Bosch, asking me to wash your dirty laundry."

I realized what he was mad about.

"The plate number?"

"Yeah, the plate number. As if you didn't know. It belongs to your ex-wife, man, and I really don't appreciate being pulled into your bullshit. I mean, either kill her or get over her, you know what I mean?"

I agreed that I knew what he meant but not what he had suggested. I could tell that I had seriously put him out with the plate check.

"Roy, all I can tell you is that I didn't know. I'm sorry. You're right. I shouldn't drag you in and I am sorry I did."

There was silence and I thought that I had placated him.

"Roy?"

"What?"

"Did you write down the address from the registration?"

"You fucking asshole."

He vented for another minute but eventually, grudgingly gave me the address Eleanor's car was registered to. There was no apartment number with it. It looked like she had not only come up a level in wheels. She was living in a house now.

"Thanks, Roy. It's the last time on that. I promise. Anything come up on the other thing I asked about?"

"Nothing good, nothing useful. The guy's record is pretty clean. There is some juvenile stuff but it's all sealed. I didn't go any further with it."

"Okay."

I wondered if the juvenile stuff involved his former Beverly Hills High classmates and now partners.

"The only other thing is that he's a junior. There is another Linus Simonson on the computer. Going by the age it looks like Daddy."

"What's he on there for?"

"He's got an IRS rap and a bankruptcy. It's all old stuff."

"How old?"

"The IRS came first, like they usually do. That was in 'ninety-four. The old man went bankrupt two years later. Who is this guy Linus and why did you want me to check him for a tail?"

I didn't answer as I found myself looking into a Most Wanted picture on the post office wall. A serial rapist. But I wasn't really looking at him. I was looking at Linus. I was working the interior circuits as another piece fell into place. Linus said he wasn't going to make the same mistakes as his father, who had gone belly-up and broke, an

IRS collar around his neck. The question that poked through all of that was, how does a guy with no job and no backing from Daddy parlay the thirty grand he's got in his pocket into the purchase and major renovation of a bar? And then another, and then another.

Loans maybe — if he qualified. Or maybe with a $2 million bank withdrawal.

"Bosch, you there?"

I came out of it.

"Yeah, I'm here."

"I asked you a question. Who is this guy? Is he on the movie deal?"

"It's looking like it, Roy. What are you doing tomorrow morning?"

"I'm doing what I'm always doing. Why?"

"If you want a piece of this be at my lawyer's office at nine. And don't be late."

"Is this guy connected to Marty? If he's the guy I don't want a piece. I want all of it."

"I don't know yet. But he'll get us closer, that's for sure."

Lindell wanted to ask more questions but I cut him off. I had more calls to make. I gave him Langwiser's name and address and he finally said he would be at the law office at nine. I hung up and then called Sandor Szatmari and left a message inviting him to the same meeting.

Lastly I called Kiz Rider in the administration office at Parker Center and extended the invitation to her as well. She went from zero to sixty on the anger speedometer in about five seconds.

"Harry, I warned you about this. You are going to find yourself in a lot of trouble. You can't just work a case and then call in a gang bang when you think it's time we were made privy to your private investigations."

"Kiz, I already did. You just have to decide if you want to be there or not. There will be a nice piece of this for somebody at the LAPD. As far as I'm thinking, it might as well be you. But if you're not interested, I'll call RHD."

"Goddamnit, Harry."

"In or out?"

There was a long pause.

"I'm in. But, Harry, I'm not going to protect you."

"I wouldn't expect it."

"Who is your lawyer?"

I gave her the information and was ready to hang up. I felt a sense of dread about the damage to our relationship. It seemed permanent to me.

"Okay, see you then," I finally said.

"Yes, you will," she replied sternly.

I remembered something I needed.

"Oh, and Kiz? See if you can find the original of the currency report. It should be in the murder book."

"What currency report?"

I explained and she said she would look for it. I thanked her and hung up. I went out to my car and grabbed the parking ticket off the windshield. I got in and threw it over my shoulder into the backseat for good luck.

It was almost seven on the dashboard clock. I knew things didn't get going in the Hollywood club scene until ten or later. But I had forward momentum and didn't want it to ebb away while I just went home and waited. I sat there thinking with my hand over the top of the wheel, ticking my fingertips on the dashboard. Soon they were going through the phrasing that Quentin McKinzie had taught me, and when I realized this, I knew how I could spend the next few hours. I opened up the cell phone again.

37

Sugar Ray McK was waiting for me in his chair in his room at the Splendid Age. The only indication that he knew he was going out was the porkpie hat he was wearing. He once told me he only wore it when he went out to hear music, which meant he rarely wore it anymore. Under the brim his eyes were sharper than I had seen them in a long while.

"This is going to be fun, dog," he said and I wondered if he'd been watching too much MTV.

"I hope they've got a decent crew for the first set. I didn't even check."

"Don't worry. It'll be fine."

He drew out the last word.

"Before we go can I borrow that magnifying glass you use to read the TV guide?"

"Sure can. What do you need?"

He dug the glass out of a pocket on the arm of his chair while I took the last page of the currency report out of my shirt pocket and unfolded it. Sugar Ray handed me the glass and I went over to the bed table and turned on the lamp. I held the page over the top of the shade and then studied Jocelyn Jones's signature with the magnifier. I got a confirmation of something I had seen earlier while in her office.

"What is it, Harry?" Sugar Ray asked.

I handed him the glass back and started refolding the paper.

"Just something I've been working on. Something called forger's tremor."

"Hmmm. Man, I got tremors all over."

I smiled at him.

"We've all got 'em, one way or the other. Come on, let's go. Let's hear some music."

"I'm going. You turn that lamp off. That costs money."

We headed out. As we went down the hallway I thought of Melissa Royal and wondered if she might be visiting her mother. I doubted it. A moment of dread spiked me because I knew the day was coming when I would have to sit down with Melissa and tell her I was the wrong guy.

A porter from the center helped me get Sugar Ray into the car. The Mercedes SUV was probably too high for him to climb into. I realized I would have to think about that if I took him out on any more field trips.

We went over to the Baked Potato and had dinner and watched the first set of the first act, a quartet of journeymen called Four Squared. They were decent but maybe a little tired. They were partial to Billy Strayhorn's stuff and so am I, so it didn't matter.

It didn't matter to Sugar Ray either. His face lit up and he kept the beat in his shoulders as he listened. He never spoke while they played and he clapped with enthusiasm after every song. Reverence is what I saw in his eyes. Reverence for the sound and the form.

The players didn't recognize him. Few people would now that he was down to just skin and bones. But that didn't bother Sugar Ray. It didn't diminish our evening by one note.

After the first set, I could see him starting to flag. It was after nine and time for him to sleep and dream. He'd told me once that he still could play in his dreams. I thought we should all be so lucky.

It was also time for me to look into the face of the man who had taken Angella Benton from this world. I had no badge and no official standing. But I knew things and believed that I still stood for her. I spoke for her. In the morning they could take it all away from me, make me sit down and watch from the sidelines. But I still had until then. And I knew I was not going home just yet. I was going to confront Linus Simonson and take his measure. I was going to let him know who put the bead on him. And I was going to give him the chance to answer for Angella Benton.

When we got back to the Splendid Age I left Sugar Ray dozing in the front seat while I went in to get the porter. Getting him into the Mercedes outside the Baked Potato by myself had been a chore.

I gently shook him awake and then we got him down onto the sidewalk. We walked him in and then down the hall to his room. Sitting on his bed, trying to shake off the sleep, he asked me where I'd been.

"I've been right here with you, Sugar Ray."

"You've been practicing?"

"Every chance I get."

I realized that he may have already forgotten our evening's outing. He may have thought I was there for a lesson. I felt bad about him being robbed of the memory so soon.

"Sugar Ray, I've gotta go. I've got some work to do."

"Okay, Henry."

"It's Harry."

"That's what I said."

"Oh. You want me to turn on the box or are you going to go to sleep?"

"Nah, put the box on for me if you don't mind. That'd be good."

I turned on the television that was mounted on the wall. It was on CNN and Sugar Ray said to leave it there. I went over and squeezed his shoulder and then headed for the door.

"'Lush Life,'" he said to my back.

I turned around to look at him. He was smiling. "Lush Life" was the last song of the set we had heard. He did remember.

"I love that song," he said.

"Yeah, me too."

I left him to his memories of a lush life while I headed out into the night to see a king about a stolen life. I was unarmed but unafraid. I was in a state of grace. I carried the last prayer of Angella Benton with me.

38

Shortly after ten o'clock I approached the doorway to Nat's on Cherokee, a half block south of Hollywood Boulevard. It was still early but there was no line of people waiting to get in. There was no velvet rope. There was no doorman selecting who got in and who didn't. There was no collector of a cover charge. When I got inside, there also were almost no customers.

I had been in Nat's on numerous occasions in its former incarnation as a dive bar populated by a clientele as devoted to alcohol as any other aspect of life. It wasn't a pickup spot — unless you counted the prostitutes who cooled their heels at the bar. It wasn't a celebrity-watching spot. It was a drinking spot and that was the sum of its entire purpose, and as such it had an honest character. As I walked in and saw all the polished brass and rich woods I realized that what it had now was glamour and that was never the same or as long-lasting as character. It didn't matter how many people lined up on opening night. The place wasn't going to go the distance. I knew that within fifteen seconds. The place was doomed before the first citron martini was poured shaken not stirred into its frosted glass and placed on a black napkin.

I went right to the bar where there were three patrons who looked like tourists in from Florida after a dose of much needed California Cool. The bartender was tall and thin and wore the requisite black jeans and tight body shirt that allowed her nipples to introduce themselves to the customers. She had a black-ink snake wrapped around one bicep, its forked red tongue licking the crook of her elbow, where the needle scars were evident. Her hair was shorter than mine and on the nape of her neck a bar code was tattooed. It made me think of how much I enjoyed discovering Eleanor Wish's neck the night before.

"There's a ten-dollar cover," the bartender said. "What can I get you?"

I remembered from the magazine article that it used to be $20.

"What does it cover? This place is dead."

"Stick around. That's ten dollars."

I made no move to give her the money. I leaned on the bar and spoke quietly.

"Where's Linus?"

"He's not here tonight."

"Then where is he? I need to talk to him."

"He's probably at Chet's. That's where he keeps his office. He doesn't usually start bopping around to the places until after midnight. Are you going to pay the ten?"

"I don't think so. I'm leaving."

She frowned.

"You're a cop, aren't you?"

I smiled proudly.

"Going on twenty-eight years."

I left off the part about the twenty-eight years coming

before I retired. I figured she'd get on the phone and send the word a cop was coming. That might work in my favor. I reached in my pocket and pulled out a ten. I tossed it onto the bar.

"That's not the cover. That's for you. Get a haircut."

She put an exaggerated smile on her face, one that showed she had a nice set of dimples. She snatched the ten.

"Thanks, Dad."

I smiled as I walked out.

It took me fifteen minutes to get over to Chet's on Santa Monica near LaBrea. I had the address thanks to *Los Angeles Magazine,* which had conveniently put a listing of all of the Four Kings establishments in a box on the last page of the story.

Again there was no line and few customers. I was beginning to think that once you are declared cool in the tourist books and magazines, then you're dead in the water. Chet's was almost a carbon copy of Nat's, right down to the sullen bartender with the not-so-subtle nipples and tattoos. The one thing I liked about the place was the music. Chet Baker's "Cool Burnin'" was playing when I walked in and I thought maybe the kings might have some taste after all.

The bartender was déjà vu all over again — tall, thin and in black, except her bicep tattoo was Marilyn Monroe's face circa "Happy Birthday, Mr. President."

"You the cop?" she asked before I said a word.

"You've been talking to your sister. I guess she told you I don't pay cover."

"She said something about that."

"Where's Linus?"

"He's in his office. I told him you were coming."

"That was nice of you."

I stepped away from the bar but pointed at her tattoo.

"Your mom?"

"Hey, come here, take a look."

I leaned back over the bar. She bent her elbow and flexed her muscles repeatedly. Marilyn's cheeks puffed up and then down as the bicep beneath expanded and contracted.

"Kind of looks like she's giving a blow job, doesn't it?" the bartender said.

"That's real cute," I said. "I bet you show that to all the boys."

"Is it worth ten bucks?"

I almost told her I knew places where I could get the real thing for a ten but let it go. I left her there and found my way to a hallway behind the bar. There were doors for the rest rooms and then a door marked "Management Only." I didn't knock. I just went through and it only led to a continuation of the hallway and more doors. The third door down said "Linus" on it. I opened that one without knocking, too.

Linus Simonson was sitting behind a cluttered desk. I recognized him from the magazine photo. He had a bottle of Scotch whiskey and a snifter on the desk. There was a black leather couch in the office and on it sat a man I also recognized from the magazine as one of the partners. His name was James Oliphant. He had his feet up on a coffee table and looked like he wasn't the least bit concerned by a visit from a man he'd been told was a cop.

"Hey, man, you the cop," Simonson said as he waved me in. "Close the door."

I stepped in and introduced myself. I didn't say I was a cop.

"Well, I'm Linus and that there's Jim. What's up? What can we do for you?"

I held my hands out as though I had nothing to hide.

"I'm not sure what you can do for me. I just wanted to drop by and sort of introduce myself. I'm working on the Angella Benton case and of course that includes the BankLA case so . . . here I am."

"Oh, man, BankLA. That's some serious ancient history there."

He looked at his partner and laughed.

"That was like another lifetime ago. I don't want to go there, man. That's a bad memory."

"Yeah, well, not as bad for you as it was for Angella Benton."

Simonson suddenly got serious and leaned forward on his desk.

"I don't get this, man. What are you doing here? You're not a cop. Cops come in twos. If you *are* a cop, then you aren't legit. What do you want? Let me see a badge."

"I didn't tell anybody I had a badge. I was a cop, but not now. In fact, I thought maybe you'd recognize me from that other lifetime you were talking about."

Simonson looked at Oliphant and smirked.

"Recognize you from what?"

"I was there that day you took it in the ass. I'm talking about the bullet. But then again, you were rolling around and screaming so much you probably didn't have time to look at me."

But Simonson's eyes widened in recognition. Maybe not physical recognition but recognition of who I was and what I had done.

"Shit, you're the guy. You're the cop that was there. You're the one who shot —"

He stopped himself from saying a name. He looked at Oliphant.

"He's the one who hit one of the robbers."

I looked at Oliphant and I saw recognition — physical recognition — and maybe something like hate or anger in his eyes.

"That's not known for sure because we never got the robber. But, yeah, I think I hit him. That was me."

I said it with a smile of pride. I kept it on my face as I turned back to Simonson.

"Who are you working for?" Simonson asked.

"Me? I'm working for somebody who isn't going to stop, who isn't going to let up. Not for a minute. He's going to find out who put Angella Benton down on the tile and he'll go at it until he either dies or he knows."

Simonson smirked again arrogantly.

"Well, good luck to you and him, Mr. Bosch. I think you ought to go now. We're kind of busy here."

I nodded to him and then looked at Oliphant, giving him the best deadeye in my repertoire.

"Then I guess I'll see you boys around."

I went through the door and down the hallway back to the bar. Chet Baker was now singing "My Funny Valentine." As I headed for the main door I noticed the bartender flexing her bicep for two men sitting at the bar where I had stood. They were laughing. I recognized them as the remaining two kings from the magazine photo.

They stopped laughing when they saw me and I felt their eyes on me all the way out the door.

39

On the way home I stopped at the twenty-four-hour Ralph's on Sunset and bought a bag of coffee. I didn't expect that I'd be getting much sleep between the night and the multi-agency confab the following morning.

On the drive up the hill to my house there are too many curves to use the rearview mirror to check for a tail. But there is one sweeping curve halfway up that allows you to look to your right out the passenger window and across the drop-off to the road you just covered. It's always been my habit to slow at this spot and check for a trailer.

This night I slowed more than usual and watched a little longer. I didn't expect my visit to Chet's to be taken as anything other than a threat and I wasn't wrong. As I looked across the drop-off I saw a car with no lights on round the hill and move into the sweeping curve. I eased the gas pedal down and slowly picked up speed again. After the next curve I punched it and put a little more distance between us. I pulled all the way into the carport next to my house and quickly got out with the bag from the store. I moved into the darkest corner of the carport and waited. I heard the trail car before I saw it. Then I watched it glide by. A long Jaguar. Someone was lighting a cigarette in the backseat, and in the glow from the flame I saw the car was full. The four kings were coming for me.

After the Jag had gone by I saw the bushes across the street glow red and I knew they were stopping just past my house. I moved to the door that led into the kitchen and went inside, making sure to lock the door afterward.

This was the moment when people without badges called the police for help. It's when they desperately whispered, *"Hurry, please! They are coming!"* But badge or no badge, I knew that was not an option for me now. This was my play and I didn't care in that moment about what authority I had or didn't have.

I had not carried a gun since the night I left my badge and service pistol in a drawer at Hollywood Division and walked out. But I had a weapon. I'd bought a Glock P7 for personal protection. It was wrapped in an oil rag and in a box on the shelf of the walk-in closet in the bedroom. I put the bag from Ralph's down on the counter and moved into the hallway and down to the bedroom without turning on any lights.

When I opened the closet door I was suddenly shoved backwards with great force by a man who had been waiting in there for me. I hit the opposite wall and slid to the floor. He was on me immediately, straddling and pushing the barrel of a pistol up under my jaw. I managed to look up and in the pale light coming in through the French door leading to the deck I could see who it was.

"Milton. What the —"

"Shut up, asshole. You surprised to see me? Did you think I was going to let them wash me down the toilet without doing something about it?"

"I don't know what you're talking about. Listen, there are people —"

"I said, shut the fuck up. I want the disks, you understand? I want the original data chip."

"Listen to me! There are people about to come in here for me. They want —"

He shoved the barrel in so deep under my jaw that I had to stop talking. The pain sent shards of red glass across my vision. Milton held the gun there and leaned down, his breath in my face as he spoke.

"I've got your gun right here, Bosch. And I'm going to turn you into another suicide statistic if you don't —"

There was a sudden crashing sound from the hallway and I knew it was the front door coming in off its hinges. Then there were footsteps. Milton jumped up off of me and stepped through the bedroom door into the hallway. Almost immediately, there was the booming thunder of a shotgun blast and Milton was slammed back against the wall, his eyes wide with the terror of knowing he was dying. He then slid down the wall, his heels pushing back the hallway rug to reveal the handle of the trapdoor that led beneath the house.

I knew they had mistaken him for me. It was a break worth a few seconds at the most. I rolled over and quickly moved to the French door. As I opened it I heard someone's panicked voice call out from the hallway.

"It's not him!"

The door squealed when I opened it, its hinges protesting from lack of use. I quickly crossed the deck and went over the railing like a cowboy mounting a stolen horse. I went down the railing until I was hanging from the deck, twenty feet above the sharply sloping ground below. In the dim moonlight I looked for one of the iron support beams that held the deck and house to the side of the hill. I was intimately familiar with the design of the house from having supervised its reconstruction from the ground up after the 'ninety-four earthquake.

I had to move six feet along the edge of the deck before I could reach in and grab hold of one of the support beams. I wrapped my arms and legs around it and slid down to the ground. As I went down I heard their footsteps on the deck above me.

"He went down there! He went down there!"

"Where? I don't see —"

"He went down there! You two go. We'll take the street."

I was on the ground beneath the shelter of the deck. I knew if I stepped out and tried to make my way down the steep slope to one of the streets or houses in the canyon below I would be exposed to my armed pursuers. Instead I turned and climbed up the hill under the house and further into the shelter of the structure. I knew there was a trench dug into the ground up there, where the sewer main had to be replaced after the quake. Above me there would also be the trapdoor that opened in the hallway. But I had designed it during the rebuilding of the house as an escape route, not a means of ingress. It was locked from inside and no use to me at the moment.

I moved up the hill, found the trench and rolled into it. I blindly moved my hands around at the bottom, looking for a weapon. All I found were cracked pieces of the old sewer main. I found one shard that was triangular and might work as a weapon. It would have to do.

Two men moved like shadows down the support beams to the ground below the deck. The moonlight reflected off the steel of their pistols. The reflections also showed me that one had on eyeglasses and I remembered him from the magazine story and photo. His name was Bernard Banks, known as B.B. King among the night crawlers. He had been at the bar at Chet's when I had left.

The two shadows exchanged whispers and then split up, one moving down the hill and to the left, the other — Banks — maintaining his position. It was some kind of tactical strategy in which one would hopefully chase me into the waiting pistol of the other.

From my angle above him Banks was a hard target silhouetted by the lights from the canyon below. He was fifteen feet from me but I had nothing to use as a weapon except a shard of old iron pipe. Still, it was enough. I had survived more missions into the tunnels of Vietnam than I could remember. I'd once spent a whole night in the elephant grass with the enemy moving all around me. And I had lived and worked for twenty-five-plus years on the streets of this city with a badge. This kid was going to be no match for me. I knew none of them would be.

When Banks turned to look down the canyon slope, I rose up in the trench and threw the pipe shard into the brush out to his right. It made a sound like an animal moving through high grass. As he turned, tensed and raised his weapon I slid over the top of the trench and started moving down the slope toward him, all the while keeping one of the iron beams between us as a sound and visual blind.

I got to the beam and he still had not turned from the direction of the sounds in the brush. He was just putting the misdirection together and finally turning back when I got to him. My left fist hit him squarely between the eyes while my right closed over the gun and I put a finger through the trigger guard. I had actually been aiming for his mouth but the punch broke his glasses in half at the bridge and staggered him just the same. I pivoted and swung him in a 180-degree arc, gathering momentum and putting him headfirst into one of the support beams. His skull made a sound like a water balloon breaking and the iron beam hummed like a tuning fork. He dropped to the ground like a bag of wet laundry.

I put his gun into the waistband of my pants and then turned him over. The blood on his face looked black in the moonlight. I quickly propped his back against the beam, brought his knees up and folded his arms on top of them. I leaned his face down on his arms.

Soon I heard the other one call for him from further down the hillside.

"B.B., you got him? Hey, Beeb!"

I backed away from Banks and crouched in the bushes ten feet away. I pulled the gun from my pants. In the moonlight I could not tell the make. It was a black steel pistol with no safety. Probably a Glock. I then realized it was probably my own gun. It must have been the one Milton had shoved into my neck. Banks had taken it from his body.

I heard the other one approaching in the brush. He was coming from my left and would cross within five feet of me when he approached Banks. I waited until I heard him and knew he was close.

"Banks, what are you doing? You pussy, get up and —"

He shut up when he felt the barrel of the gun against his neck.

"Drop the gun or you die right here."

I heard it hit the ground. With my free hand I reached up and grabbed the back of his collar and pulled him around and then back underneath the shelter of the deck where we couldn't be seen from above. We were both facing the lights of the canyon and the freeway below. He was the fourth king, the one in the magazine picture who had the bar towel over his shoulder. I couldn't remember his name in all of the excitement. He'd been sitting at the bar at Chet's with Banks.

"What's your name, asshole?"

"Jimmy Fazio. Look, I —"

"Shut up."

He was quiet. I leaned forward and whispered into his ear.

"Look at the lights. You are going to die here, Jimmy Fazio. The lights are the last thing you'll ever see."

"Please . . ."

"Please? Is that what Angella Benton said? Did she say please to you?"

"No, please, no, I mean, I wasn't even there."

"Convince me."

He didn't say anything.

"Or die."

"Okay, it wasn't me. Please believe me. It was Linus and Vaughn. It was their idea and they did it without even telling the rest of us. We couldn't stop it because we didn't know about it."

"Yeah, what else? You're only alive because you're talking."

"That's why we shot Vaughn. Linus said we had to because he was going to take the money and pin the girl on Linus."

"What about Linus getting shot? Was that part of the plan?"

He shook his head.

"That wasn't supposed to happen but we figured out how to make it work. Like a cover for us buying the clubs."

"Yeah, it worked all right. What about Marty Gessler and Jack Dorsey?"

"Who?"

I jammed the gun's muzzle hard into his neck.

"Don't give me that shit. I want the whole goddamn story."

"I don't —"

"Faz! You fucking coward!"

The voice came from above us. I looked up and saw the upper body of a man hanging down over the edge of the deck. His arms were extended, two hands on a gun. I let go of my captive and dove left just as the gunfire erupted. The shooter was Oliphant. He screamed as he fired. Just blindly screamed. The whole shelter area beneath the house lit up with the flashes. Slugs ricocheted off the iron beams. I came up on the side of one of the beams and fired three times in a quick burst at him. His shout cut off and I knew I'd hit him. I watched as he dropped his gun, lost his balance and fell the twenty feet down, making a heavy thud in the bushes.

I looked around for Fazio and found him on the ground near Banks. He'd been hit in the upper chest but was still alive. It was too dark to see his eyes but I knew they were open and panicked, looking at me for help. I grabbed his jaw and turned his face to mine.

"Can you talk?"

"Uh . . . it hurts."

"Yeah, it does, doesn't it? Tell me about the FBI agent. Where is she? What happened to her?"

"Uh . . ."

"Who killed the cop? Was that Linus, too?"

"Linus . . ."

"Is that a yes? Did Linus do it?"

He didn't answer. I was losing him. I lightly patted his cheeks and then shook him by the collar.

"Come on, man, stay with me. Was that a yes? Fazio, did Linus Simonson kill the cop?"

Nothing. He was gone. Then a voice came from behind me.

"I think that would be a yes."

I turned. It was Simonson. He had found the trapdoor and come down out of the house behind me. He was holding a sawed-off shotgun. I slowly stood up, leaving my gun on the ground next to Fazio's body and raising my hands. I backed away from Simonson, stepping further down the hill.

"Cops on the payroll are always a pain in the ass," he said. "I had to put an end to that pronto."

I took another step backwards, but for every step I took, Simonson did likewise. The shotgun was only three feet away. I knew I'd be unable to escape its kill range if I tried to make a move. All I could do was play for time. Somebody in the neighborhood had to have heard the shots and made a call.

Simonson aimed the weapon at my heart.

"I'm going to enjoy this. This one's for Cozy."

"Cozy?" I asked, though I had already put it together. "Who the hell is Cozy?"

"You hit him that day. With your bullets. And he didn't make it."

"What happened to him?"

"What do you think happened? He died in the back of the van."

"You buried him? Where?"

"Not me. I was sort of busy that day, remember? They buried him. Cozy liked boats. They gave him a burial at sea, you could say."

I took another step back. Simonson followed. I was walking out from beneath the deck. If the cops ever showed up they could put a bead on him from above.

"What about the FBI agent? What happened to Marty Gessler?"

"See that's the thing. When Dorsey told me about her and what the plan was, that was when I knew he had to go. I mean, he was —"

The shotgun suddenly pointed skyward as the foot Simonson had put his weight down on went out from under him. He took a classic pratfall, landing on his back. I was on him then like a wild man. We rolled and fought for control of the shotgun. He was younger and stronger and quickly was able to hold the top position. But he was an inexperienced fighter. His focus was on controlling the struggle rather than on simply overpowering his opponent.

I had my left hand wrapped around the snubbed barrel while the other was gripped at the trigger guard. I managed to squeeze my thumb into the guard behind his finger. I closed my eyes and an image came to me. Angella Benton's hands. The image from memory and dreams. I channeled all my strength into my left arm and pushed. The angle of the gun shifted. I closed my eyes and depressed the trigger with my thumb. The loudest sound I have ever heard in my life roared through my head as the shotgun discharged. My face felt like it had caught on fire. I opened my eyes and looked up at Simonson and saw that he no longer had a face.

He rolled off of me and an inhuman sound gurgled from the pulp that had been his face. His legs kicked like he was riding an invisible bicycle. He rolled back and forth as his hands balled into fists as tight as stones, and then he stopped and went still.

Slowly, I sat up, registering what had happened. I touched my own face and found it intact. I was burned from the discharge gases but otherwise I was okay. My ears were ringing and for once I couldn't hear the ever present sound of the freeway below.

I saw a glint in the brush and reached for the object. It was a water bottle. It was full, unopened. I realized that Simonson had slipped on the water bottle I had knocked off the deck a few days before. And it had saved my life. I twisted the cap off the bottle and poured water over my face, washing away the blood and the sting of the burn.

"Don't move!"

I looked up from my position and saw a man leaning over the deck railing, pointing another gun at me. The moon reflected off the badge on his uniform. The cops had finally arrived. I dropped the bottle and spread my hands wide.

"Don't worry," I said. "I'm not moving."

I leaned back, my arms still spread. My head rested on the ground and I pulled great gulps of air into my lungs. The ringing in my ears was still there but I could now also hear my heart as it slowed its cadence to the normal beat of life. I looked up into the dark, sacred night, to the place where those not saved on earth wait for the rest of us above. Not yet, I thought. No, not yet.

40

While the cop on the deck above kept his gun on me his partner dropped through the trapdoor and made his way down the slope to me. He had a flashlight in one hand and a gun in the other and the wild eyes of a man who has no idea what he has stepped into.

"Roll over and put your hands behind your back," he ordered, adrenaline drawing his voice high and tight.

I did as I was instructed and he put his flashlight down on the ground as he cuffed my wrists, thankfully not in the style of the FBI. I tried to calmly talk to him.

"Just so you know, I —"

"I don't want to know anything from you."

"— I'm LAPD retired. Out of Hollywood. Pulled the pin last year after twenty-five-plus."

"Good for you. Why don't you save it for the suits?"

My house was in North Hollywood Division. I knew there was no reason why they should know me or care.

"Hey," said the one from above. "What's his name? Put the light on him."

The man on the ground put the light in my face from a foot away. It was blinding.

"What's your name?"

"Harry Bosch. I worked homicide."

"Har—"

"I know who he is, Swanny. He's all right. Get the light out of his face."

Swanny took the light away.

"Yeah, fine. But the cuffs stay on. The suits can sort it all — ah, Jesus!"

He had put his light on the faceless body in the brush to my left. Linus Simonson, or what was left of him.

"Don't puke, Swanny," came the voice from above. "It's a crime scene."

"Fuck you, Hurwitz, I'm not gonna puke."

I heard him moving around. I tried to lift my head to watch him but the brush was too tall. I could only listen. It sounded like he was moving from body to body. I was right.

"Hey, we got a live one down here! Call it in."

That would be Banks, I assumed. I was glad to hear it. I had the feeling I was going to need a survivor to back up my account. I figured that with Banks facing the fall by himself for the whole thing, he would cut a deal to save his ass and tell the story.

I rolled over and sat up. The cop was kneeling next to Banks on the dirt below the deck. He looked over at me.

"I didn't tell you to move."

"I couldn't breathe with my face in the dirt."

"Don't fucking move again."

"Hey, Swanny," Hurwitz called down. "The stiff in the house? He's got a badge. FBI."

"Holy shit!"

"Yeah, holy shit."

And they were right. It was a holy shit case. Within the hour the place was swarmed. By the LAPD. By the LAFD. By the FBI. By the media. By my count, there were six helicopters circling in the sky through most of the night, the cacophony so loud I found myself preferring the shotgun blast ringing in my ears.

The LAFD used a chopper to bring Banks up out of the canyon on a stretcher. When they were done with him I called the paramedics over and they put a clear aloe-based gel over the gas burns on my face. They gave me an aspirin and told me the injuries were minor and that there would be no scarring. It felt to me like I'd had my face laser-peeled by a blind surgeon.

I was uncuffed long enough to climb up the slope and then up through the trapdoor. In my house I was recuffed and made to sit on a couch in the living room. From there I could see Milton's legs extending from the hallway as a crime scene team hovered over him.

Once all of the suits started showing up it started getting serious. Most of them followed the same pattern. They came in, somberly studied Milton's body, then walked through the living room without looking at me and out onto the deck, where they looked down at the other three bodies. Then they came back in, looked at me without saying a word and went into the kitchen, where somebody had taken it upon himself to open up my new bag of coffee and put the percolator into heavy rotation.

This went on for at least two hours. At first I didn't know any of them because they were North Hollywood detectives. But then the command decision was made to shift the investigation — LAPD's part of it — to Robbery-

Homicide Division. When the RHD dicks started showing up it started getting like old-home week. I knew many of them and had even worked side by side with some. It wasn't until Kiz Rider showed up from the chief's office that anybody thought to take the cuffs off my wrists. She angrily demanded that I be released from the bindings and when nobody made a move to do it, she did it herself.

"You okay, Harry?"

"I think I am now."

"Your face is red and kind of puffy. You want me to call paramedics?"

"They already checked me out. Minor burns from getting too close to the wrong end of a shotgun."

"How do you want to do this? You know the score. You want to get a lawyer or can we talk?"

"I'll talk to you, Kiz. I'll tell you the whole story. Otherwise, I'll take the lawyer."

"I'm not in RHD anymore, Harry. You know that."

"You should be and you know that."

"But I'm not."

"Well, that's the deal, Kiz. Take it or leave it. I've got a good lawyer."

She thought about it for a few moments.

"All right, wait here for a minute and I'll be right back."

She went out the front door to consult with the powers that be about my offer. While she was gone and I was waiting I saw Special Agent John Peoples come in and crouch next to Milton's body. He then looked over at me and held my eyes. If he was trying to send me a message I wasn't sure exactly what it was. But he knew I held something of his in the balance. His future.

Rider came back inside and over to me.

"This is the deal. It's turning into a major gang bang. We've got FBI all over this. The guy on the floor is apparently from a terrorism squad and that trumps all. They're not going to let you and me waltz off into the sunset."

"Okay, this is what I'll do. I'll talk to you and one agent. I want it to be Roy Lindell. Wake him up and bring him in and I'll lay it all out for everybody. It's got to be you and Roy or I lawyer up and everybody can figure it out for themselves."

She nodded and turned and went back out. I noticed that Peoples was no longer in the hallway but I hadn't seen him leave.

This time Rider was gone for a half hour. But when she came back she strode in with a command presence. I knew before she told me that the deal had been made. The case was hers, at least on the LAPD side of the ledger.

"Okay, we're going to go down the hill to North Hollywood Division. We'll use a room there and they'll tape it for us. Lindell is on his way there. This way everybody's happy and everybody's got a piece."

That was always the way. You had to walk the gauntlet of departmental and intra-agency politics just to get the job done. I was glad I no longer had a part of it.

"You can stand up now, Harry," Rider said. "I'll drive."

I stood up.

"I want to go out on the deck first. I want to look down there."

She let me go. I walked across the deck and looked down over the railing. Below, large crime scene lights had been erected. The slope was like an anthill with crime scene techs working all over the place. Crews from the medical examiner's office were huddled over the bodies. Above it all the helicopters moved in a loud, multilevel choreography. I knew that whatever relationships I'd previously had with my neighbors were surely gone now.

"Know what, Kiz?"

"What, Harry?"

"I think it's time to sell this place."

"Yeah, good luck with that, Harry."

She took me by the arm and pulled me away from the railing.

41

The North Hollywood station was the newest in the city. It was built post–earthquake and Rodney King riots. On the outside it was a brick fortress designed to withstand both tectonic and social upheavals. On the inside it was state-of-the-art electronics and comfort. I was sat in the center seat of a table in a large interview room. I could not see the microphones and the camera but I knew they were there. I also knew I had to be careful. I had made a bad deal. If a quarter century in the cops had taught me anything, it was not to talk to cops without a lawyer's advice. And here I was about to do just that. I was about to open up to two people predisposed to believe me and to want to help me. But that wouldn't matter. What would matter was the tape. I had to step carefully and make sure I said nothing that could come back on me when the tape was reviewed by those who were not my friends.

Kizmin Rider started things off by entering all three of our names into the record, reporting the date, time and location, and then reading me my constitutionally guaranteed right to a lawyer and to hold my tongue if I wished.

She then asked me to acknowledge both orally and in writing that I understood these rights and was willingly waiving them. I did so. I had taught her well.

She then got right to it.

"Okay, Harry, you have four people including a federal agent dead at your house, not to mention a fifth man in a coma. You want to tell us all about it?"

"I killed two of them — in self-defense. And the guy in the coma, I did that too."

"Okay, tell us what happened."

I began the story at the Baked Potato and took it from there. I mentioned Sugar Ray, the quartet, the porter, the bartenders and their tattoos. I even described the cashier I had bought the coffee from at Ralph's. I used as much detail as I could remember because I knew that the details would convince them once they checked it all out. I knew from experience that conversation was hearsay, it wasn't provable one way or the other. So if you were going to tell a story about what people said and how they said it — especially people who were no longer alive — then you'd best salt the story with the things that could be checked and proven. The details. Safety and salvation were in the details.

So I put everything I could remember on the tape, right down to the Marilyn Monroe tattoo. That one made Roy Lindell laugh but Rider didn't see the humor in it.

I walked them through the story, describing things as they had happened. I offered no background story because I knew that would come out in the questioning that would follow. I wanted them to have a moment-by-moment and detail-by-detail account of what had happened. I did not lie in what I told them but I didn't tell them everything. I still wasn't sure how to play the Milton angle. I would wait for a signal from Lindell on that. I was sure he had been given his orders long before he got to the station.

I held the Milton details out for Lindell. The detail I held out for myself was what I had seen when I closed my eyes before pressing the shotgun's trigger. I kept the image of Angella Benton's hands to myself.

"And that's it," I said when I was done. "Then the uniforms showed up and here we are."

Rider had been jotting down notes occasionally on a legal pad. She put her pad down and looked at me. She seemed stunned by the story. She probably believed I was very lucky to have survived it.

"Thank you, Harry. That was certainly a close call for you."

"It was about five close calls."

"Um, I think we're going to take a break for a few minutes. Agent Lindell and I are going to step out and talk about this and then I'm sure we will come back with some questions."

I smiled.

"I'm sure you will."

"Can we get you anything?"

"Coffee would be nice. I've been up all night and at the house they wouldn't give me any from my own machine."

"Coffee coming up."

She and Lindell got up and left the room. A few minutes later a North Hollywood detective I didn't know came in with a cup of black coffee. He told me to hang in there and left.

When Rider and Lindell came back in I noticed that there were more notes on her pad. She kept the lead and started out doing the talking again.

"We need to clear up a couple things first," she said.

"Okay."

"You said that Agent Milton was already in your house when you came in."

"That's right."

I looked at Lindell and then back at Rider.

"You said you were in the process of informing him that you believed you had been followed home when the front door was kicked in by the intruders."

"Correct."

"He stepped into the hall to investigate and was immediately hit with a blast from a shotgun, presumably fired by Linus Simonson."

"Right again."

"What was Agent Milton doing in your house if you weren't there?"

Before I could speak Lindell blurted out a question.

"He did have permission to be there, didn't he?"

"Hey, how about we take one question at a time?" I said.

I looked at Lindell again and his eyes turned down to the table. He couldn't look at me. Judging by his question, which was really a statement disguised as a question, Lindell was revealing to me what he wanted me to say. I believed at that point that he was making an offer of trade. He was almost certainly in trouble with the bureau for his aid to me during my investigation. And as such, he now had his orders: keep the bureau's nose clean on this, or there would be consequences for him and possibly for me. So what Lindell was saying to me was that if I told the story in a way that helped him accomplish that objective — without legally compromising myself — then we would both be better off.

The truth was I didn't mind sparing Milton posthumous controversy and shame. As far as I was concerned he'd already gotten what he deserved and then some. Going after him now would be vindictive and I didn't need to be vindictive to a dead man. I had other things to do and wanted to preserve my ability to do them.

There was Special Agent Peoples and his BAM squad but there was too much gray between them and Milton's actions. I had Milton on tape, not Peoples. Using one to try to get to the other was a tough road to drive. I decided in that moment to let the dead man sleep and to live to drive another day.

"What was Agent Milton doing in your house if you weren't there?" Rider repeated.

I looked back at her.

"He was waiting for me."

"To do what?"

"I had told him to meet me there but I got delayed because I went and bought the coffee on my way home."

"Why was he meeting you so late at night?"

"Because I had information that would clear some things up for him."

"What was that information?"

"It was about how a terrorist involved in a case he was working ended up with a hundred-dollar bill that supposedly came from the movie set heist I was investigating and had been warned off of. I told him I had put things together and found that the two cases were actually unrelated. I invited him to come to my lawyer's office in the morning when you two were going to come and I'd explain it all to everybody. But he didn't want to wait so I told him to meet me at the house."

"And what, you left him a key?"

"No, I didn't. But I must've left the door unlocked because he was inside when I got home. I guess you could say he had permission because I invited him to the house but I didn't exactly tell him to go inside. He just sort of did that on his own when he beat me to the house."

"Agent Milton had a number of miniaturized listening devices in the pocket of his coat. Do you know anything about that or why he had them?"

My guess was that he had removed them from my house but I didn't say this.

"No idea," I said. "You would've had to ask him, I guess."

"What about his car? It was found parked about a block north of your house on Woodrow Wilson. In fact, it was further away from your house than the car the four assailants used. Any idea why Milton would park so far from your house if he was invited to be there?"

"No, not really. Like I said, I guess he's the only one who knew that."

"Exactly."

I could see her getting heated. Her eyes grew sharper and she seemed to be trying to read the looks I was giving Lindell. She knew there was a play on but she was smart enough not to mention anything on camera. I had taught her well.

"Okay, I'll tell you what, Harry. You told us every detail about what happened last night but not how it fits into anything. Before all the shit hit the fan you called the big meeting for this morning in order to lay it all out for us. So go ahead and do it now. Tell us what you've got."

"You mean from the beginning?"

"From the beginning."

I nodded.

"Okay, well, I guess you could say it all started with Ray Vaughn and Linus Simonson deciding to rip off the cash shipment to the movie set. There was some sort of connection between them. One of their former colleagues at the bank said she thought Vaughn was gay and Simonson had said he was making a move on him. Anyway, whether Simonson drew Vaughn in or it was the other way around, they decided to take the money. They planned it out and then Simonson recruited his four pals for the heavy work. It went from there."

"What about Angella Benton?" Rider asked.

"I'm getting to that. Without telling the others, Vaughn and Linus decided they needed a device, something that would make the cops think the heist came from inside the movie company, not the bank. So they picked her. She'd come to the bank as a liaison once with documents pertaining to the loan. So they knew a case could be made that she knew about the money. They picked her and probably watched her for a couple days and then figured out when she was most vulnerable and when to do it. They killed her and one of them put the semen on her so it would look like a sex case at first and it wouldn't immediately reflect on the movie company or the plan to shoot scenes with real money. That would come later. After the heist."

"So she was just a device is what you are saying," Rider said dejectedly. "Her life taken simply because she fit into the plan."

I nodded somberly.

"What a wonderful world, right?"

"Okay, go on. Did they both do it?"

"I don't know, maybe. Simonson had an alibi for that night but it was cleared by Jack Dorsey, and we'll get to him in a minute. But my guess is that they did it together. It would take two to completely overpower her without a struggle."

"The jizz," Rider said. "We can see if it matches one of them. Since Vaughn was killed during the robbery and Simonson was shot, it was never thought to type them against the semen collected at the murder scene."

I shook my head.

"I have a feeling that it won't match either one of them."

"Then who did it come from?"

"We may never know. Remember the spatter evidence? We decided the semen was brought to the scene and dripped onto the body. Who knows where they got it. Maybe from one of themselves but if they were smart they wouldn't have left their own. Why leave a direct tie to the crime?"

"So, what, they just go up to a stranger and ask him to jerk off in a cup for them?" Lindell asked incredulously.

"It wouldn't be that hard to get," Rider said. "Go into any alley in Hollywood and you'll find a loaded condom. And if Vaughn was gay, then it could have come from one of his partners and the partner might not have ever known it."

I nodded. I had been thinking the same thing.

"Exactly. And that's probably why he was killed. Simonson double-crossed him. He told his guys to make sure they took him out during the robbery. It would mean more money for them and a link to the Benton case eliminated."

"Jesus, these are cold-blooded fucks," Lindell said.

I could tell he was thinking about Marty Gessler and her unknown fate.

"Simonson further secured the operation and the future use of the money by switching the currency report he and another BankLA employee had put together. You could say he unmarked the bills."

"How?" Rider asked.

"I thought at first that he probably just put wrong currency numbers into the report he and another bank employee made in the vault. But I guess that would have been too risky because she wasn't in on it and she might have decided to double-check the numbers. So I think what he did was create a second, phony report on his computer. It listed currency numbers he just made up. He then printed it out and forged his coworker's signature on it and turned it in to the vice president for his signature. From there it went to the insurance company and then to the cops after the heist and eventually to the FBI."

"You told me to bring the original to the meeting we were supposed to have this morning," Rider said. "Why?"

"You know what forger's tremor is? It's something you can see in a signature that has been forged by tracing. He traced his coworker's signature off the original or real currency report. In the photocopy of the one he turned in I could see hesitation marks. Her signature would have been one smooth, uninterrupted scrawl. But it looks like whoever signed that page never lifted the pen but stopped and started after almost every letter. It's a tell and I think the original will show it beyond a doubt."

"How was that missed?"

I shrugged.

"Maybe it wasn't."

"Dorsey and Cross."

"I think Dorsey. I don't know about Cross. Cross helped me with this. In fact, he called me and gave me the jump start on it."

Lindell leaned forward. We were getting to the part about Marty Gessler and he wanted to get it right.

"So Simonson turns in a report with made-up numbers and then his buddies go and rip off the delivery and kill Vaughn in the process. Intentionally."

"That's right."

"What about Simonson? He got shot, too. Were they trying to cut him out, too?"

"No, that wasn't supposed to happen. Not according to Fazio. At least that was what he was saying to me before he got nailed last night. It sounded like Simonson getting shot was just dumb luck. A ricochet. If Banks comes out of his sleep with his brain intact maybe he can tell you about that. I have a feeling he'll want to talk. He'll want to spread the blame around."

"Don't worry, if he comes out of it, we'll be there. But the early word from the hospital is that that's a big if."

"The thing about that ricochet is that it actually helped them. It gave Simonson a valid out from the bank. No suspicion there. Then he hid the purchase and renovation of the bars behind a settlement from the bank. The truth was he didn't make enough off the settlement to put in a new beer cooler."

"How do you know that?"

"I just know."

"All right, let's get back to the heist for a minute," Lindell said. "So other than Simonson taking a slug in the ass, the heist goes off as planned. All the cops —"

"Not exactly," Rider said. "Harry was there. He nailed one of the robbers."

I nodded.

"And he apparently died in the van during the getaway. Simonson told me the others took him out on a boat or something and buried him at sea. His name was Cozy. They named one of the bars after him."

"Okay," Lindell said. "But when the dust settles from this thing, all the cops have is Angella Benton dead and a phony list of numbers that nobody knows is phony. Then nine months sail by and lo and behold one of those numbers scores a hit when Marty Gessler puts it into her computer."

I nodded. Lindell knew where it was going.

"Wait a minute," Rider said. "I'm not tracking this part."

Lindell and I took five minutes to fill her in on Marty Gessler's computer program that tracked currency numbers and what her discovery meant.

"Got it," Rider said. "She came up with the first inference that something was wrong. She came up with a hit that didn't work because the hundred-dollar bill in question was already in evidence lockup. It could not have been taken during the movie set heist."

"Exactly," I said. "One of the numbers Simonson made up just happened to be on a bill already accounted for. The same thing would later happen when they arrested Mousouwa Aziz at the border. One of the hundreds he was carrying matched Simonson's phony list. That brought Milton and the Homeland Security heavies into it and it was all bullshit. The truth was, there was no connection between the two cases."

Which meant I had spent the night in federal lockup for nothing and Milton had been killed while pursuing what amounted to nothing, a wild goose chase. I tried not to think about this and moved on with the story.

"When Marty Gessler got that hit, she called up Jack Dorsey because his name was on the list when it was circulated to other law enforcement agencies. It went from there."

"You're saying that Dorsey then put two and two together and came up with Simonson," Lindell said. "Maybe he knew about the forgery or maybe he knew about something else. But he knew enough to know. He went to Simonson and cut himself in."

I noticed that we were all nodding. The story worked.

"Dorsey had money problems," I added. "The insurance investigator on this did routine background checks on all the cops involved. Dorsey was in debt up to his neck, had two kids in college and two still to go."

"Everybody's got money problems," Rider said angrily. "It's no excuse."

That made us all silent for a long moment and then I took up the story again.

"There was just one problem at that point."

"Agent Gessler," Rider said. "She knew too much. She had to disappear."

Rider didn't know anything about Lindell's relationship with Gessler, and Lindell did little to reveal it. He just sat quietly, his eyes down. I moved the story forward.

"My guess is that Simonson and his guys played Dorsey along while they took care of the Gessler problem. Dorsey knew what they did, but what could he do or say about it? He was in too deep. Then Simonson took care of him in Nat's. Cross and the bartender were window dressing."

Rider squinted her eyes and shook her head.

"What?" Lindell asked.

"Doesn't work for me," she said. "There's a disconnect there. With Gessler, she's gone without a trace. Very smooth. Three years later and who knows where the body is?"

I was cringing for Lindell's sake but tried not to show it.

"But with Dorsey, it's a shoot-out at the OK Corral. Dorsey, Cross, the bartender. Two completely different styles. One smooth as smoke, the other a blood bath."

"Well," I said, "with Dorsey, they wanted it to look like a robbery gone wrong. If he just disappeared, then the obvious thing to do would be to go back over the old cases.

Simonson didn't want that. So he orchestrated thc big blowout so the investigators would think robbery."

"I still don't buy it. I think they're different. Look, I don't remember all the details but didn't Marty Gessler disappear while driving home through the Sepulveda Pass?"

"That's right. Somebody bumped her and she pulled over."

"Okay, then here's an armed and trained agent. Are you going to tell me Simonson and these guys got her to pull over by bumping her car and then they got the best of her? Uh-uh, guys. I say, no way. Not without a fight. Not without somebody seeing something. I think she stopped because she felt safe. She stopped for a cop."

She pointed at me and nodded when she said the last line. Lindell brought a fist down hard on the table. Rider had convinced him. I had defended my theory but now saw the cracks in it. I started thinking Rider might be right.

I noticed Rider looking at Lindell. She was finally picking up the vibe.

"You really knew her, didn't you?" she asked.

Lindell just nodded to the question. Then he brought his eyes up to stare angrily at me.

"And you blew it, Bosch," he said.

"I blew it? What are you talking about?"

"With your little stunt last night. Going in there like fucking Steve McQueen. What did you think, that they'd be so spooked they'd march right down to Parker Center and turn themselves in?"

"Roy," Rider said, "I think we —"

"You wanted to provoke them, didn't you? You wanted them to come after you."

"That's crazy," I said calmly. "Four against one? The only reason I'm alive right now and talking to you is because I saw them tailing me and because Milton distracted them long enough for me to get out of the house."

"Yeah, that's just it. You saw the tail. You saw it because you were looking for it and you were looking for it because you wanted it. You blew it, Bosch. If that kid in the hospital doesn't wake up with a working brain, then we'll never know what happened to Marty or where —"

He stopped before his voice lost it. He stopped speaking but didn't stop staring at me.

"Guys," Rider said quietly, "let's take a break here. Let's stop questioning motives and accusing. We all want the same thing here."

Lindell slowly and emphatically shook his head.

"No, not Harry Bosch," he said quietly, his eyes still on mine. "It's always just what he wants. He's always been a private investigator, even when he carried a badge."

I looked from Lindell to Rider. She didn't say anything but her eyes dropped away from mine, and in their movement was a tell. I saw her confirmation.

42

It was dawn by the time I got back to my house. The place was still a swarm of police and media activity and the police would not let me back in. The house and canyon comprised a major crime scene and as such they had commandeered custody of it. I was told to try back in a day, maybe two. They would not even let me go back inside to get fresh clothes or any other belongings. I was strictly persona non grata. I was asked to stay away. The one concession I was able to talk my way into was my car. Two uniform cops — Hurwitz and Swanny, who had caught the precious overtime assignment — cleared room for me among the police and media vehicles and I backed the Mercedes out of the carport and took off.

The adrenaline rush that came with the near-death experience of the night before had long since ebbed away. I was exhausted but had no place to go. I drove aimlessly along Mulholland until I came to Laurel Canyon Boulevard and then took a right and drove down into the Valley.

I started getting a sense of where I was headed but knew it was too early. When I got to Ventura I took another right and pulled into the parking lot at the Dupar's. I decided that I needed some high octane, and coffee and pancakes would fit the bill. Before getting out of the car I got the cell phone out and turned it on. I called the numbers I had for Janis Langwiser and Sandor Szatmari and got no answers but left messages that the morning meeting was canceled because of circumstances beyond my control.

The phone's screen showed that I had messages waiting. I called to pick them up and listened to four messages left through the night by Keisha Russell, the *Times* reporter. She started out very cool and concerned about my well-being and wanting to talk to me at my convenience to make sure I was okay. By the third message her voice had taken on a high-pitched urgency, and in the fourth she demanded that I make good on our deal in which I promised to talk to her if anything happened with what I was working on.

"Something's obviously happened now, Harry. You've got four on the floor on Woodrow Wilson. *Call* me like you *promised* me you would."

"Yes, dear," I said as I erased the message.

The last message was from Alexander Taylor, the box office champion. There was a proprietary tone to his voice. He wanted me to know that this story was his.

"Mr. Bosch, I see you are all over the news. I am assuming that the nastiness on the hill last night is related to my heist. There were four robbers; the news says there are four dead men on your property. I want you to know that the offer I made still stands. But I'll double it. One hundred thousand as an option on the story. The back end is open to negotiation and we can talk about that when I hear back from you. I will give you my assistant's private number. Call me back. I'll be waiting."

He gave a number but I didn't bother writing it down. I thought about the money for all of five seconds and then erased the message and closed the phone.

As I walked into the restaurant I wondered about what constituted circumstances beyond my control and what Lindell had said at the end of the interview in North Hollywood. I thought about fighting monsters and what had been said about me and to me in the past, and what I had said to Peoples in that restaurant booth just a few nights earlier. I wondered if a subtle slide into the abyss was any different from the kind of swan dive Milton had taken.

I knew I would have to think about this and the motives behind my actions of the last ten hours. But I soon decided it would have to keep. There was still a mystery to solve and as soon as I refueled I was going after it.

I sat at the counter and ordered the number two special without looking at a menu. The waitress with the wide hips poured my coffee and was about to put the order in at the kitchen window when somebody took the stool next to me and said, "I'll have coffee, too."

I recognized the voice and turned and saw Keisha Russell smiling at me as she put her bag down on the floor between us. She had followed me down the hill.

"I should've known."

"Harry, if you don't want to be followed all you have to do is return your calls."

"I just got your messages five minutes ago, Keisha."

"Well, now you don't have to call me back."

"I'm not talking to you. Not yet."

"Harry, your house is like a war zone. Bodies all over. Are you all right?"

"I'm sitting here, aren't I? I'm all right. But I still can't talk to you. I don't know how this is going to play out and

I'm not going to say anything that shows up in the paper and might be at odds with the official line. That's suicide."

"You mean you don't want to tell me the truth just in case what they put out isn't."

"Keisha, you know me. I will talk to you when I can. Why don't you let me have my coffee and eat in peace now?"

"Just answer one question. It's not even a question. Just confirm for me that whatever happened up there is related to what you called me about. About Martha Gessler."

I shook my head in frustration. I knew I wasn't going to be able to shake her without giving her something.

"Actually, I can't confirm that, and that's the truth. But, look, if I give you something that will help you, will you let me be until there is a time I can talk about it?"

Before she answered, the waitress slid a plate in front of me. I looked down at a short stack of buttered pancakes with a fried egg and two pieces of bacon forming an X on top. She then put down a small pitcher of maple syrup. I grabbed it and started pouring syrup over everything.

"My God," Russell said. "You eat that and I'm not sure there will ever be a time you can talk about it. You are killing yourself, Harry."

I looked up at the waitress, who was standing there writing up my check. I gave her a what-are-you-going-to-do smile and shrugged.

"Are you paying for her coffee?" she asked.

"Sure."

She put the bill down on the counter and walked away. I looked at Russell.

"Why don't you say that louder next time?"

"Sorry, Harry, but I don't want you to get fat and old and ugly. You're my bud. I want you around."

I saw through all of that. She hid her motives the way the bartenders I'd seen the night before hid their nipples.

"Do we have a deal? I give you something and you hit the road, leave me alone?"

She took a sip from her free coffee and smiled.

"Deal."

"Go pull your clips on the Angella Benton case."

She narrowed her eyes. She didn't remember it.

"You didn't do much with it at first, then it blew up big when it was connected to the movie set heist over on Selma. Eidolon Productions? Ring a bell?"

She almost came off her stool.

"Are you fucking kidding me?" she said a little too loud. "The four on the floor are those guys?"

"Not quite. Three of them are those guys. Plus the one they took to the hospital."

"Then who is the fourth?"

"I gave you what I'm giving you, Keisha. I'm going to eat now."

I turned to my plate and started cutting my food up.

"This is so cool!" she said. "This is going to be big."

As if four bodies in the Cahuenga Pass wasn't already big. I took my first bite and the syrup hit me like a sugar bullet.

"Great," I said.

She reached down to her bag and started getting up.

"I've gotta go, Harry. Thanks for the coffee."

"One last thing."

I took another bite and turned to her and started talking with my mouth full.

"Check out *Los Angeles Magazine* seven months ago. They did this story on these four guys who own all the hot bars in Hollywood. It called them the kings of the night crawlers. Check it out."

Her eyes widened.

"You're kidding."

"No, check it out."

She leaned down and kissed me on the cheek. She had never done that before, when I carried a badge.

"Thanks, Harry. I'll call you."

"I bet you will."

I watched her glide quickly through the restaurant and out. I turned back to my plate. The egg had been over easy and cutting it up had made a mess of things. But at that moment it tasted like the best thing I had ever eaten.

Finally alone, I considered the question Kiz Rider had raised during the interview about how the style of the Marty Gessler disappearance was so different from the massacre at Nat's. I was now sure Rider was right. The crimes had been designed, if not carried out, by different perpetrators.

"Dorsey," I said out loud.

Maybe too loud. A man three stools down turned and looked at me until I turned and stared him back to his coffee cup.

Most of my records and notes were in the house and not attainable. I had the murder book in the Mercedes but it contained nothing from the Gessler case. From memory I worked on the details of the FBI agent's disappearance. The car left at the airport. The use of her credit card up near the desert to buy more gas than her car could hold. I tried to fit these facts under the new heading of Dorsey. It was hard to make it work. Dorsey had been working crimes from one side of the law for nearly thirty years. He was too smart, he had seen too much, to leave a trail like that.

But by the time I finished my plate I thought I had something. Something that worked. I looked around to make sure the man three stools down and nobody else was looking at me. I poured a little more syrup onto my plate and then dipped my fork into it and ate it. I was about to dip again when the wide hips of the waitress appeared in front of me.

"Finished?"

"Uh, yes, sure. Thank you."

"More coffee?"

"Can I get a to-go cup?"

"Yes, you may."

She took the plate and my syrup away. I thought about my next moves until she came back with the coffee and reworked my bill. I left two bucks on the counter and took the bill to the cashier, where I noticed bottles of the restaurant's syrup were on display and for sale. The cashier noticed my gaze.

"How about a bottle of syrup to go?"

I was tempted but decided to stick with the coffee.

"Nah, I think I've had enough sweetness for today. Thanks."

"You need sweetness. It's a nasty world out there."

I agreed with her, paid my bill and left with my cup of harsh black coffee. Back in the car I opened the phone and called Roy Lindell's cell number.

"This is Roy."

"This is Bosch. We still talking?"

"What do you want, an apology? Fuck you, you're not getting one."

"No, I can live without an apology from you, Roy. So fuck you, too. I want to know if you still want to find her."

There was no need to use a name.

"What do you think, Bosch?"

"Okay, then."

I thought for a moment about how to do this.

"Bosch, you still there?"

"Yeah, listen, I've got to go see somebody right now. Can you meet me in two hours?"

"Two hours. Where?"

"You know where Bronson Canyon is?"

"Above Hollywood, right?"

"Yeah, Griffith Park. Meet me at the end of Bronson Canyon. Two hours. If you're not there, I won't wait."

"What's up there? What do you have?"

"Right now just a hunch. You going to meet me?"

There was a pause.

"I'll be there, Bosch. What should I bring?"

Good question. I tried to think of what we'd need.

"Bring flashlights and a bolt cutter. I guess you better bring a shovel too, Roy."

That brought another pause before he replied.

"What are you bringing?"

"I guess just my hunch for now."

"Where are we going up there?"

"I'll tell you when I see you. I'll show you."

I closed the phone then.

43

The garage door at Lawton Cross's house was closed. The van was parked in the driveway but there were no other vehicles. Kiz Rider hadn't gotten there yet. Nobody had. I pulled in behind the van and got out and knocked on the front door. It didn't take too long for Danny Cross to answer it.

"Harry," she said. "We were just watching it on the TV. Are you all right?"

"Never better."

"Are they the ones? The ones who did this to Law?"

She had a pleading look in her eyes. I nodded.

"It was them. The one who was in the bar that day, who shot Law, I took his face off with his own shotgun. Does that make you happy, Danny?"

She pressed her lips together in an effort to hold back tears.

"Revenge tastes sweet, doesn't it? Just like pancake syrup."

I reached out and put my hand on her shoulder but not to comfort her. I gently pushed her to the side of the doorway and stepped in. Rather than head left toward

Lawton Cross's sitting room I went to the right. I went into the kitchen and found the door to the garage. I went to the file cabinets in front of the Malibu and pulled the file on the Antonio Markwell case, the abduction-murder that had made Cross and Dorsey in the department.

I returned to the house and entered the sitting room. I didn't know where Danny had gone but her husband was waiting for me.

"Harry, you're all over the tube," he said.

I looked up at the television screen. It was a helicopter view of my house. I could see all the official cars and media vans on the street in front. I could see the black tarps covering the bodies in the back. I hit the power button with the side of my fist and the screen went blank. I turned back to Cross and dropped the Markwell file on his lap. He couldn't move. All he could do was lower his eyes to it and try to read the tab.

"How does it feel? Does it give you a hard-on watching what you did? In your case, a make-believe hard-on?"

"Harry, I —"

"Where is she, Law?"

"Where is who? Harry, I don't know what —"

"Sure you do. You know exactly what I'm talking about. You sat there like a puppet but the whole time you were pulling the strings. My strings."

"Harry, please."

"Don't 'Harry, please' me. You wanted revenge on them and I was your ticket. Well, you got it, partner. I took care of all of them, just like you thought. Like you hoped. You played me just right."

He didn't say anything. His eyes were cast down, away from mine.

"Now there's one thing I want from you. I want to know where you and Jack hid Marty Gessler. I want to bring her home."

He remained silent, his eyes away from me. I reached down and took the file off his lap. On the bureau I opened it and started leafing through the documents.

"You know, I didn't see it until somebody I taught the job to saw it first," I said as I looked through the file. "She's the one who said it had to be a cop. It was the only way Gessler could've been taken so easily. And she was right. Those four punks didn't have the steel."

I gestured toward the empty television screen.

"I mean, look what happened when they came for me."

I found what I was looking for in the file. A map of Griffith Park. I started unfolding it. Its creases cracked and split. It had been folded in the file for maybe five years. It was marked by the location where Antonio Markwell's body had been found in Bronson Canyon.

"Once I started in that direction, then I began to see it. The gas had always been a problem. Somebody used her card and they bought more gas than her car could hold. That was a mistake, Law. A big one. Not buying the gas. That was part of the misdirection. But getting so much of it. The bureau thought maybe it was a truck, that they were looking for a trucker. But now I'm thinking Crown Vic. The Police Interceptor model they make for all the departments. The cars with extra-capacity gas tanks so you don't get caught out there on the hunt without any juice."

I had delicately spread the map open. It depicted the many winding roads and footpaths of the huge mountain park. It showed the public road up through Bronson Canyon and then the fire road which extended further up into the rocky terrain. It showed the area of caves and tunnels left behind when the canyon had been a quarry, its rock payload crushed and used for railroad beds across the west. I laid the map across Cross's lap and over his dead arms.

"The way I figure it, you guys followed her from Westwood. Then in the Pass you pulled her over in one of the quiet spots. Used the blue light on your Crown Vic and she thought, *No problem, they're cops.* But then you put her in the trunk of that big car with the big gas tank. One of you drove her car to the airport and the other followed and picked him up. Probably you backed her car into another car or a pillar or something somewhere. Nice touch. Sell the misdirection. Then you drive up to the desert and use the gas card. Again, sell that misdirection. And then you turn around and take her back to the real hiding place. Which one of you did it, Law? Which one actually took from her everything she had or would ever have?"

I didn't expect an answer and didn't get one. I pointed to the map.

"That's my bet. You guys went to a place you were familiar with, a place nobody would be looking for Marty Gessler because they'd all be looking up in the desert. You wanted her hidden but you wanted access to her, right? You wanted to know exactly where she was. She was your ace in the hole, right? You would use her to get to them. Marty and her computer. The connection was on that box. Find her and find the box, the connection would be made and there'd be a knock on Linus Simonson's door."

I paused to give him a chance to protest, to tell me to get the hell out or call me a liar. But he didn't do any of that. He didn't say a word.

"It all seemed to work," I said. "And then that day at Nat's you guys were supposed to cut the deal, right? Shake hands and share the wealth? Only Linus Simonson had other ideas about that. Turned out he didn't want to share anything and he'd take his chances with Gessler's computer. That must have shocked you. There you two were, waiting in there, probably already counting your money. And he comes in and opens up on you . . .

"I think you should've seen it coming, Law."

I leaned down and tapped the map with a finger.

"Bronson Canyon. All those tunnels, caves. Where you found the boy."

My eyes came up from the map.

"That's my guess. They've got the roads going up there locked. But you two had a key, didn't you? From the boy's case. You kept that key and then it came in handy. Where is she?"

Cross finally brought his eyes up to mine and spoke.

"Look what they did to me," he said. "They deserved what they got."

I nodded in agreement.

"And you deserved what you got. Where is she?"

His eyes turned and he looked up at the empty TV. He said nothing. Anger bloomed inside of me. I thought of Milton squeezing the air tubes shut. Of becoming a monster, of becoming the thing I hunted. I took a step toward his chair and looked down on him with eyes dark with rage. Slowly I raised my hands toward his face.

"Tell him."

I turned and Danny Cross was in the doorway. I didn't know how long she had been there or what she had heard. I didn't know if it was a story that was new to her or not. All I knew is that she brought me back from the edge of the abyss. I turned and looked back at Lawton Cross. His eyes were on his wife and his frozen face still somehow took on an expression of sadness and misery.

"Tell him, Lawton," she said. "Or I won't be there beside you."

A look of fear immediately took over his face. Then there was pleading in his eyes.

"You promise to stay with me?"

"I promise."

His eyes dropped to the map spread across the chair.

"You don't need this," he said. "Just go up there. You go in the big cave and then take the tunnel on the right. It comes to an open clearing. Somebody told us they call it The Devil's Punchbowl. Anyway, that's where we found him. She's there now."

He could no longer hold my eyes and looked away, back down at the map.

"Where do I look, Lawton?"

"Where the kid was. That family marked the spot. You'll know when you get there."

I nodded. I understood. Slowly I took the map from him and refolded it. I watched him as I did it. He seemed becalmed, his face now returned to expressionless. I'd seen the look a thousand times before in the eyes and faces of those who have confessed. A lifting of the burden.

There was nothing else to say. I slipped the map back into the file and took it with me as I left the room. Danny Cross remained just outside the door, looking in at her husband. I stopped as I passed her.

"He's a black hole," I said. "He'll suck you in and take you down. Save yourself, Danny."

"How?"

"You know how."

I left her there and went out. I got in my car and started driving south toward Hollywood and the secret the hills had hidden for so long.

44

It wasn't raining yet but the sky was full of the low rumbling of thunder by the time I got to Hollywood. From the freeway I took Franklin over to Bronson and then up into the hills. Bronson Canyon had been in more movies than I had probably seen in my whole life. Its rugged terrain and jagged rock outcroppings formed the backdrop of countless westerns and more than a few low-budget interplanetary explorations. I had been there as a kid and I had been there on cases. I knew that if you weren't careful you could get lost on the trails or in the caves and quarried-out spaces. The rock facings would begin to crowd you and after a while they all looked the same. You could lose your bearings. In that sameness was the danger.

I took the park road up until it terminated at the fire road. Entrance to this dirt and crushed-gravel extension was blocked by a steel gate with a padlock on it. The key to that lock resided with the fire department and the city's film bureau, but thanks to Lawton Cross I knew better than that.

I got there before Lindell and I was tempted not to wait. It would be a long walk up to the caves on foot, but my anger had forged into resolve and momentum. Sitting at the locked gate was not the way to stoke those fires and keep them burning. I wanted to get up into the hills and get it over with. I pulled out the cell phone and called him to see where he was.

"Right behind you."

I checked the mirror. He was coming around the last bend in a federal Crown Vic. It made me think about how he would react when he found out the last clue I had put together had been so close all along.

"It's about time," I said.

I hung up and got out of the Mercedes. When Lindell pulled up I leaned into his window.

"Did you bring the bolt cutter?"

Lindell looked out the windshield at the gate.

"For that? I'm not going to cut that. They'll climb all over me if I break their lock."

"Roy, I thought you were a big-time federal agent. Give me the cutter, I'll do it."

"And you can take all the heat. Just tell them you had a hunch."

I threw him a look, hoping to communicate that I was operating on more than a hunch now. He popped the trunk lid and I went back and pulled out the bolt cutter he had probably checked out of the federal equipment shed. He stayed in the car while I walked over and cut the lock and pushed the gate open.

I walked by his window on the way back to the trunk.

"By any means, Roy," I said as I passed. "I think I'm getting the idea why you weren't picked for the squad."

I threw the tool in the trunk, slammed it and told him to follow me up the hill.

We drove up the winding road, the gravel crunching under our wheels sounding like the rain that was still coming. The road up took a final 180 and terminated in front of the main tunnel entrance, a fifteen-foot-high opening cut into a granite deposit the size of an office building. I parked next to Lindell and met him at the trunk. He'd brought two shovels and two flashlights. As I was reaching in for mine he put his hand on my arm.

"Okay, Bosch, what are we doing?"

"She's here. We're going to go in and find her."

"Confirmed?"

I looked at him and nodded. In my life I have told a lot of people — too many to count — about loved ones they weren't going to see alive again. I knew Lindell had long ago given up hope for Marty Gessler, but the final confirmation is still never easy to get. Or to give.

"Yes, confirmed. Lawton Cross told me."

Lindell nodded and turned away from the trunk. He looked up at the crest of the granite mountain. I busied myself with getting the tools from the trunk and checking to see if my cell phone was catching a signal. Over my shoulder I heard him say, "It's going to rain."

"Yeah," I said. "Let's go."

I handed him a light and a shovel and we approached the mouth of the tunnel.

"He's going to pay for this," Lindell said.

I nodded. I didn't bother to tell him that Lawton Cross had already been paying for it every day of his life.

The tunnel was big. Shaquille O'Neal could walk through with Wilt Chamberlain on his shoulders. It was nothing like the stale, claustrophobic systems I had crawled through thirty-five years before. The air inside was fresh. It smelled clean. Ten feet in we put on the lights, and in another fifty feet the channel curved and we were out of sight of the entrance. I remembered Cross's directions and kept to the right, moving slowly.

We came to a central cavern and stopped. There were three tributary tunnels. I focused my light on the third opening and knew it was the way. I then turned my light off and told Lindell to do the same.

"Why? What's going on?"

"Nothing. Just turn it off for a second."

He did and I waited a moment for my eyes to adjust to the darkness. My vision and focus came back and I could pick up the outline of the rock walls and jutting surfaces. I could see the light that had followed us in.

"What is it?" Lindell asked.

"Lost light. I wanted to see the lost light."

"What?"

"You can always find it. Even in the dark, even underground."

I snapped my light back on, careful not to hit Lindell in the face with the beam, and headed toward the third tributary tunnel.

This time we needed to duck and proceed in single file as the tunnel grew smaller and more cramped. The channel curved to the right and soon we could see light ahead. An opening. We moved through and came out into an open bowl, a granite stadium chiseled out decades before. The Devil's Punchbowl.

Over time the bottom of the bowl had filled with a layer of run-off granite debris and dust, a layer just thick enough for brush to put down roots and for a body to be buried. It was here that Dorsey and Cross had been led to the body of

Antonio Markwell and where they would come back again with Marty Gessler. I found myself wondering how long she had been alive on that night three years ago. Had she been pushed at gunpoint through the tunnel or dragged, already dead, to her final resting spot?

Neither answer was any comfort. I looked back at Lindell as he came out of the tunnel into the opening. His face was ghostly white and I guessed that he might have been considering the same thing.

"Where?" he asked.

I turned from him and scanned the bottom of the bowl and then I saw it. A tiny white cross rising in the brown-and-yellow brush line by the granite facing.

"There."

Lindell took the lead and walked quickly to the cross. He lifted it out of the ground without a second thought and tossed it to the side. He was already putting his shovel into the ground when I got there. I looked down at the cross. It was made from an old picket fence. At its center point was a photo of a young boy. A school photo framed with popsicle sticks. Antonio Markwell was long gone from this life and this spot but his family had marked it as a holy ground. Dorsey and Cross had then used it because they knew the ground here would never be disturbed by trespassers.

I leaned down and picked the tiny cross up. I leaned it against the granite wall, and then I went to work with my borrowed shovel.

We didn't really dig with the shovels. We scraped at the surface, both of us instinctively reluctant to drive the point of the blade down too deeply.

In less than five minutes we found her. One final scrape of Lindell's shovel revealed a thick plastic tarp. We put the shovels aside and we both squatted to look. The plastic was opaque, like a shower curtain. But through it was the distinct outline of a hand. A small withered hand. A woman's hand.

"Okay, Roy, we found her. Maybe we should back out of here now. Make the calls."

"No, I want to do this. I . . ."

He didn't finish. He put his hand on my chest and gently pushed me back away. He then crouched over the spot and started digging with his hands, his arms moving quickly, as though he thought he was in a race against time, that he was trying to save her before she suffocated.

"I'm sorry, Roy," I said to his back but I don't think he heard me.

In a few minutes he had uncovered most of the plastic. From her face down to her hips. The plastic had apparently slowed but not stopped decay. The air in the bowl took on a musty smell. Moving back closer and peering over Lindell's shoulder I could see that Agent Martha Gessler had been wrapped and buried fully clothed, with her arms crossed in front of her. Only half of her face was dimly visible through the plastic. The rest was hidden in blackness; blood in the folds of the plastic. I guessed that they had killed her with a head shot.

"Her computer is here," Lindell said.

I stepped further forward to see. I could make out the outline of a laptop computer. It was wrapped in its own plastic and left on her chest.

"It holds the connection to Simonson," I said, though that was obvious by now. "It was their edge. They wanted the body and the laptop someplace where they could get to it. They thought it would keep Simonson and the others in line. But they were wrong."

I saw Lindell's shoulders start to shake but I knew he was no longer digging.

"Give me a minute, Harry," he said, his voice straining.

"Sure, Roy. I'm going to make my way back to the cars and call some people. I left my cell phone."

Whether he knew I had lied or not, he didn't object. I picked up one of the flashlights and headed back. On my way back through the smaller tunnel I could hear the big man crying behind me. The sound was somehow picked up and intensified as it came into the tunnel. It was like he was right next to me. It was like he was inside my head. I moved faster. I got to the main channel and was almost running by the time I got to the entrance. When I finally came out into the light it was raining.

45

The following afternoon I took another Southwest jet from Burbank to Las Vegas. I still wasn't allowed back into my house and wasn't sure I ever wanted to go back anyway. I was still a key part of the investigation but nobody had specifically told me not to leave town. They only say that sort of stuff in movies, anyway.

As usual the flight was full. People going to the cathedrals of greed. Bringing their stores of cash and hope. It made me think of Simonson and Dorsey and Cross and Angella Benton and what part greed and luck had played in their lives. Most of all I thought of Marty Gessler and the bad luck she had. Left to molder for more than three years in that place. She had simply made a phone call to a cop, and that had brought about her own destruction. Good intentions. Trust. What a way to go. What a wonderful world.

This time I rented a car at McCarran and I fought my own way through the traffic. The address Lindell had gotten for me off the license plate number I had given him was located on the northwest side of the city. It was out near the end of the sprawl. For now, at least. It belonged to a house that was newly built and large. It had a French Provincial style to it. I think it did, at least. I'm not that good at that sort of thing.

The two-car garage was closed but off to the side of the circular driveway was a car that wasn't the one I had been in with Eleanor. It was a Toyota, maybe five years old with a lot of miles on it. I could tell. I am good at that sort of thing.

I parked the rental at the edge of the circle and slowly got out. I don't know, maybe I thought if I took my time somebody would open the door and invite me in and all my qualms would be eased.

But it didn't happen. I got to the door and had to push the button and knew I would probably have to push my way in. Figuratively. I heard a chime sound from inside and I waited. Before I needed to ring again the door was answered by a woman, a Latina who looked to be in her sixties. She was small and had a kind but worn face. She looked like she felt bad about the shotgun burns on my face. She didn't wear a uniform of any type but I was guessing she was the maid. Eleanor with a maid. I had a hard time picturing that.

"Is Eleanor Wish here?"

"Can I say who it is, please?"

Her English was good and carried only a slight accent.

"Tell her it's her husband."

I saw the alarm go off in her eyes and I realized that I had been stupid.

"Former husband," I said quickly. "Just tell her it's Harry."

"Please wait."

I nodded and she closed the door. I heard her lock it. As I waited I could feel the heat working through my clothes, penetrating my scalp. All around me the sun was reflecting brightly. It was almost five minutes before the door was opened again and Eleanor stood there.

"Harry, are you all right?"

"I'm fine."

"I saw everything on TV. CNN."

I just nodded to that.

"It's so sad about Marty Gessler."

"Yeah."

And then nothing for a long moment before she finally spoke.

"What are you doing here, Harry?"

"I don't know. I just wanted to see you."

"How did you find this place?"

I shrugged.

"I'm a detective. Was, at least."

"You should have called me first."

"I know. I should have done a lot of things but I didn't, Eleanor. I'm sorry, okay? Sorry for everything. Are you going to let me in or should I just melt out here in the sun?"

"Before you come in I have to tell you, this is not how I wanted to do this."

I felt a deep downward tug in my chest as she stepped back and opened the door. She raised her hand in a welcoming gesture and I stepped into a foyer area that had arched doorways leading in three different directions.

"It's not how you wanted to do what?" I asked.

"Let's go into the living room," she said.

We took the middle arch and stepped into a large room that was neat and nicely furnished. In one corner was a baby grand piano that caught my eye. Eleanor didn't play, unless she had taken it up since she'd left me.

"You want something to drink, Harry?"

"Um, water would be good. It's hot out there."

"It usually is. Stay here and I'll be right back."

I nodded and she left me there. I looked around the room. I recognized none of the furniture from the apartment where I had once visited her. Everything was different, everything was new. The rear wall of the room was comprised of sliding glass doors that looked upon a screened-in pool area. I noticed that surrounding the pool was a white plastic safety fence that people with children put up as a precaution.

Something suddenly began to click about all of Eleanor's mysteries. The obtuse answers, the car trunk that couldn't be opened. People carry fold-up strollers in their trunks. People with children.

"Harry?"

I turned. Eleanor was there. And standing next to her was a little girl with dark hair and eyes. They held hands. I looked from Eleanor to the girl and then back and forth again. The girl had Eleanor's features. The same wave in her hair, the same full lips and bobbed nose. There was something about her demeanor that was the same, too. The way she looked at me.

But the eyes weren't Eleanor's. They were the eyes I saw when I looked in the mirror. They came from me.

A sudden rush of feelings welled up in me, not all of them good. But now I could not take my eyes off the girl.

"Eleanor . . . ?"

"This is Maddie."

"Maddie?"

"Short for Madeline."

"Madeline. How old?"

"She's almost four now."

My mind shifted back. I remembered the last time we'd

been together before Eleanor left for good. In the house on the hill. It could have happened then. Eleanor seemed to read my thoughts.

"It was like it was supposed to be. Like something was supposed to make sure we never . . ."

She didn't finish.

"Why didn't you tell me?"

"I wanted it to be the right time."

"When was that going to be?"

"Now, I guess. You are a detective. I guess I wanted you to find out about it."

"That's not right."

"What would have been right?"

Twin skyrockets were going off inside me. One left a trail of red, the other green. They were going different ways. One anger, one warmth. One led to the heart's dark abyss, a devil's punchbowl filled with recriminations and revenge I could dip my cup fully into. The other led away from all of that. To Paradise Road. To bright, blessed days and dark, sacred nights. It led to the place where lost light came from. My lost light.

I knew I could choose one path but not both. I looked up from the girl to Eleanor. She had tears on her face and yet a smile. I knew then what path to choose and that there is no end to things of the heart. I stepped forward and squatted down in front of the girl. I knew from dealing with young witnesses that it was best to approach them on their level.

"Hello, Maddie," I said to my daughter.

She turned her face and pushed it into her mother's leg.

"I'm too shy," she said.

"That's okay, Maddie. I'm pretty shy myself. Can I just hold your hand?"

She let go of her mother's hand and extended hers to me. I took it and she wrapped her tiny fingers around my index finger. I shifted forward until my knees were on the floor and I was sitting back on my heels. She peeked her eyes out at me. She didn't seem scared. Just cautious. I raised my other hand and she gave me her other hand, the fingers wrapping the same way around my one.

I leaned forward and raised her tiny fists and held them against my closed eyes. In that moment I knew all the mysteries were solved. That I was home. That I was saved.

ACKNOWLEDGMENTS

The author would like to gratefully acknowledge the following people for their work in improving and correcting this novel: Michael Pietsch, Pamela Marshall, Philip Spitzer, Joel Gotler, Terrill Lee Lankford, James Swain, Jane Davis, Jerry Hooten, Carolyn Chriss, Linda Connelly and Mary Lavelle.

Michael Connelly is a former journalist and author of the bestselling series of Harry Bosch novels and the bestselling novels *Chasing the Dime, The Poet, Void Moon,* and *Blood Work,* which was made into a movie starring Clint Eastwood. Connelly has won numerous awards for his journalism and novels, including an Edgar Award.